TAP

Green Ivy Publishing
1 Lincoln Centre
18W140 Butterfield Road
Suite 1500
Oakbrook Terrace IL 60181-4843
www.greenivybooks.com

ISBN: 978-1-945379-53-6

Cover art by:That_Kei_Guy

Acknowledgments

Thank you, Sandy Ferguson and Nathaniel Watkins, the real Dinred and Hayden. I tried.

I

"Watson, stay with me!"

Watson's ears rang loudly, and blood dripped from his tongue. His vision, still blurred from a blinding flash, attempted to focus on the figure in front of him. He was finally able to see it. There stood a wolf man, furry head and ears, tail stiff. He was padded in armor, from his toes to his collar, with boots and shin guards, gauntlets of steel, cloth gloves, and a cuirass of thin metal, strong as tough iron. He was armed with a rifle, and he had a look of horror, sorrow, and death on his face.

"Watson! Get up and shoot!" His commander's voice cracked as he yelled.

Watson felt the blood drip from his head, and he had a blown ear drum. He fell back when he attempted to get to his feet. His right foot stung deeply, and the pain, once absent in ignorance, now shot up his leg. He looked down and was unable to see what was left. His boot and greave were all but destroyed. His armor was punctured, and he could feel the blood dribbling down his fur. But he was able to breathe; he could still be a threat.

He reached to his right to grab his trusty pistol from the dirt. It was large, as any weapon with a .50-caliber chamber should be. He grasped the handle and took off the safety. The ringing slowly left, allowing him to get a sense of his surroundings. His ear was soon flooded with the sounds of bullets spewing out of nozzles. His lungs filled with a gasp as his eyes focused. He was at the bottom of a muddy trench. His sights were filled with wolfen taking cover behind a wall of dirt and debris. Behind him a medic was doing his best to seal a bleeding wound on a soldier who didn't have the strength to struggle.

Watson could see the medic try to get the corpse's attention, getting riled up as the eyes refused to respond. He couldn't hear what he was saying over the gunfire.

"Watson, you had better be dead." The closest wolfen howled at him. Watson still lay in the mud, clutching his pistol. "Get up and shoot," the wolfen said. "That's an order."

Watson was unsure if his comrade had noticed his condition, or if he even cared. He couldn't argue. He crawled, digging his fingers into the muck and dirt as he clawed his way up the wall. The gun trembled in Watson's hand. Outside the trenches was the grass and dew of the cold tundra. On the horizon was a thick wall of smoke with a few breaks in it. The soldiers fired blindly into it, as futile as it was.

Hailstorms of bullets were traced through the air from the smokescreen, whizzing past Watson. A few others weren't lucky enough to be missed. At least three new bodies hit the trench floors. He fired his weapon in the smoke where the bullets came from. The onslaught of bullets refused to stop. In one of the breaks in the smoke, Watson was able see what he was up against.

A thick metal beast with cannons and treads, it was size of a large vehicle. Beside it were several infantry men in lighter armor than Watson's. A flash came from the enormous barrel mounted on top of the tank.

Debris filled the air as several shells plummeted and ricocheted off the ground. A high explosive round burst in the trench a few meters from Watson. The force knocked him back, removing the air from his lungs. He struggled to breathe and coughed up blood. An organ had ruptured. Internal bleeding. He was a dead man.

He twisted his body, looking for the medic. There was no medic anymore. There was nothing at all. It was silent. For a moment he thought his ears had been all but shredded, and he was mostly right.

But that wasn't the reason behind the silence, and Watson knew it. He heard another gunshot.

Watson's hand twitched. It bore no weight. The gun was missing.

"Damn you!" one final wolfen shouted as he stood on the trench walls firing his pistol. "Damn all of you!"

He continued shouting, even when he was out of ammo. A loud thud hushed him, and a tank shell landed under his feet. He flew back into the trench a leg short of a full person. His body lay limp and emotionless. His dead stare faced Watson for what felt like an eternity of stillness.

The air, the ground, all quiet. Watson couldn't feel anything. His spine was broken below his ribs. It felt like his fur and armor were stained, and not with the blood of his enemy.

The sounds of engines and treads grew closer as the tanks and troop marched across the field. Watson lay still, hoping there was the slightest chance he wouldn't be tortured if he played dead. Moments after the sounds started approaching, they stopped. A figure dropped from the trench walls and landed near Watson. It was a soldier, his whole body covered in silver metal power armor. His limbs were bulky, but not compared to his upper body, which held the reactor. The soldier's head and neck appeared to be hidden behind his shoulder pads. When Watson finally got a glimpse of his head, he saw that it was covered by a metal helmet with two glowing red slits for eyes and a beak with a yellow stripe across it. On the back of the helmet, layers and layers of feathers rested among each other as they cascaded down his back. The soldier leaned down and grabbed the wolfen beside him and, with a twitch of his arm, a blade jutted out of the top of the dead wolfen's gauntlet. With a fluid punch he stabbed the corpse of the wolfen commander. Blood dripped from the neck instead of spraying; the heart hadn't beaten in some time.

A loud thump diverted Watson's attention. Above him was another soldier in similar armor. Watson heard the gears grind as the soldier lifted his leg and slammed it onto his chest. Watson gasped as his ribs were crushed under the titanic weight.

"Heretic," the Seraph muttered through his mask. The talons at the base of his leg pinched and pierced his metal armor. Watson was conscious until the Seraph grasped his heart and squeezed the blood out of it.

2

"We're losing him!"

Kabol's heart raced at the nurse's voice. Below his hands was a dying leona entrusted to his care. His body, once twisted and contorted, lay flat on the surgery bed. His chest was damaged, and his ribs had punctured his lungs.

The beeping heart rate on the monitor was anything but normal as the organ struggled for the oxygen it had been so deprived of. The transfusions of blood had done very little to replace what had been lost.

Kabol looked around, his heart beating faster than the patient's. "We need to keep him breathing. Where's the breathing tube I ordered?"

"It's on the way!" another nurse called.

"Stay with me." Kabol tilted the cat's head and parted his jaws.. He breathed into his mouth, watching in horror as his chest didn't rise. Another breath, and another, resulted in wasted effort.

Kabol heard the sorrow-filled, single-toned song of the dead. The monitor showed a flat line accompanied by a long and agonizing beep. He had failed.

⚬⟡⟡⚬

Kabol sipped his tea while leaning back in his rocking chair. The summer breeze made his ears twitch. He was trying to enjoy the peaceful, overcast afternoon on his balcony. His feline tail curled beside his lap and between his legs, and he was careful to keep it out of the way. The two-story house was tightly squeezed among the others on this side of the street, almost creating a single building. Below him, beyond the railings, a stream split a stone path. Its surface seemed soft and inviting. The path was meters long, and both ends led to the parking lots in the front of his house.

The air was clear today, so Kabol could see the palace off in the distance. He enjoyed the days he could see it. The majestic towers, of a gothic age, were christened in gold statues and lined with silver idols and symbols across their majestic, stained glass windows. When the sky was clear, the sun would reflect its glimmering wonder on his rocking chair. His balcony was unique in that way.

He finished his cup of tea, despising its flat taste. Sugar had been so highly taxed that he'd almost grown accustomed to having none, although that didn't mean he had to like it. The war had yet to truly affect New Albion other than through taxes and tariffs.

Next to Kabol sat a letter on a glass table. It had been sent to all houses, from the monarchy, reassuring the leonas and their canine neighbors that this wasn't their war and would not be in the foreseeable future. Next to it was a newspaper. The beige tint revealed its age. The front-page article was in bold letters: "Avon Nations Declare War."

Kabol had kept it for more than keepsake. The memories of stunned faces and looks of worry at the hospital, as he had read it aloud at work, was something he didn't want to forget soon. He couldn't believe it himself; it felt like it had come from nowhere. The tensions were all on the mainland of Europa, southeast of New Albion. Kabol had tried to pay attention to these conflicts, to little avail.

A soft thud on wood made his ear jerk. Behind him, in the dining room, his wife Dinred was setting up plates. She was an average-sized leona, a few inches shorter than he was. She was five feet tall and slim. Her black hair was down behind her shoulders. Her fur was white, with no markings to intrude on her figure, unlike Kabol's dark gray pelt. He had white diamonds on his knees and elbows, the front and back of his torso, and the tip of his tail. The marking on his face was also a diamond; it stretched to his brow and neck. It was positioned in such a way that it looked like a triangle until someone looked at the bottom of his jaw. His brown hair was fancily groomed on the sides with some strands hanging down the right side of his forehead.

His eyes were the most noticeable thing about him. Others believed them to be a dark shade of amber, but they were red as blood. He believed it was just a defect in the pigment in his irises. They always caught someone's attention, but it was nothing too rare. He was sure he'd seen it in two or three patients.

Dinred's eyes were a rather deep green, and Kabol couldn't stop himself from smiling whenever he looked into them. He rose from his chair, carried his belongings through the sliding door into the house, and set them aside. Dinred took notice. "Evening, Love. Did you enjoy your tea?"

"It was tolerable," he muttered. He might as well not have had any tea at all. He took a seat at the dinner table, and Dinred placed a bowl of soup on his plate. Kabol thanked her as she went back to her own bowl.

"I'm sorry to hear that," Dinred said softly. She placed her elbows on the table and looked rather sad as she picked up her spoon and began to eat.

"Don't be, and never you mind." Kabol smiled before putting his spoon on the table.

"Elbows off, Dear, it's rude," she said.

Kabol started eating. "So, how was your day?"

"It was... troubling," she began. "I was watching the news—"

"When has that ever been a good idea?" Kabol interrupted. Dinred gave him a smirk and a tilt of her head. He snickered. "I'm sorry. Please continue."

"I was watching the news. The reporter said terrible battles had happened."

What a shock! Kabol thought.

"Said the Avon aren't even slowing down, and the wolfen are calling for help but we aren't answering."

"Why is that?" Kabol dipped his spoon into the soup and scraped the edge of his bowl with it. "Say it with me."

"Not our war." They said, in unison, the very thing the monarchy and bureaucrats had told everyone.

He remembered the Avon religion before the war. Its followers believed that any man of Avian kind was favored by a god, as they were essentially the species of the heavens. Next came the foxen, then the leona, and so forth, naming every species, with the last being the wolfen, who were seen mostly as barbarians. Those who went to war with nations they thought were populated with the lowest form of life had never truly piqued Kabol's interest, and religion was something he preferred to keep his distance from.

"You don't seem happy, Dear." Dinred's concern sounded as cold as it was sincere.

"I can't say that I'm too fond of how today has been turning out." Kabol bowed his head, ruminating on his failure. "I know you don't like it when I tell you about my work, and how much the details can sicken you, so I'll keep it simple. I lost someone."

"I understand." Dinred was silent after that, taking a full minute for her own thoughts. She started twirling the spoon in her bowl. "I want to dance."

Kabol's ears perked up at the sound of her cheery attitude. He was almost impressed that she could turn his misery aside so easily. "Can't you wait until the coronation?"

"I want to dance now." She pouted, crossing her arms.

"But I haven't even finished eating."

Dinred didn't accept that answer. She got up and headed toward her husband with a smile. "You can eat any time you want. You can only dance for so long."

"But there isn't any music." Kabol got up to play her game. Dinred wrapped his hands around her hips and rested her head on his shoulder. She cradled their bodies together, humming a tune. It was soft and gentle with a calming melody. Kabol remembered hearing her hum it before. On nights when she'd helped the servants and handmaidens, they'd all hummed the hymn of slaves of old: "Tea for One." He was rarely home to hear it, but when he was, he felt out of the picture. It got to a part where the rhythm picked up, and the subtle hint of a jazzy tone seeped in. Kabol whistled in tune to her humming. He knew, at least, this part.

When the beat became clearer, Kabol held Dinred's hand above her as she twirled away from him, and when her hand tightened he tugged, spinning her back into his arms. He dipped her head and torso down and gently pulled her up. She spun once more, crossing her arms in front of her chest, her back facing Kabol, who had wrapped his arms around her waist.

Kabol fell into total bliss. All of his worries, fears, and tantrums drained from his body in her warm embrace, making a smile curl on his face.

A purr found its way out of her chest, and she rubbed her head against his chin. Her tail wrapped around his legs, and she whispered, "I love you so much, Kabol."

His eyes were closed, helping him cherish this embrace. "I love you so much more, Dinred." He let her go with a chipper smile and sat down. "That song is old." Sarcasm crept into his voice.

"Well, your mother is old, but you still listen to her." Dinred stuck out her tongue and sat down to enjoy her meal.

While sipping a spoonful of soup, Kabol could hear someone at the door of the room. It was one of his maids, Isabelle. She was a mutt, a golden retriever with tan ears that bent forward. She was wearing an apron with her maid outfit, even though it was her day off. "Kabol, sir, you have a guest."

"I'll be there soon enough." He sipped more broth.

The mutt stood there hesitantly. "He looks very important."

"Did he say what it was about?"

"I couldn't understand what he said."

Kabol stood up from the table and tossed his spoon in the bowl. "Well, let's look at the bright side. I just might finish my soup before dawn."

Isabelle hugged the wall to let her master pass. "He's in the drawing—"

"I know where he is," Kabol interrupted, passing through the door. He sauntered through the Victorian halls, upset that he couldn't finish a single bowl of soup without being disturbed. He felt hot with anger, and his warm clothes, quilted with wool, did little to help. He sighed deeply and put on a smile before walking down the stairs.

He had much to smile about, especially in contrast to his

youth. In the end it was his choice how to act. Being disrespectful to a guest because he hadn't finished eating would be rude. The stained glass window behind him reflected on the walls beside him. The walls themselves were decorated down to the millimeter. Gold vines littered the green wallpaper, on the walls and ceilings, from the front door to the kitchens, from the stairs to the bathrooms, and, basically, anywhere else a guest may look. It was a welcome change from the coal mines where he'd spent his childhood.

Kabol saw himself in a mirror next to the hat rack. On the rack was the trusty tan fedora he never left home without. Next to the rack, a door led to the kitchenette, furbished with marble counters and steel ovens. He turned the corner into the guest room. In there stood a mutt, almost a foot taller than Kabol.

He was a pit bull with white fur covering his bald head. His left ear was bent while the right one stood high. He fiddled with a decorative clock, careful not to let his claws touch it, before finding something else of interest. His brown eyes lingered on an oil painting, on fine cloth, of Kabol standing behind his sitting wife.

Kabol looked at the pit bull. What piqued his interest was a familiar radiance. A presence he had once known was under the faded gray camouflage fatigues. Kabol cleared his throat, catching his guest's attention.

The man spun around and smiled. He spoke in his Northern Deutschland tongue. "Kabol! Long time, no see."

"Ansgar!" Kabol purred, happy he still remembered a language other than English but even happier to meet his old friend from medical school. Kabol couldn't help himself and hugged the mutt before starting to speak in his dialect. "My, why haven't I seen you in almost a year? I almost thought you had forgotten about me."

"Been looking for work." Ansgar looked around in awe. "This

country is Utopia compared to Deutschland. Just look at this place. My eyes hurt looking at all the shiny things. You hit it off big."

"What's with the outfit? Are you really a soldier, or are you just wearing that?"

"Medic."

"Is that so? How did you find me? And what brings you to New Albion if you serve Deutschland?"

"Well, I was helping at the hospital. I saw your name on one of the photos and went asking for you, and a nurse told me where you lived." Ansgar fidgeted and his voice sounded a bit unsteady. "About the second part, I've volunteered to help the wolfen. They brought me here to ship me off to the east, to Swethin."

"Swethin?" Kabol tilted his head. *The war is that close to home? It's only been a few months, and already the wolfen have lost half their motherland.* "How did the wolfen lose so much land? Aren't they bred to fight?"

"Hey." Ansgar pointed his finger at Kabol. "That's racist. Besides, their excuse was they were caught off guard. The Avon declared war after the bombs fell. And they didn't lose much land." Ansgar stepped beside Kabol, held his hand in the air, and made a vertical stroke. "This is the front line. Avon forces split wolfen forces." He moved his hand to the right. "Main wolfen force defending." He moved the hand past the invisible line. "Main Avon force attacking." He moved his hand to the left and up. "Swethin, large wolfen forces trapped. They overcame their pride and requested help."

Kabol nodded his head. "So are all the canines and mutts trying to help, or just the armed forces?"

Ansgar nodded and smirked. "Yes."

Kabol rolled his eyes. "Is it a good idea to involve yourselves in a holy war?"

"No. However, we aren't involving ourselves entirely. We are just sending medics and boats. And we cannot take them directly to Deutschland. They have us blockaded."

"So where are you taking them?"

"Kabol, who is it?" Dinred stood at the base of the stairs, hand on the decorated pylon. Kabol motioned for her to enter. When she saw the canine next to him, without a maid's outfit, she seemed rather surprised. Such a sight was rare in her house. As she entered the drawing room, she held out her hand. "Hello, my name is Dinred. And you are?"

Ansgar shook her hand. "Moin! Guten abend, Dinred, ich heiße Ansgar."

Dinred looked uneasy. She leaned toward Kabol and whispered, "He sounds angry. Did I do something wrong?"

Kabol held in a laugh while Ansgar shook his head and said, "Ich verstehe das nicht."

Kabol nudged Dinred. "That's Ansgar, and you don't have to whisper. He doesn't understand English." He turned to the pit bull and, in the English tongue, said, "Go die in a fire, Ansgar, you stupid mutt."

"Ja," he replied. "Ich heiße… called Ansgar. Entshuldigong." He bowed his head slightly and turned to Kabol. "I have to go report back to headquarters. It was nice seeing you; we should catch up some time."

"I'd like that very much." Kabol showed him to the door. "Auf Wiedersehen." He turned to Dinred. "That means goodbye."

"Goodbye!" Dinred called when the mutt was halfway to the gate.

The pit bull turned around and waved. "Goodbye." The canine put on his cover and went on his way.

Kabol closed the door and looked at his silver pocket watch. His tail swayed in annoyance. "Dinred, the coronation is going to start in a few hours. Best get dressed."

3

Kabol checked his pocket watch once more. "We're going to be late," he called through the doors of his chamber.

"Don't come in! She's changing!" Isabelle called back.

"I've seen it all before, and she's completely covered by fur," Kabol muttered and rolled his eyes. He could not see why Isabelle was Dinred's favorite, even if she had been a gift from the royal family, when all she did was back talk. Technically she was Kabol's favorite as well, as she was the only servant whose name he could remember.

He had never understood why it took Dinred so long, or why it took two people, for her to change. Kabol was already tucked into a dark brown vest, red plaid scarf, and thick wool raincoat with a handkerchief by his heart. He put on his leather gloves, thinking it would be senseless to wait outside the doors when there were plenty of chairs downstairs.

On his way down the adorned steps, with the engraved railing, he heard a ruckus from the living room but paid it little mind. It was one of the servants, perchance. Once his foot touched the floor, he stumbled upon a maid who was running. She collided with him hard, knocking him against the railing.

The maid, a simple canine like all the others, fell onto her rump and rubbed her head where it had rammed into Kabol's chin. She gasped. "I'm sorry, Master. I wasn't looking where I was going."

Kabol held out his hand while he got a good look at her. She wasn't an average pooch, but instead, a foxen. A red coat surrounding a white underbelly made her teal eyes stand out from under her bangs.

"It's fine. Think nothing of it." Kabol helped her to her feet, noticing that her claws weren't trimmed and were somewhat sharp. "Just be more careful. Also get your nails trimmed immediately. We're civilized here, so you don't need them."

"I'm sorry, Master, I'm new." Her ears were flattened in embarrassment.

"I can see that, very blatantly." Kabol never liked hearing the word 'Master' coming from a subordinate's mouth, whether it was etiquette or not. "What seems to be the hurry?"

"I'm sorry; you'll have to excuse me." She bowed and ran off, batting Kabol with her thick, bushy tail.

Kabol's ears twitched in frustration. He took a deep breath and exhaled slowly. Tonight would be a good night, and he got to decide whether to enjoy it or not. He was not going to linger on petty things such as unruliness from the new girl, at least not today.

Kabol heard a whistle from upstairs. He turned his sights on Isabelle, at the top of the staircase. She bowed her head deeply and mimicked a romantic accent. "Le mademoiselle is ready."

She backed away to reveal the white cat in an elegant hooded dress. It was dark as the night sky with golden silk sewn in like moss clinging to a chapel. Her hood was down, and she wore silver lace and a locket around her neck. Her hands and arms were hidden in thin black cotton. Her waist was shrouded in a frilled skirt.

She stepped carefully down the stairs, maintaining her poise and wary of the dress. Kabol couldn't resist a smile. "As beautiful as the day we met."

Dinred leaned in and kissed the bottom of his chin. She dragged a finger across his chest and walked toward the door. "Flattery doesn't suit you, Love."

Kabol nodded at Isabelle, appreciating a job well done. The mutt replied with a thumbs up and a grin. Kabol snagged his fedora and followed his wife out. The air was damp and cool, rumored to be the first sign it was going to rain soon. He despised the constant cloudy weather; he sometimes forgot what the sun felt like.

"Sir!" Kabol turned around at the sound of his maid's voice, and she tossed him an umbrella. "I'll hold down the fort. Have a nice night."

He thanked her with a two-finger salute and walked out through the iron gates.

The palace garden was enveloped with roses and statues. Commotion filled the air as the party had long since started. Kabol's ears were immobile, sticking from two slits in his hat. Silence was another plane of existence at parties. The music ringing from the speakers was bearable solely for its classical pulse. It originated from a live orchestra playing inside.

The small talk didn't sound as soothing among the leona and, on occasion, the servants, who were of both the cat and dog species. Dinred tugged his arm, wrapping her own around it. The gathering was held mostly inside, a place Kabol was not willing to go. Outside was more peaceful, even when swarmed by guests and cupbearers.

Kabol glared at the table of sweets and polished flasks. *So this is what stature gets you? The good old days are dead and gone, aren't they?*

Dinred squeezed his arm. "Lighten up, will you? We've been here for almost an hour, and you still haven't figured out it's a party?"

"You're the aristocrat. I'm just a doctor. These are all your friends. And I'm oh so glad to see that, ninety-eight years after Cerberus' reign, all the rich still have their commodities dipped in gold. Somehow flaunting them is considered a party. Such progress."

"So you refuse to enjoy yourself? How does that help?" Dinred teased.

"Yeah. A little hypocritical aren't you, Sergeant Anton?" a voice said behind him.

Kabol turned around, ready to sharpen his tongue against the insulting cur. "What did you call me?"

"Sergeant. Anton." The mutt smiled. His voice was rough as sandpaper. He had white fur and hair brushed back behind his bent black ears. His muzzle was encased by a light azure arch traveling from his nose to his chin.

Kabol glared into his blue eyes before realizing who it was. "Hayden?" The canine was dressed in attire less appealing than Kabol's, but proper enough that he seemed to have had no trouble getting in. Kabol was amused. He'd been almost unable to recognize him without a uniform on.

"The greatest. The one. The only." Hayden smiled again. "Trying to bite my head off?"

"No… Well, yes I was, but what are you doing here?" Kabol was tempted to hug the mutt.

"Enjoying myself. You'd think the novelty of the medals would've worn off by now." He fiddled with a straw in his drink. "It hasn't. How did you get in here? You off guard duty?"

Kabol shook his head. "No, I'm through with hurting people." He tried changing the subject, wishing he hadn't let an old friend see him at this kind of party. "I didn't plan on seeing you here. This is quite unanticipated." Kabol batted his tail, unable to hide his nervousness in front of his old colleague.

"Whoa. Six whole syllables. That's a record. I never figured you'd be out here. I knew you never liked playing soldier, but to find you here? You moved up in the world." He turned to look away. "I need to get back to a friend."

"Friend? Do you mean Ben?" Kabol's ears would've perked up if they had not been constrained.

"Inaan, yeah. He's…" Hayden pointed deeper into the gardens and circled his finger.

Dinred wrapped her arms around Kabol's waist and gave him a kiss on the cheek. "Who's your friend here? An old war hero?"

Hayden sulked. "Nah. Went to war. Killed a couple of people. Lived to tell about it. Heroes are the ones that die."

"He's great company, as you may have guessed," Kabol joked.

"Funny." Hayden glanced at him with a false smile. The pooch bowed his head and left toward the empty gardens and statues.

Dinred released Kabol and handed him a glass of brandy from a servant's tray.

Kabol led her to a table away from the rabble and pulled up a chair. "He can be unappreciative like that sometimes. I'll go apologize."

Dinred held his hand tightly and hesitated before letting go. "Don't be too long."

Kabol kissed her on the forehead, satisfied by the reassuring purr in her chest. He followed the path Hayden had taken. It was lined with hedges and stone figures of cherubs and angels. Much of it was dark. He wondered if he was not allowed to be there. However, dimly lit lampposts soon appeared, scattered along the path, and next to them speakers echoed the orchestra's soft violins.

He came to a plaza. A large fountain stood before him, entrenched in black roses. Hard metal benches faced the stone statue at the center of the fountain.

In the center, a wolfen sat among a throne of skeletons woven together by thorns. The man was covered in archaic power armor, with a bulky chest and appendages. On his shoulders were the skulls of feral wolves without bottom jaws. His eyes were not of common stone, but precious red gems. The rubies glistened in the lamplight.

Just at the foot of the fountain was a plaque: "Ode to Our Savior, the Daemon Cerberus."

He was no demon, just a man, Kabol thought, distraught at how poetry and art were the bane of history.

Something caught his attention. Behind the statue lay two paths. On the path to the right, a man peered at a small statuette. He was a leona with purple hair, most likely dyed, and bright-yellow fur with two spikes of white on his face pointing to his nose. His attire was appalling. He wore an open vest, without a shirt and jeans to boot. His belly bore a white oval that disappeared past his hips. He was making faces at a baby fox clinging to its neglectful mother's dress.

That can't be right. Kabol walked stealthily toward the man, who pulled a bag out of his pocket and placed stick-on googly eyes on the faces of the child and mother.

"Are you daft?" Kabol raised his voice, almost angry, making the man jump and backhand the eyes off the stone.

The cat had no brows, and his irises were small and as white as the rest of his eyes. "Oh Kabol, it's you!" He pounced and hugged him. "I missed you, Buddy. How have you been? Did you find Hayden?"

"Rather suddenly, Ben. Uh… How did you get in here dressed like that? Actually, how did you get in here at all?"

"I snuck in." He put on a smug smile.

"How? There are guards everywhere—"

"I know! Crazy, right?" He scratched his head and tilted it to the side. A white hand was placed on his shoulder, making him jump.

"There you are. I told you to stay home, Inaan," Hayden growled.

Inaan flattened his ears and fiddled with his tail. "So you managed to find me?"

"Wasn't hard. Followed the trail." Hayden pointed behind him. Every stone structure had the playful eyes stuck on them. Even a stone pylon with a horizontal crack had been vandalized with mocking peepers. "Clean up that mess. I'm taking you home before the police do."

Ben did what he'd been told without a word of protest.

Kabol crossed his arms. "Some things never change."

Hayden covered his face with his palm. "I know. I have to live with him."

Ben placed his elbow upon Hayden's shoulder, leaned on it, and faced Kabol. "He still acts like a warrant officer. Ain't that right, Hayden?"

Hayden didn't say a word. He only glanced at his shoulder before glaring at Ben. The yellow cat got the message, and his hand slowly slid off. He backed away to continue removing the fake eyes. Hayden continued talking to the gray cat. "I feel like I need to buy a leash and a muzzle for him sometimes. At least he didn't get hurt. Go and enjoy yourself, Sarge."

"Don't call me that. It's 'Doctor' now. Truly, just call me Kabol."

Hayden smirked and huffed. "Sure. Right. I guess." He turned around and flicked his hand, two fingers blindly pointing out. "I'll see you around, Doctor Sergeant Anton."

Kabol had nothing to say. He merely smiled, reminded of old times. "I missed you…" he muttered to himself.

Kabol turned tail and headed back to Dinred. A couple was now sitting at one of the benches in front of the fountain. One was an orange foxen. Her head rested against a taller brown leona's shoulder. He wore a guard's uniform. A metal lunch case sat next to his feet. Perhaps it was his time off. The man had his eyes closed, and the woman was gazing at him, beaming. Kabol ignored them. He has his own wife to get to.

After a short walk, he was able to see her. She had a crescent on her plate, between her relaxed arms that angled skyward on the table, and her head rested against her hands.

"Elbows off, Dear…" Kabol bumped the legs of the table with his umbrella and, seeing her face brighten up, he continued. "It's rude."

"I know you don't really mean that." She rose from her seat and hugged him.

Kabol cherished her warmth and whispered, "I love you."

"I love you more," she whispered back, locking her eyes with his. He'd seen this before. He'd been challenged.

"Impossible. For I love you as surely as the sun rises, then sets in envy because its beauty cannot compare to thee."

Dinred poked her husband's chest with two fingers. "English hath not the words I wish to express. To describe my love would be like to pour an entire sea into a goblet. Your touch be so divine, I feel as if I must wash my hands before I dare lay a finger. Your eyes, may I say, bare the very soul I yearn for."

Kabol hummed, attempting to think of another simile to keep the game going, keeping his mind off the distasteful surroundings. His mind was empty. "All right, you win this round."

She was about to launch into another show of wit and cheesy romance, but the music stopped, and a voice boomed from the speakers.

"Ladies and gentlemen, may we have your attention?" The crowds stopped talking, and heads turned toward the large glass doors at the top of a staircase. "We will begin the coronation soon. You're welcome to gather in the throne room. In the meantime, please stand for the national anthem."

Kabol stood up, took his hat off, and placed it over his heart.

Before the song began, Dinred grabbed his arm and yanked him toward the gardens. The lights dimmed further as she dragged him in front of the fountain. As the music began to play, she wrapped her arms around him and burrowed her head into his chest.

Kabol purred in her embrace. For a moment, she looked up and locked eyes with him. "I'm sorry you don't like it here."

Kabol kissed her forehead. "It's not your fault I'm bothered by such. I know it's a new monarch, but shouldn't we celebrate Princess Mary's crowning after she does some good?"

"Oh, shut up." She hugged him tightly. "It's the first time a mutt's been crowned since forever. Here, I'll teach you how to enjoy yourself."

The anthem of New Albion began to sing through the speakers. Kabol whirled her around, and they danced as they had practiced. They danced like no one was watching while, at the same time, they danced as if the world admired them. He dipped her back and quickly pulled her up, gently enough that their noses touched with ease.

Her gaze was fixed on his eyes once more, flattering him with a warm smile. Behind her, the guard was resting.

"What's wrong, Dear?" she asked.

"That man's not standing." Kabol felt like he had oversimplified it. Something was off. Where was the foxen? "And I think his wife abandoned him."

"Maybe she went inside. And who cares if he's not standing for this? We're dancing to it."

Despite these valid arguments, Kabol still felt uncertain. Perhaps he was too concerned. "He could get fired. Or court marshaled. At the least, he's asleep on guard duty." Kabol let go of her and strode toward the sleeping man. "Excuse me, Sir." Kabol didn't know what he was thinking; his voice was almost as soft as the music. He looked at his watch. "Sir, you need to get up. The hour's almost over. You'll want to be at your post for the changing…"

A sudden thought struck him. He figured out what had made this man so eerie, what had made him questionable to look at. It wasn't his sloppy posture in sleep or his complete disregard of his oaths.

It was his absent breathing, his still chest.

Kabol rejected the thought. He got closer to the man. "Sir!" He placed two fingers on his neck. Kabol was horrified. There was no pulse.

4

Don't panic, Kabol reassured himself. *Call the guard, and get Dinred out.*

"Dinred, go to the car. We're leaving," he managed to mutter. The anthem died down, touching its last notes. "Go now!"

It took a moment for the urgency in Kabol's voice to compel her to go. Before she could move, a bright light flashed in the distance.

Kabol and Dinred had a clear view of the source. They had seen an explosion, miles away, through the railed fence. Soon another fiery inferno rose next to it. Another, then another and, within a few seconds, and entire district had been leveled.

Kabol, experienced at sights like these, rushed to Dinred. "Cover your ears!"

He pushed both of them to the ground, away from the light. The deafening roar of a shockwave soon hit them.

⁂

Marshal Gavin burst through the doors to the control room, spilling the coffee in his hands. The whole room was alive with people rushing from console to console. Lights flickered from the white computers, monitors, and systems surrounding a group of displays in the center of the room. Gavin growled, "What the hell is going on? Ensign, assessment!"

The white room had a clear view of London from atop the palace. An entire block had been demolished, and the surrounding area had been split apart by flames. A leona in uniform turned from the blinking consoles. All of the computers beeped and scanned as if it were a normal day on the isle. "Oi! The cor bloody radar dinnit pick up a blip, Marshal." He pointed at the circular screen. "There ain't a thing in the sky that isn't ours."

The ensign's voice was just barely audible over the commotion of other people scurrying from monitor to monitor. "There's still no word from Southend-on-sea," another ensign called out. "Their comm's maintenance should have been done by now."

The Marshal studied the radar on the screen carefully. "If Southend is under attack, what does that tell us?"

"Sir!" The second ensign pointed at his screen. "We've received an encoded message. It's from Southend." He stood next to her and leaned over her shoulder. Her fingers battered against the keyboard in front of him. "It's a video."

"On the monitor, now!" he commanded and backed up to the center of the room. All heads turned to face the images on screen. The video was fuzzy at best, dreadful at the least, but Gavin was able to see what was being broadcasted.

His fur bristled and a cold shiver ran up his spine. Buildings lay wasted on a scorched horizon. The setting sun was clouded by dark smoke. Silver-armored figures stormed over bloodied walls. Above it all was a massive war machine of Avian design.

At least a few kilometers long, it soared above the ruined landscape, propelled by multiple large thrusters and engines. Streams of bullets rained from its cannons. Shells plummeted from its rail guns onto the ruins below. Several hundred smaller aircrafts swarmed the skies destroying whatever resistance was met.

Gavin tried his best to hide his shock in front of his subordinates. Their faces said it all. One of the ensigns muttered a curse, another sat back covering his mouth, and the one from the radar couldn't breathe correctly.

Gavin stood there silently for what seemed like an eternity before turning around and pointing at an operator. "Sound the alarms. I want all birds in the air. We're evacuating now! Civilians and non-combat personnel are top priority. All other hands grab a gun."

"Sir, what's the rally point?" one of the operators asked, among the phones, pressing the silent alarms.

"Marshal!" The officer at the communications raised his hand. "I'm getting several more messages. Grimsby and Hull, Ipswitch, the whole coast is under siege!"

"Get everyone out of Albion. Get the royal family on the first craft out of the isle; they aren't safe here, and who knows where else is under attack." Gavin turned toward the double doors he had burst through. Half his coffee was on the floor. "Get all ships away from that Nimbus-class destroyer."

"They're requesting a rally point," an operator called.

"We're heading to our allies past the channel: Deutschland, Gaul, Burgundy, anywhere! We'll regroup and formulate an idea when we're safe from the warship. Warn the Sea Wall about incoming refugees and help them do what they can to gain a perimeter. Tell them to turn those 2k shell cannons inward. It's the only hope of stopping that monster."

One of the officers followed the brown leona out of the room. Gavin could hear the youth in the gray one's voice. "Sir, with all due respect, shouldn't we hold the isle?"

Gavin picked up the pace down the short hallway. The shiny chrome-framed doors of the elevator were in sight. "Ensign, I don't know if you've seen a Nimbus-class warship in combat, but they rarely lose."

"Then how do we stop it?"

"We can't." Gavin stopped just in front of the lift and faced the young man. It hummed without a button being pushed. "We haven't the means to take it on alone, and that thing will be on us within the hour."

The lift dinged, and Gavin turned to face the parting doors. The lift was empty. The ringing faded into a beeping. Gavin saw an open case with a cylinder and several wires attached. The beeping became faster until he was blinded and burned by a flash of fire.

Another burst of fire made Kabol grasp his wife more tightly. Glass rained down from the shattered windows. Kabol shielded Dinred from the oncoming glass, pushing her below his hovering chest. He felt the stained glass crystals sprinkle onto him, and his ear bled due to the smaller shards. His hat protected most of his head.

An air siren was broadcasted. He could hear screams and the sounds of toppling wood and metal. His nose was filled with the scent of phosphorous; the inside of the building was ablaze. Kabol didn't dare take a look, fearing more glass might fall. The faces of the damned were left unseen. The heat from the fire was almost unbearable as it sped across the floors.

Kabol pulled Dinred away from the bushes by the windows. "Cover your ears!" Fear surged within his chest, and his heart began to pound loudly. He could feel it in his ears. As they fled the gardens, figures alight fled through the doors. Kabol's eardrums rang as loudly as their bloodcurdling cries.

He made his way out through the black iron gates as the guards abandoned their posts. Others were fleeing from the scene—leonas, mutts, and foxen alike—but too few were making it out. *Where do I go?*

The car? No. Those would be their next targets. What are they targeting? The royals or the rich?

His mind raced. He turned to Dinred, who moved her mouth in an attempt to speak. The ringing in his ears made her sound mute. Slowly, but surely, the ringing died enough for him to hear.

"Kabol!" Dinred squeezed his arms tightly. The fear in her eyes spoke for itself. She hadn't had the luxury of being deaf for the past few minutes. Adrenaline was perhaps the only thing keeping her from trembling. She tugged again. "What's happening?"

"We have to leave." He was barely able to keep his voice from cracking with fear. He pulled her off the palace grounds and toward the other side of the street. "We have to go as far as we can from any form of military."

Dinred frowned. "What do you mean? They can protect us!"

"We don't know how many bombs are left, or who's behind this! We need to find someplace where we can't—"

"Isabelle!" Dinred interrupted, pulling herself from Kabol's grasp. "What about Isabelle? We can't just leave her."

Kabol pointed at the burning palace. He opened his mouth to say something, but the only thing that came out was ragged breathing. He dropped his arm, placing it to his side. He couldn't bear the thought of Isabelle's corpse, and he knew Dinred would never forgive him if he let that mutt die.

"The hospital," Kabol muttered, becoming aware of its benign presence. He clutched his wife's arm and pulled her close. "Listen to me. Get to the hospital. You'll be safe there. Replace the dress as soon as possible. We don't know what's going on, but it's not the best time to look like you have money."

Dinred had never looked more terrified.

"I'm going to get Isabelle, and I'll meet you there." Kabol hugged her more tightly than he'd ever hugged her before. The palace was little more than an inferno. The streets were abandoned, and the air was tainted with the shouts of the fleeing. He felt like his heart was about to burst out of his chest, and he could feel her trembling. Anger filled him; instinct told him to lash out against whatever may threaten her.

He released her, seeing her sorrowful face illuminated by the palace fires. He forced himself to step away from her. She stood there, frozen in fear perhaps. He pointed in the direction of the hospital. "Go. Go!"

"I love you!" she called.

"I love you too." He didn't want to leave her, but the feeling of necessity clung to him. He wasn't satisfied until she was out of his sight. He fled toward home.

5

The sky began to turn a hue of amber as new flames spread across the horizon.

The burning buildings were disintegrating beyond recognition. Kabol barely knew where he was. If it weren't for the familiar stone path and deep stream, he'd be lost. *Fire doesn't spread this fast. The explosions were nowhere near here. How did they—?*

The sounds of propellers were closing in, grabbing the leona's attention. A police chopper flew into view from the distance. The speakers were barely audible as the copilot gave out orders. "Attention, all citizens. We are commencing an evacuation. All civilians in this area please report to one of the following locations: St. Amelie Hospital, The Regent's Park, and Bryony Commons. Please report there immediately."

Kabol felt relief flow over him. He was less than a few miles from the hospital. He turned back to the houses. Isabelle was smart enough to leave in case of a fire, but something felt wrong when he stared into the flames. All that he had worked for was burning in that fire, but all of it could be replaced, so that wasn't it.

Still, the feeling of loss crept into him. Among the fires from the balcony, he could see a limp, charred body hanging over the railing. He charged in, closing the distance, until he could confirm what it truly was. A corpse burned beyond recognition.

"Isabelle!" His desperation seeped into his voice.

"Kabol!"

He gasped. He would recognize that voice anywhere. The corpse wasn't her. Isabelle was still alive! He called her name again, rushing to the back door. With a strong kick, the weakened hinges let loose. The wooden slab fell over, revealing a hallway beside a burning staircase. Directly in front of him, down the hall, the mirror and hat rack were charred and alight. "Isabelle!"

A mutt appeared through the arched doorway to the kitchen, next to the rack. The retriever was panting, and she looked around wide eyed. At the sound of any cracks in the ceiling above, she wouldn't second guess fleeing. Kabol darted into the hall, grabbed the girl by her apron, and dragged her past the burning wallpaper.

The cracks began to grow louder before turning into snaps. Kabol quickened his pace and dove out the back door with Isabelle. After escaping the smoke-filled house, she was still gasping for breath. Kabol got to his feet and dragged the coughing girl away as the roof caved in. Embers shot out like wasps from a nest, spreading in every direction before floating up.

Kabol, for the first time in an hour, felt safe. He looked at Isabelle, who still held the newspaper in her hands. She stared at the blazing building and coughed. "The others…"

"They had to have escaped." For a moment, anger surged within him. "Why were you still in there? You could have been killed! What happened?"

"The fox… She lit the fire… Slit his throat—" Isabelle managed to say before turning to vomit.

Kabol rubbed her back and kept her steady as he looked toward the smoldering corpse. Kabol heard the sound of another helicopter. Its blades were steadily coming closer. Down the stream appeared the metal craft. Kabol stood up and helped Isabelle to her feet, relieved that the pilot of the steel bird was able to see them. The relief didn't last long.

After a closer look, he realized the chopper wasn't of Albion design. It had two propellers separated horizontally from its axis. It was thin with a curved cockpit and a carriage on its belly. "No," Kabol growled, turning both of them around. It was the Avon.

The chopper maintained its elevation, and a figure in silvery power armor dropped from the carriage before it flew away. The figure glimmered in the light. Kabol was unable to get a good look at it, but he knew it was death.

"This way!" He dragged Isabelle into one of the nearby buildings that had been set alight. It wasn't as much of an inferno as his own home, but it was dangerous enough that maybe the soldier wouldn't follow. The house was similar to his own, other than a few rooms and the unfamiliar furniture.

The only thing that he needed to worry about was the smoke. He guided Isabelle through the dark smoke, both of them ducking their heads, and pulled her through the fire. "Try not to breathe," he warned her. The heat was unbearable, but Kabol was determined to get her to safety. He'd heard what Avon were capable of. He'd take his chances with the fire.

The first room he found himself in was full of chairs aligned next to a long table. The next room led out the front door. Kabol dragged Isabelle through the room and under the arch, only to be met with a burning sensation. The room began to heat up even more. Oil poured down the stairs, and following it was a sea of fire. He hastened and was just able to get through the door before the oil lit the entire floor ablaze.

"Are you all right?" Kabol asked Isabelle when they were a safe distance from the house.

"Are you crazy?" She coughed. "You pulled me out of a burning building, and the first thing you do is drag me through another one?"

"I panicked. And the first thing you do when in a burning building is to grab a newspaper?" Kabol snapped back.

"I panicked." She went into a coughing fit.

Kabol ignored her snide attitude. He was just happy to see her alive. "Listen. Are you able to stand?"

Isabelle nodded, getting on her feet.

"We need to get to the hospital. They're evacuating citizens to the hospital, and Dinred is waiting for us." Kabol heard a clanging of metal and wood, and he turned around to see the soldier, on top of the burning house, following him.

"Isabelle, take care of Dinred, make sure she is safe, run as fast as you can." She hesitated, about to speak, but Kabol snapped, "Go!"

The Avon turned his beaked head toward Kabol. A yellow stripe adorned his helmet, and his eyes bled red light through the smoke. Gray feathers from the back of his head dripped past his shoulders. The number of feathers hanging off the back of his helmet showed how experienced he was. They reached his waist, signifying his exceptional expertise. A bandolier secured explosives and rations to his waist, along with a knife sprouting from the shoulder.

He was a Seraph. Avon's angel of death.

Kabol heard Isabelle scurry off over the sound of his terrified heart pounding blood through his ears. He felt like he was going to die. His empty hands felt cold, and his heart felt like it would burst.

He's going to follow us. I can't let that happen.

The Seraph jumped from the building, landed hard on the stone surface below, and marched steadily toward Kabol.

"What do you want, Avon?" Kabol held his ground. "There are

no wolfen here."

The Seraph pressed the side of his helmet, turning off the blood-red slits, and pointed toward Kabol, perhaps gesturing to the fleeing mutt behind him. "Civilian, give her to me. I will forgive your insolence." His voice was modulated, through the armor, to sound more menacing.

"Why?" Kabol growled. His blood raced with anxiety, but he refused to allow the Seraph to know his fear. This wasn't his first time fighting something in power armor, but it was the first time his life had been on the line. *One false move…* No, he couldn't afford to think like that.

"I do not wish to harm her; I merely would like to speak with her." He began to circle to Kabol's left.

Kabol eyed the power armor, remembering his training. *The hinges and neck. The armor is as ceremonial as it is combat effective; that terrible balance may just give me a chance.* Kabol shook his head. *I don't want to kill this man if I don't have to. Please don't make me kill you.* "Good sir, surely you lie."

The Seraph's arms twitched, and long blades sprouted from the thick gauntlets. Without warning, the Seraph charged. Kabol leaned to the side, and the point of the blade barely scraped his right shoulder. Kabol rushed toward the exposed side of the Seraph.

The Seraph, surprised, turned his back to Kabol and swung his left arm behind him. The leona ducked and the blade missed its target. Now the Seraph's arms were spread apart and his chest exposed. Kabol, without stopping the flow of movement, reached and grabbed the handle of the knife. With a hard yank, he unclipped it from the sheath. But he pulled too hard, making him take a step back. Kabol used both hands to plunge the dagger toward the exposed shoulder, by the neck.

The Seraph gasped and, in a panic, placed his left hand in the path of the blade. He screamed as the blade cleaved into his thick talon-like palm and dug into his wrist under the armor. With another hard yank, the blade sliced through his palm. The Seraph, in a fury, swung his other arm and smacked Kabol's head.

Kabol was knocked down, and the Seraph grasped his wrist, screaming in pain. Kabol tried to get up, but the armored soldier took the opportunity to kick him straight in the chin.

He rolled and tried to crawl away, but with the senses knocked out of him and his vision blurred, he couldn't get far before the Seraph's foot was on top of him. He struggled fruitlessly, realizing he was on his stomach in midst of a fight. He could feel the talons on his back. Kabol let out a painful gasp and moan. The cool metal-tipped claws dug into his waist, drawing warm blood and staining his clothes.

Instead of feeling his spine being snapped and crushed, he heard the sounds of gunfire filling his ears. The weight lifted off him, and the Seraph stepped back. Most of the bullets ricocheted off his armor as he turned and fled. The ones that didn't embedded themselves in the armor, unable to pierce it entirely. Some, however, lodged in the hinges of the appendages. The Avon shielded his neck with his arms and fled. Kabol's vision was blurry and his ears returned to a light ringing pitch. Despite this, he reached for the knife on the ground.

By the time Kabol grasped the hilt, the Avian soldier had fled into the burning house. Kabol was unable to get up. Every time he got to his hands and knees, his strength failed him. He rolled to his back, and his vision weakened.

Red smoke and pink light appeared in a figure's hand before a glowing flare was dropped on the ground. The last thing Kabol heard before blacking out was his old friend's voice softly saying, "Pick him up."

6

Ziyad watched the toppling city below. His hand bled, dripping on the windows under the catwalk as he tightly grasped the cold metal railings. The windowed corridor gave him a clear view of London. Shells plunged into empty houses, churches, and military targets. The hums of the engines nearby silenced the two-meter-long shells shortly after they were fired. Ziyad was livid.

In the skies were transport crafts and he had seen, with his own eyes, that they were unhindered in their flight. He didn't need the binoculars embedded in his helmet to see the ships fly over the fire like ants on a flashlight. Ziyad grasped the rail even more tightly, nearly trembling in anger. An hour after he'd been wounded, his white skin and feathers were still stained in his gore. His fury outweighed his pain. He marched down the hallway toward the golden engraved door.

In front of the door were two honor guards, in power armor similar to his own, and a foxen who was smaller than he was, wearing a cuirass of his own race's design with a knee-length brown cape draped over his left shoulder. The red foxen had white-tipped ears on his hairless head and a mischievous smile. His hazel eyes blinked at Ziyad. He waved his hand and spoke with a cross between a Roman and Albion accent, in the English tongue nonetheless. "Hello, Ziyad, my feathered friend."

Ziyad despised English, even though he'd spoken it all his life. It was a challenge to pronounce the words using mostly the tip of his tongue, but he didn't expect a foxen to understand his language. Ziyad hummed, in a low growl, "Cypher, I am not in the mood to deal with you. Where is he?"

Cypher shrugged. "Where is who? There are plenty of 'hes' here. Please be specific."

"You know who I am referring to!" Ziyad burned with rage, disappointed an equal was in his way and not someone he could simply yell at. "Where is Naseer?"

"Let me go ahead and check to see if he's available," Cypher volunteered before staring at nothing behind Ziyad. Ziyad clenched his fists and narrowed his eyes. After the foxen had stared into space for a moment he said, "Nope, sorry. The Father is busy initiating new recruits."

Ziyad stepped forward, ready to unsheathe his blades. "If I had half a mind to deal with you—"

"Mind you…" Cypher slid his right hand under the cape and pulled out a rapier before Ziyad could take another step. With every syllable, he touched Ziyad's shoulder plates with the tip of the sword. "It is not the best idea to interrupt initiation." Cypher rolled his eyes and sheathed his weapon. "Actually, on second thought, I want to see what happens." Cypher took a step toward him and gestured for him to enter.

Ziyad strode up to the double doors, unlocking them from an electronic panel in the center of the gates, and they slid open. The room was large enough to fit more than five hundred people in the ground floor. It had three other entrances, an equal distance apart, for each level. Like an amphitheater, or the colosseum, the floors stacked higher into three stories with slanted platforms, containing rows of benches, facing the center of the room. The altar's floor was made of hard, thick glass shielded from the world below by triangular metal sheets.

In the center of the room nine foxen in civilian clothes were lined up in military fashion.

In front of them was an Avian in ceremonial power armor similar to Ziyad's. His feathers reached almost to his ankles, and his helmet and armor bristled with engraved golden vines and thorns. His head was cocked to its side, and black eye slits stared at Ziyad. He spoke in a well-trained voice. "Ziyad, dearest child. You break tradition?"

Ziyad bowed his head slightly before answering. "Father, with respect, I must ask why you have given orders not to fire on the transports."

"So you cannot wait? You are bleeding all over the sanctuary." Naseer waved his hand, as if he were pushing the problem away. "Never mind. Today is blessed in good cheer. Let me finish and I shall answer all questions."

Ziyad grunted and sat on a nearby pew.

"Well that was anticlimactic," Cypher muttered before closing the door.

Naseer turned back to the nine foxen in front of him, gesturing dramatically. "Now then, fellow Avon, you come to me with a city drowned in chaos seeking our favor. You ask if you may join our ranks, and we would be foolish not to accept. Such impressive cunning is what defeated the Daemon. However, the ranks of Honor, Seraph, and Godsend are reserved for those who have shown impeccable loyalty. Setting buildings ablaze, anyone can do. We must ask much more from you. Nonetheless, you will not go unrewarded. We will give you the means and many more opportunities to demonstrate your loyalty. We shall even give you the armor, but the title shall remain absent." The Father stepped down from the altar. "Are there any questions?"

One foxen, the farthest to the right, stepped forward. He sounded distraught, almost unable to speak. "What about my sister Maria's title?"

Naseer spoke softly. "The palace. She gave everything she had, even her life, proving that her loyalty outweighed such a luxury. It is confirmed that the royal bloodline is severed. Maria made history and she will be remembered, in the records, as a Godsend."

The fox silently hung his head.

Naseer continued to speak softly. "I may not know how you feel, but if you need time alone, we understand."

The foxen nodded and hid himself among the empty pews. Ziyad forgot his anger when he looked at the poor man's weeping face. As his anger faded, he became aware of the pain in his hand. He unhooked a bag from his bandolier and injected painkillers in his palm, relishing the relief. However, any attempts to move his hand were futile. The blade had done far more damage to Ziyad's wrist than he had realized. He'd take care of it later.

Naseer paced in front of the foxen, who became silent. He gestured to the door beside Ziyad, clicked the side of his helmet, and ordered that the door open. "Head to the armory. Cypher will show you the way. He will help fit your armor."

The foxen, save for the one who was alone in the pews, headed for the doors. Ziyad refused to turn his head, not wanting to risk locking eyes with Cypher. Naseer remained in the center of the room and when the door closed, Ziyad marched toward him. He pressed multiple buttons on the tablet on the altar. The metal sheets below opened, revealing a palace in flames.

"Look at it, Ziyad." Naseer stared at the scene almost greedily. "In all of history, this has only happened once before. This sight may not ever be seen again in hundreds of years."

Ziyad was silent. Another chopper flew, unharmed, out of view.

"Something troubles you, Child." Naseer began speaking in avian tongue. "Tara Nuul," he said, calling him a stupid child in the holiest of languages. "Why are you not in the medical bay?"

"When I heard you were letting the leona get away," Ziyad said, not letting strife seep into his voice, "I had to see you and ask you why."

"Civilians," the Father answered, admiring the wasted city. He took off his helmet and placed it on the altar. "Civilians, dear child. Atasha, cares little for them, sera."

"We should crush them, now!" the Seraph snapped.

"Dearest child…" Naseer turned his dark green-feathered head. His eyes, deep amber, burned with disbelief. "How dare you suggest that? Have you forgotten why they aren't a slave race? Even though they rose against the Daemon himself? They are like us; they've earned his respect through will, cunning, and persistence in combat." He turned his gaze back to the city below. Shells continued to create a wall of fire around empty houses. "They have nowhere to go. No country to fight for, no monarch to lead them, no soldiers to die with, and no friends to turn to. But if Europa finds out we've slaughtered an entire country of innocents, sympathy will brew. It will make the Cleansing even harder. Besides, the leona are, at least, sophisticated. Not barbaric like the wolves."

Ziyad saw a helicopter, on a pad, that hadn't taken off. It was atop a medium-sized building with a larger parking lot than most. "Why aren't all of them leaving?"

Naseer smirked. "I believe that's my fault. I ordered the capture of hospitals. What can I say? We need doctors. And parliament isn't going anywhere, either. Besides, the mutts are going to be left here, scrambling for any ship they can find. They'll have to go somewhere, and it is best that we keep a keen eye on them. They can be even more unpredictable."

"How do you know those canines are going to be left behind?" Ziyad asked even though he could guess the answer.

"Atasha, there are only so many transports, and so few for the lower class," Naseer said.

Ziyad remembered the stories of old. When the Daemon reigned over a few of the industrial nations of Asia, he ignored his exile and returned to Europa. The wolfen everywhere he went—from Swethin, to Russia, to Sparta—took a knee the moment he arrived. However, their canine brothers refused to bow. Within a month, all rebellions within these nations were crushed. Ever since, the dogs had been treated like slaves, losing the respect of most sentient life.

The leonas recognized the warmonger for what he was and refused to give into his rule without a fight. Ziyad's own ancestors fought in that war. The leona tribes in Africa had been thought to be easy prey, but their sophisticated kin in Britannia fought by their sides.

They stood by each other and clashed to the death, earning the respect of the Daemon. When integrated into his empire, they were the ones who inherited half their nations and were assigned to keep the mutts on a leash. And now he was going to war with them.

Ziyad saw some merit to the argument, but he refused to let up. "The wolfen menace is not here. Why bring the *Basilicus*?"

"Tash'tata," He playfully insulted his subordinate's common sense. "You know that answer. Look at them. They flee at the mere sight of a Nimbus. Without our firing a shot, they've lost their capital and monarchy. And they are smart to do so, or else they'd die tired. We must prepare for they will come back, and in much greater numbers." He took a deep breath and smiled. "This war is not close to being over, but it's a good start for us. The leona would have almost become a worthy opponent."

"Then kill them now," Ziyad said.

"Dearest child, are you deaf?" The Father pointed toward the doors. "Leave me."

7

Dinred shuddered in the cool dark room.

For the past hour she had felt the ground shake as the city was shelled. She didn't have time to replace her clothes, but she wasn't the only overdressed person in the room. Silhouettes clustered on the floor of the waiting room. The electricity was out, and the only lights were in the hallways, running on backup power, and were dimmed. The children and adolescents were under the tables and chairs, leaving the adults at the mercy of the lights if they shattered. Dinred was accompanied by Isabelle, who had given her white apron to a group of children in the corner to hide under.

Even though everyone in the room could be killed by a single shell, she was more worried about Kabol than about herself. Isabelle had stormed through the doors just before the bombs dropped and the power went out. That had been almost an hour ago, and Isabelle had stayed silent since then.

Soon the thundering sounds began to fade. The ground stopped shaking. A few mutts poked their heads out from under the table to look around. For a moment it was completely silent. The room was still, the lights either dim or out.

One of the mutts gasped, and Dinred shot her attention to the doorway. There stood a silhouette of a man, or what may have been a man. His eyes were two deep, glowing green slits. His foreign voice sounded almost distorted through the metal and speakers in his helmet. "Everyone stay down."

Dinred couldn't put her finger on what kind of accent it was, but she knew it didn't belong to Europa. The lights shot back on. Most of the people in the room scurried away from the soldier, or what Dinred presumed was a soldier and not a creature.

With the lights on she could see the armor he wore reflecting the light. From the back of his helmet, layers of feathers trickled down to his waist. His loud footsteps told her that the armor must have been even heavier than it looked. Still, Dinred didn't know what she was looking at. He seemed more machine than organic.

The ironclad beast reared its beaked head, scanning the room. "Are there any soldiers posted here?"

The room stayed silent.

The soldier nodded and looked around. "All right." He left through the hall from whence he had come, gesturing toward the other end. "Atasha. Ri'ct ta natatune."

Two soldiers, a foxen and an Avian, ran past him. The Avon, weighed down by heavy armor, stayed behind and circled the room. A radio played, at a low volume, below his chest plate. It was in the Avian language, and Dinred couldn't understand a word.

She was too scared to even attempt to whisper to her colleague.

Isabelle, on the other hand, was brave enough to stand up. "What are you going to do with us?"

The Avon shot her a glance. His English sounded broken, as if he knew what to say but hadn't practiced it. "We're going to detain you. Make sure you don't cause trouble until we sort things out." His radio started chattering again. He stopped and listened to it and raised his hand. "Everyone in this room is under house arrest. No leaving the hospital until we know who you are."

His radio began chattering again before going silent. The lights flickered after another thud outside, this time much closer. The soldier's radio started to talk again. The Avon replied, placing a finger on the side of his helmet. Soon, loud popping was heard, in a rapid repeating rhythm, from the floor above them. Gunshots.

Some of the mutts whimpered. The Avon held up a hand, either telling everyone to be quiet or showing he didn't plan to harm anyone. The gunshots' rhythm became irregular as more bullets flew through the air. Isabelle forgot her brave posture and hid next to Dinred. The Avon was unfazed. He stood tall above the rest without fear.

The radio went off again. The bullets soon stopped. The Avon clicked his helmet and responded, looking around the room as if he sought something in particular. His metallic glare rested on Dinred. "You, Cat. Stand up."

Dinred was hesitant. She was unsure about his intentions. What did he plan to do if she got up? What would he do if she didn't?

The Avon pointed to her and whistled. "You. White cat. Get up. Bring the mutt if you must."

Dinred stood up. The mutt at her side refused to move, shaking her head. Dinred pulled Isabelle's hand, whispering for her to follow. She finally stood up. They treaded carefully among the frightened bodies on the floor.

The Avon went to the door and pointed down the hall. "Someone requested a nurse. One that isn't a mutt. You'll do. Go to the stairs."

Dinred nudged Isabelle with her elbow and told her to follow her. Isabelle's ears were flat and her tail was curled in submission. Dinred did her best not to mimic this pose. Her mother had taught her to always be better than a mutt. She had said she'd stand out. It seemed she had been right.

Dinred walked down the hallways. It felt wrong seeing the halls devoid of life. The doors were shut, and any windows into the rooms were covered with curtains. When she neared the end of the corridor, she heard someone calling out. The noise seemed to be coming from a staircase at the end of the hall. It was in heavily slurred English, repeating, "I surrender." Another heavily armored soldier, quite similar to the first one, stood in front of the staircase with two foxen soldiers, in normal military gear, and a male mutt nurse.

The top of the Avon's helmet was on a chair he had pulled from a room. Its slits were black and unpowered, and there was a yellow stripe across the beak.

The Avian turned around. His beak was dull gray, his eyes dark brown bordering on black, and his feathers white as snow. His armor covered everything from the lower beak down. His shoulder was bleeding through a hole in his under-armor.

"I'm trying to help you," the nurse told the Avian.

The bird withdrew his arm. "I'm a Seraph. I will not let your filthy mutt hands touch me." He turned his gaze to Dinred and pointed at her. "Leona, do you know anything about removing a bullet from a flesh wound?"

Dinred shook her head. "I don't. I'm sorry."

The Seraph motioned for her to come closer. "Don't worry. I'll show you how." The calls in English, from up the staircase, were growing closer. The English sounded more slurred and desperate. Then it was replaced by thudding and cries. Down the stairs toppled a white-furred mutt in the armor of a foreign soldier. Dinred held in a gasp. It was the pit bull from earlier that day. She tried her best to remember his name. He was in the Deutschland armor. It was green and covered only his torso, elbows, knees, and shins. He pointed to the bag slung over his shoulder, showing a red medic's cross in a white circle on the green exterior.

He got to his knees and raised his hands in the air as he started begging. "I surrender." He said it only once correctly; the rest sounded slurred beyond comprehension. He looked at the cat, looking confused and hopeful. "Dinred?"

She did her best not to react to her name. She didn't want to know what would happen if the soldiers found out they knew each other.

"Dinred?" The Seraph crossed his arms and held his chin. "Dinred? I am unaware what that word means. What does that mean?"

Dinred tried not to look hesitant and did her best to think of something on the spot. "It's a formal leona greeting. He must have heard it somewhere before."

The Avian turned back to the mutt. "I see. Give me a weapon." One of the soldiers handed him a small pistol, and he pointed it at the mutt's shoulder. "Dinred."

The hound emitted a loud whimper as a flash from the muzzle of the barrel planted a bullet in him. He whimpered and squealed as he grabbed his wounded shoulder. He wailed and rolled on the floor in deep pain as blood gushed out of the wound under his palm.

The Seraph handed a combat knife to Dinred. "Get your mutt to cover his loud mouth. I shall show you what to do with the blade. Mutt, quiet him."

Isabelle hesitated, but the Seraph's glare prompted her to obey.

With the mutt's mouth held shut, the Seraph continued. "Good. Now, Cat, go into a room and get a bandage."

Dinred ran to a nearby closet and searched frantically for any bindings. After a few moments, she found a large roll of white paper. She returned to the howling mutt and the soldiers. One of the soldiers handed a lighter and blade, from the mutt's medical bag, to the Seraph.

"Good," the Seraph said. "Now, wrap the wound. Put pressure

on it. Stop the bleeding." Dinred wrapped the bandages around his shoulder. The mutt whimpered but tried not to squirm. "You'll be fine, Dog. Put pressure on him, Miss." The Seraph rested his hand on her shoulder.

Dinred pushed down, feeling the blood between the bandages. She felt dismayed. Nothing was happening—the bandages weren't doing anything. "He's still bleeding!"

"Stay calm, Cat. I thought I must've hit an artery." The Seraph was heating the tip of the knife with the lighter. She didn't know how hot the lighter was, but the blade was almost changing color. "Sounds like we need to cauterize the wound."

The wounded mutt, after hearing the bird speak, and understanding the universal signs of a hot piece of metal near a bleeding wound, shook his head and tried to kick away those whom held him down. The bird pierced the bandages with the knife. Dinred could hear a searing noise as flesh and blood begin to boil.

The mutt grabbed Isabelle's arm. His breathing lost its rhythm, and he clenched her arm tightly. The Avian grabbed Dinred's hand and placed it on the hilt of the knife. "Now hook the blade on the bullet. Pull it out."

Dinred tried her best to find the bottom of the bullet. She wanted to vomit at the smell of seared flesh. She wanted nothing to do with the mutts or Avian, but the apathy in the bird's words were more putrid than the wound. She found the bullet and was perhaps entirely lucky that, when she pushed the knife's hilt down, the bullet fell out of the wound.

"Very good," the Avian said. "Almost a fine job."

The mutt was silent, and his eyes were closed. His chest still moved and his breathing seemed to be fine, but he was unresponsive to anything.

"Dog." The Avian looked at Isabelle. "He needs to breathe. Let him go. Cat, stand. Now that you've seen firsthand how *not* to pull a bullet out, I want you to come with me so that the mutt nurses will tell you how to properly do it."

"Why did you make me do this if it was all wrong?" Dinred demanded.

"I wanted to put a bullet in him." The Avian looked at one of the foxen soldiers, who was searching the body. He pulled out a book from the bag around his waist. The Seraph asked, "So who is he?"

The soldier growled, "Thing's in German. But I think this one line, 'Ich… Hei Be? Ansgar.'"

Ick house called Ansgar. "I think that means he's called Ansgar," Dinred said. She turned to the Avian, who raised an eyebrow. She shrugged and began to lie. "My husband spoke to a lot of people from Deutschland."

The Seraph held his gaze. "What is your name?"

Dinred said the first thing that came to her mind. "Mary."

The Seraph looked intrigued. He crossed his arms. "A leona with an actual, normal name? You're lying."

Isabelle ran to Dinred's side and held her arm. "It's short for Marineet."

The Seraph nodded. He grabbed his helmet, opened the door to a nearby room, and motioned for her to follow him. "Nurse, help Mary get my wound clean. Corporal Geovanni, get the medic some actual medical attention. Mary, come."

Isabelle raised her hand as if she were in grade school. "What about me? What do I do?"

The Seraph shot her a glance. "You can stay the hell out of my room."

He sat on the bed in the examining room and began removing his armor. It was easier to remove than it looked. Just a few clicks in certain places, and the armor almost fell apart. He looked quite skinny without the armor on. The only thing on his torso was the under-armor suit, which hugged his body so tightly Dinred could see curvatures of his muscles. It must have been made out of a material she had never seen before.

The Avian spoke, grabbing Dinred's attention. "Before the subject gets too stale, my name is Ziyad."

8

Kabol held his posture straight.

He had arrived in Gaul only to find out his wife wasn't among the refugees. He couldn't remember much from that night, while at the same time he felt as if he could describe everything in detail.

The last thing he remembered before passing out was Hayden shooting the Seraph with a foreign machine gun and getting an evacuation chopper's attention with a flare. Ben had been there as well. Kabol remembered what had happened before the chopper: The Seraph had almost killed him.

He thought it was entirely luck that he had managed to plunge the knife into his hand. The Seraph had to have underestimated him. Who would think a civilian knew that kind of pugilism? It wouldn't happen again. After that, he remembered waking up in one of the refugee camps along the coast of Gaul and the Netherlands.

The queen was dead, what was left of parliament wasn't among the rabble, and half of the military leaders were either deceased or captured. It had only been three days.

They had attacked everywhere along the coast from the east. Only a few commanders had managed to escape. They had put their heads together and thought of the brilliant strategy of going back. Kabol wouldn't have it any other way.

Now he found himself drafted into the ranks of a platoon of cadets. It was one of many. He didn't mind the draft; he'd have volunteered. He was willing to do anything to get back home, back to Dinred.

Kabol was standing at attention. His heels connected and his legs were straight with his knees unlocked. To his right was Hayden, who had volunteered an hour before his name had been called. To his left was Ben, who had been told, in a futile effort, to stand somewhere else. Still, he was surrounded by allied recruits. All in all, there was a new army the Avon would have to fight. It included a hundred and fifty thousand upset conscripts.

The Master Sergeant marched to the podium in front of the cadets. A black and tan canine of the German shepherd breed, he wore a dark brown trench coat with a matching shirt and pants and a bald head to top it off. His hands were folded behind his straight back, and he narrowed his eyes at the crowd in front of him.

Beside him was a row of inspectors. Each one was a lower ranked officer, each one a different breed of canine.

The Sergeant's eyes were filled with sincere anger. He got to the microphone and barked, "I asked what was left of New Albion's command to draft me some fierce killing machines straight from hell. From what I can tell, such leonas don't exist." His manner of speaking was well versed and educated, and his accent bore only a hint of German, though he was obviously mimicking Albion's accent. "Instead, they sent me a whole lot of pissants that probably don't know what a bullet tastes like. Hell, I bet the greatest achievement any of you have ever accomplished was creating a clear stream of piss. Hell, I bet none of you are man enough to step in the shower before turning it on. Let me tell you what's going to happen. I have three months to train you. This is not enough time to train you to be any kind of killing machines. If I was given every day of the week for two years, you twinkle-toed morons would still not be able to kill a dying rat on the street."

Kabol knew what the Sergeant was doing. He was insulting the recruits as a means of breaking their spirits so he could build them up from scratch. He'd been through it before, but nothing like this. He did his best not to let the anger, and the failed attempts of humor, get to him.

The Sergeant's glare burned hotter than the sun. He coughed what seemed to be a laugh and continued. "Due to the time restraints, I, Master Sergeant Kai, have been forced to up the training's difficulty. I will make you all into mighty death machines of war. I will make you look like you can stick a hand in a blender and make the inanimate object beg for mercy. I will tear you down, break you, and make you so fearsome the enemy will wish they'd have one last chance to fondle their own urine-soaked crap as if it was the last thing they'd get to love. I will make you remember your one true order is to kill them all, and you will live it like it is your birthright. Do you understand me?"

"Sir, yes, Sir," the recruits said in unison.

"That's what I thought. Inspectors." Kai nodded to the hounds next to him. The Sergeant jumped off the platform and headed directly for a leona in front of him. "Stand at ease! What's your story?"

Kabol ignored the Sergeant's rant and leaned over to Hayden. "What do you make of this?"

Hayden spoke, barely moving his lips. "Don't let him see you move. Speak under your breath. He's trying to scare us. See who breaks. Have you heard of Kai? Respectable. Humorous. He was on his way to Marshal until—" Hayden held his mouth shut as Kai looked among the ranks. Kabol could barely hear Hayden as the Sergeant and the other inspectors were still yelling at the pathetic excuses of cadets in front of them. Hayden continued, "Until an incident happened that changed him."

"Incident?"

"Friendly fire. He got his toe shot off," Hayden said under his breath. "Ever since then, he has been different. They won't allow him to see combat anymore. He beat the messenger half to death. Now he doesn't have an inside voice. At least he found his calling."

The Sergeant spent more than half an hour degrading whatever troops he came across. He'd spin the troops to face the back of the lines as soon as he was finished with the random compilations of similes and metaphors he considered insulting. Soon enough, he got to Ben.

"What the hell am I looking at?" Sergeant Kai barked. "Why in the holy hell's bells is your fur dyed yellow?"

"Sir!" Ben answered. "It's my favorite color, Sir!"

"Cadet, I will tell you now, I will not allow a subordinate to dye their fur. What is your natural color?"

"White, Sir." Ben seemed embarrassed.

"You will keep it white." The Sergeant barked louder. "If you ever dye it again, it will be with the blood of your enemies."

"But they don't bleed yellow," Ben responded with an almost ungodly amount of seriousness.

Sergeant Kai was unfazed by the answer. He opened his mouth. "Are you stupid? You might possibly be the dumbest man I have ever met, and I have met some pretty stupid people; I've been to London. What is your name?"

"Ben Inaan," he answered, disheartened.

"Ben? That's a stupid name. Fitting! What's your story? Why are you here?"

Ben saluted. "Ex-soldier, Sir! I am here to fight for queen and country."

"Do you think that matters to anyone?"

"You asked, so I think so?" Ben raised a brow.

"It was a trick question! Sucker punch!" Kai yelled at the top of his lungs. He threw his fist directly in front of him without taking a second to aim. It made contact with the yellow-furred cat's chin. Ben fell flat on his back, and Kai placed his boot on Ben's chest and continued to yell, looking among the remaining recruits. "First lesson to all of you: a good soldier does not think—he acts! When you're under a hailstorm of bullets while your best friend is lollygagging while on fire, you do not have time to think. Next time you hear me say 'sucker punch,' you duck. When I say 'fire,' you shoot. When I say 'dig your own grave,' you ask 'how deep?'"

Kabol's ears began to ring. He was shocked that the Sergeant had hit a cadet. He had the urge to defend his old friend and deck his superior in the nose. The Sergeant locked eyes with him, replacing his urge to fight with the urge to run.

"What is this?" Kai asked rhetorically. He inspected Kabol, removing his fedora and putting it behind his back. His eyes seemed to be drilling into Kabol's soul and trying to eat him. Kai's face looked almost as if he was offended. "An aristocrat? What's your story?"

Kabol anxiously stood at attention and saluted. "My name is Kabol Anton. Ex-military. I joined to help take back Albion—"

Before Kabol could finish he felt a pain under his chest as Kai planted his knee into his gut and knocked the air out of him. Kabol landed on his knees and held his gut, spitting out, "Why the bloody... hell?"

"Knee to the gut. Seeing as how you are an ex-soldier, I sincerely hope you did not expect the enemy to warn you of an attack. Now you listen here and you listen good. I hate you already. You're a lot like your country: ugly. You're no longer in a mansion sipping tea, wearing your suit made out of baby fox pelts sewn by the lower-class misfits over hills yonder. This is my domain; there is no council, no senate, no parliament, kings, queens, or piss-poor secretaries named Martha that can't understand what a latte is. There is, however, a God, but he's been gone for some time, and a devil dog like me smiles like the cat who just ate the canary. And by the time I am done with all of you, you will wish I'd abandoned your hide long enough to get the chance to eat slop from a pigpen like the swine you are." The Sergeant grabbed Kabol by the hair and pulled him up to eye level. "Do you understand me?"

"Yes, Sir." Kabol muttered. His body begged him to lie back on the ground, but he knew the Sergeant would most likely hit him even harder. Kai pulled Kabol's chin up before continuing to straighten out the troops.

⟫⟩ ⟨⟪

Kabol could barely stand. He had been awake and active for fifty-six hours, with food rationed, water given only to the ones who looked like they were dying, and no sleep for anyone. It was nothing but exercise. His fingers ached in the cold mud as he counted his pushups. *Thirty, thirty-one, thirty-two.* Every repetition was harder and slower than the last. It didn't help that Hayden was just finishing his fiftieth. The Sergeant didn't let anyone slow down. Kabol had learned this the hard way when he and Hayden were caught trying to pace themselves and save energy.

Kai kept treading back and forth in front of the two, seeming almost happy that Hayden had finished. Kabol's elbows locked in the freezing air. Kai placed his muddy boot on Kabol's bare back. The cold made his spine shiver, and his elbows shook then froze, refusing to bend. Kai pushed down harder until Kabol's arms couldn't hold him anymore and his chest was smothered against the mud.

His fur was stained in the cold, slick mud as Kai continued to push him down. "Now to recap, you will give it your all one hundred percent of the time. You will not conserve energy; you will not stop and let your fellow soldiers down just because you don't feel good. Now get back to sparring."

Kabol's arms felt like they wanted to drop off. He was hardly able to use them to lift himself up. He stood in a position of combat. The rules were grapple only. Most of the other cadets were sloppy and completely untrained. It was controlled savagery.

Kabol got back into a regular combat stance. Hayden, who had received the same training, did the same. Their bare feet in the mud, Kabol remembered what he had learned: *one leg out, keep them separate; chin low, don't let them hit it; knuckles in view, guard, kill.*

Hayden made the first move, forgetting his position and simply tackling Kabol with his full force. Kabol managed to keep his balance, but felt Hayden sneak a knee between his separated legs.

Kabol braced for a painful impact, holding tightly onto the mutt. Hayden used his mud-soaked pelt to his advantage and slipped from Kabol's grasp, giving way to moving his arm between the legs as well. Kabol felt Hayden's shoulder plunge into his gut and was lifted into the air. Hayden twisted his torso, allowing for enough torque to toss Kabol to the ground.

The amount of energy Hayden put into his attack made him lose his footing while Kabol landed flat on his back. He ignored the pain, seeing Hayden on the ground as well. They both scurried to their feet.

Kabol was up first. He went to grab the mutt. As he did, Hayden got a grip on him as well. They pushed against each other. Hayden was stronger, and Kabol knew it. Kabol trusted the ground under his left foot, moving his head under Hayden's arms and wrapping his right leg around Hayden's own.

Hayden made the unfortunate mistake of keeping his legs close together, allowing Kabol to easily turn his own body weight in a desperate fight against gravity. In less than a second, the mutt was on the ground.

Kabol felt the ground under his feet give way and he, too, slipped in the mud. He tried to get back up, but the mutt was already there. Hayden tackled Kabol hard enough that whatever energy the cat could muster left him entirely. Hayden seemed to be in no better condition.

They lay on their backs in silence for several seconds before Kabol burst out laughing about how much fun this was. Hayden soon followed. They both stopped when they heard Sergeant Kai's boots slop through the mud.

Kai held a whistle to his mouth and blew loudly enough that every cadet held still. Kai's attention wasn't focused on Hayden or Kabol, but on another person in the center of the recruits. "Inaan!" Kai's voice broke through the crisp air, his breath turning to fog.

Kabol saw Ben sitting, holding an officer in a choke hold. He released the hound when he saw Kai marching toward him, stood at attention, and saluted with his fingers on his nonexistent eyebrows.

"There's something on your palm." Kai pointed. Ben looked at it only for a moment. It was enough time for Kai to jump toward the leona and slap his face. Kai's voice was filled with sincere hate. "What are you doing? You must be all kinds of inbred to believe that was a smart thing to do. Now that I have everyone's attention, you can all report to the showers. You have two minutes each to wash up and then report immediately to the mess hall. There you will be assigned to the barracks." Kai blew his whistle and grabbed Ben. "Not you, Maggot. You're staying here with me."

Kabol felt Hayden slap his back. "Regrettable words. Believe me."

Kabol sat next to Hayden on a bench. He had finally received a shirt after hours of exposure to the cool air, and his pants had been replaced as well. Hayden was looking off into the distance, holding his almost empty food tray. There was a large pit full of mud lit by floodlights. Kabol saw two people inside the pit. One was running from one side to the other, and the other person was yelling—he was audible but unintelligible.

"This is unbelievable," Hayden said. "I've never seen a man yell at the top of his lungs for an hour straight."

"I wonder how Ben feels," Kabol said. The moment he sat down, his body instinctively tried to sleep.

"He's probably having the time of his life."

Hayden's words woke Kabol up, with the help of a jerk he provided himself. The cool air made this moment feel even more like a dream. He had to be occupied or else he would succumb to his exhaustion. "What barracks number you going to live in?"

"Thirteen. Baker Company," Hayden said with a mouthful of bread.

"Same." He was too tired to appreciate his luck. "I hope we get to share the same bunk bed."

"I call top bunk," Hayden said quickly and smiled.

Kabol held in a weak laugh. Perhaps it was the exhaustion in his body or the sore muscles in his arms and legs, but with Hayden and Ben by his side, he just might make it through this war.

9

Dinred's arms ached. She was slouched in her chair next to the bed where Ziyad, the injured Avian, rested. For the past several days, she'd been playing doctor for the nurses, who eyed her with distaste.

On the other side of the room, Isabelle moved some chairs next to each other to lie down, facing the wall with the TV. Ziyad said she was allowed to stay in the room, so long as she did not breathe in his general direction.

In the center of the room was the Avon, in his hospital bed, with wires and tubes against his skin and a blanket on his waist. Ziyad was not too fond of hearing how he had to stay bedridden until his infection healed, even if it was minor and the medicine would accelerate the healing process by weeks.

He'd made the most of it though. The idiot box hanging from the wall helped pass the time. On the screen was a cartoon of feral rabbits exploring space. Dinred had never heard of the show, but it seemed to be filled with slapstick humor, with no clear plot, as they traveled from planet to planet getting into surreal situations. The volume was low, making it easy for Dinred to become disinterested. She didn't understand why cartoons were on past midnight.

Ziyad laughed. "Cartoons not your thing?" he muttered.

"I grew out of them." Dinred answered as if it was instinct.

"Is a grown man not allowed to have fun? That rabbit just kicked a penguin into a volcano. Where will you ever see that again?"

Dinred didn't respond. This is the first time he had bothered to talk when he wasn't giving orders. She had no motivation to talk to him. She was being held against her will. She crossed her arms. "I can imagine better things."

"Try me."

"What if the penguin was wearing a tuxedo? And talked by playing a trumpet?" Dinred rolled her eyes, upset at herself for thinking so simply.

"Hmm… All right." He smirked. "That's only an improvement on something that already exists."

"That a bad thing? I used imagination, didn't I?"

Ziyad nodded, with a chuckle of agreement, and silently watched the television, pulling his helmet closer to him.

Dinred got a good look at the helmet. The emotionless, beaked masked looked devilish and ugly. She'd never want it in a collection, let alone on her head. The gray feathers on the back of the helmet drooped off the bed. Dinred was unable to tell if those feathers were fabricated or organic.

The Avian noticed her prying eyes. He held the helmet up. "It's a marvelous thing, the feeling behind this mask." He held it toward her. "Try it on."

"Oh, no, I couldn't." Dinred shook her head. "It wouldn't fit very well."

"I insist. You'll know what I'm talking about."

Dinred was hesitant at first but, deciding to play his game, she took the helmet and wondered how to put it on.

The first thing she noticed was the weight. It didn't look as heavy as it felt but, then again, it was made of bulletproof metal. She got a feel for the feathers on the back noticing that, behind the feathers, straps helped hold the helmet in place. The quills themselves weren't made of actual feathers, but rather an artificial material that she couldn't put her finger on. She thought it was a mixture of thread and plastic. Then she noticed how long the beak and helmet were. It looked like it would barely fit her.

Ziyad told her to swing the feathers around her shoulders and place it on her head from the back. She did as instructed, slowly covering her face with the metal mask. Her ears twitched as they poked through the feathers. She felt the weight of the helmet on her neck. The tip of the upper beak of the mask hung just outside of her snout. The helmet was more than a mask. Spectacles behind the slits allowed little visibility.

She could feel what Ziyad was referring to though. She felt like she was no longer Dinred or Mary, but rather someone more fearsome and threatening. She felt like someone else entirely. She got the sensation she could do anything. A feeling of superiority. It made her smile.

She touched the side of the helmet and clicked a button under the feathers. A quick laser scanned her face, and the spectacles snapped out of position and toward her eyes. Her vision was unobstructed, and she could see as if she didn't even have the helmet on.

She pressed the button again. The room turned a red hue, and she could see the warmth of people through walls and sound waves from a nurse's footsteps outside the door. The nurse's body was shapeless, like a cloud. The images dissipated as the nurse went farther down the hall, until she disappeared all altogether.

Dinred pressed the button again, and the room turned blue. She was unable to see the body heat through the walls. She looked at the feathered folk beside her. Instead of smoky blob, it was a more accurate representation of what Ziyad's body looked like.

One more click and the room turned into a green hue and light was magnified a thousandfold. She instinctively closed her eyes and turned her head away from the brightness, pressing the button again.

This time her vision was normal.

Ziyad clicked a button on the other side of her head. The spectacles retreated into their previous position. She removed the helmet. She handed it back and rubbed her neck. "My neck has never been this sore."

Ziyad reached over the bed and pulled out the bottom half of the helmet. He pointed to the rim on the base of the skull. A metal loop had a cushioning gel. "This, you see, supports the neck. It's designed for strength and comfort when turning the neck. The armor is heavy. Worth it, though. I essentially cannot be hurt in any area this helmet covers. The muscle suit does the same, to a lesser extent. It cannot stop AP bullets."

"AP?

"Armor piercing." He rubbed his shoulder. "Stupid dog came prepared."

"What are you going to do with him?" Dinred asked, taking her chance to get to know more about the occupiers. "Why do you despise them?"

The Avon looked at her sternly. "Atasha, Mary."

"What does that even mean?"

"Atasha. I'm sorry, force of habit; I didn't expect you to know what that meant. It's Avian. There is no one word in your language for it. It's an intense version of 'none of your business.'"

She couldn't think of a single word for that, though a crude swear followed by "off" would suffice.

Ziyad could see she was still unsatisfied. He looked at the sleeping Isabelle. "They are untouchable. Not as barbaric as the wolfen, though they lack any form of self-respect; otherwise they'd not have let leonas rule their land. For more than a century, they have been treated as second-class citizens in their own inherited nation. Despicable. At least the wolfen understand this, even if they are brutal in nature."

Dinred couldn't understand any part of his argument. She'd heard bureaucrats and politicians gripe about how mutts were constantly treated as a lower class, but without any sense of alarm, especially since her majesty, the queen, was a mutt. Though the queen was just there in case the king died and the heir was too young. And these were Old World problems since parliament would take over if the royals were killed.

A nurse entered the room and sorted some pills and capsules. Ziyad refused to acknowledge her, focusing his attention on the screen above. She placed a few bottles of medicine on a table next to him. "You're being released from the hospital. Take these three times a day for a week, and you'll be fine."

"Thank you." He spoke to her in a pleasant tone for the first time, whether he meant to or not. He turned to Dinred. "Mary, will you help me back into the armor? It'll be easier to walk out of here in it than to carry it."

Dinred agreed; it'd make it easier for him to get out of her sight.

It took a few moments, but Ziyad showed her the strips and magnetically sealed hinges that she needed to activate. For a person to do the task on their own would take three or four minutes, but with Dinred's help, it took less than one.

He put his lower chin armor on, but left the mask off. He didn't want to scare anyone on the way out. They both walked to the door of the room, and he turned to her. "You're good company. You know that?"

"OK. Thanks."

Ziyad couldn't help but smirk. Not the kind he gave before, but one that showed a hint of approval.

"Ziyad!" A red foxen in southern European armor called out to him from down the hall. His left arm was completely hidden in a brown leather cape that was draped over his shoulder and stopped past his thighs. He raised his other hand. "Hey! Heck of a way to start the invasion. You get stabbed with your own knife, you go to the hospital to fix it, and then you get shot with your own gun."

Ziyad shook his head. "I wasn't shot with my own gun."

"Oh? That's what I've been telling everyone." The foxen bared his teeth in a wide smile. "Come on, I'll buy you a drink."

Ziyad sighed and turned to Dinred. "Mary, what is your last name? You'll be better company than this joker."

"I'll tell you the next time I see you."

Ziyad continued to stare. "I don't plan on being hospitalized again any time soon."

"Shame." Dinred spoke honestly.

Ziyad laughed. "Goodbye, Mary. I do hope I see you again." Dinred headed back into the room, refusing to look at the Avian walking away. The first thing she did was turn off the TV screen, plunging the already quiet room into an eerie silence.

Isabelle turned her head. "Is he gone?"

Dinred nodded, surprised at the mutt suddenly being alive again.

Isabelle stood up quickly and closed the door. Her tail wagged anxiously, her eyes darted around the room, and her ears were high in alarm. "There's something important I need to tell you."

10

A loud crash woke Kabol up.

"Rise and shine, maggots," Kai barked as he burst through the doors of the barracks, snapping the hinges off the doors. The room was illuminated as Kai chanted, "Lights! Lights! Lights!"

Kabol jumped from the bottom bunk as the roof beams lit up. Hayden landed beside him. They both rushed to the foot of the bed.

He impulsively got dressed in his fatigues. Sergeant Kai, along with the top brass of the regime, didn't allow any New Albion soldiers to wear uniforms from Deutschland and insisted they wear New Albion's Britannian armor.

It was a tinted olive green cloth with six metal buttons. On his shoulders leather flaps were buttoned close to the neck. They were meant to bear an insignia that he didn't have. The sleeves went down to his wrists. This was something he was used to, save for the lack of cuff links. Two pockets, one per peck on the chest, and two more pockets, one on each thigh.

The only things that were missing, combat-wise, were his rifle, harness, belt, armor plates, and matching helmet. New Albion had so few uniforms after the evacuation that they are now paying Deutschland factories to produce them.

The officers wore their Deutschland gear, in contrast to Kai. The officers had gray fatigues of similar design but with fewer buttons and more pockets, and they wore their rank on their sleeves over their biceps. Kabol hadn't seen them wear any armor over their uniforms, but he had seen them wear it in field exercises. It was a light metal breastplate over a cuirass. There was no shoulder armor save for the hard leather holding up the body armor. However, separate metal plates protected the thighs and shins. All the metal plates were protected in black waterproof sleeves that kept the armor from rusting.

Kai had a more extravagant uniform that he had kept from his years at a higher rank. The brown coat's back split at his tail, and two flaps covered the backs of his legs. Behind the trench coat was a suit and tie. Nothing about his uniform implied that he was going to see battle, but its design gave off an aura of superiority and omnipotence.

It took less than a minute for Kabol to change from a white shirt and sweatpants to full on Albion fatigues. He'd had enough practice in the week he'd been there.

Two long rows of leonas faced each other as Kai paced down the barracks, tail swaying, inspecting all of the troops for anything out of the order in their uniforms. Satisfied, he called, "All of you report to the training grounds. Double time."

All of the cadets formed the ranks they had learned in the preceding nights. Kai followed, running backward and shouting a marching tune in Germanic. The other officers joined in the tune and called in cadence.

Kabol tried to understand what they were saying, but he was concentrating on not running into the person in front of him, and the sun peeking over the horizon kept getting in his eyes. His lungs were also beginning to hurt. With all these distractions he couldn't translate the words in his head. What he could understand was that they were talking about a flower or a girl named Erika.

The officers herded the recruits to the muddy pit where they'd wrestled in previous nights. Chills crawled up Kabol's spine just thinking of the cold mud.

Kai ordered the group to join another cadet and prepare to stretch and run laps at the same pace. The square was at least fifty meters long and twenty meters wide. Kai was picky; if someone wasn't running, everyone would be forced to run faster and longer. This time, however, once everyone had completed a single lap, Kai ordered everyone to fall in ranks.

The troops lined up in five rows consisting of ten people each. The officers started handing out rectangular pieces of cardboard a little bigger than their hands. When it got to Kabol, he examined it.

It was a candy bar. The chocolate was so rich that Kabol could smell the sweet flavor through the packaging. The wrapping was white with a black symbol in the center. It was a silhouette of a feral wolf's head facing left and diagonally. Its jaws were parted and between them was a single orange kolovrat, an eight-armed cross that swerved to the right, a tribute to the Avon, representing the sun, that had been deemed pagan.

"What are these for?" Kabol unraveled the paper around the chocolate bar with the rest of the unit. The bar had such fine craftsmanship the symbol was even imprinted into it by hand.

"Celebration," Hayden answered, with his bar still wrapped, watching Sergeant Kai pace between the ranks in front of him.

"Ladies, what a glorious, heartfelt day it is for the Fatherland." He pulled out a parchment he'd hidden behind his back and held it high in the air, "After news of Albion's occupation, our Roman friends had something to say." After a few seconds, he brought it to eye level. "Dear Deutschland, that's us, we, the sissies, the cowardly Romans—that's absolutely what it says—have decided, in order to reclaim our lands, to hereby annex both banks of the Rhineland.

"Our government…" The Sergeant cleared his throat, crumbling the piece of paper. "My government, the magnificent regime, took this not only as an insult, but an act of war." He tossed the paper aside. Kai did not sound fearful or sorrowful, but almost enthusiastic. "For those who lack geography skills, the Rhineland is where we are now. And the front lines are one hundred and fifty and a half kilometers in that direction, southwest or something. The Avon nations have finished their Swethin campaign and have allied themselves to the Roman cause. And as I speak, the French of Gaul are being invaded by them as well, cutting off much support from our allies."

The faces of the men were not as impassive as Kai's. War with the Avon was one thing, but war with the limitless numbers, impressive technology, and immortal tactics of Rome was a death sentence.

Hayden looked furious, molding his hands into fists as he remembered his decade-old enemies. This also tugged Kabol's heartstrings.

Kai added, "While we are between the pincers of hell, we are not alone. The wolfen are revolting in Greece. And Carthage and Cairo had their sovereign nations declare war on the Avon, for the sacking of New Albion, as well as the Romans due to their alliance. So you won't have too much to worry about it for however long it takes for the foxen to completely annihilate them."

Annihilate them? Kabol thought. Kai said it almost as if it were just another day. Kabol bit into the chocolate bar to help calm his nerves. He only got one bite before Kai snatched it from him and walked away.

"So eat this in celebration, anticipation, and give birth to a stubborn relation to our glorious nation. Amen." Kai took a bite out of Kabol's bar. "Now move out to the obstacle course. Double time, before it rains."

Before Kabol could get upset, Hayden handed him half of his candy bar. Kabol wanted to reject it; he was sure the Sergeant would be displeased if he enjoyed a treat. But Kabol gave up that thought when he remembered it was rude to reject a gift.

Hayden patted Kabol's shoulder and murmured. "I got your back."

<hr>

Kabol jumped and grabbed one of the monkey bars overhead. It was covered in layers of wet dirt, making him lose his grip and slip immediately. He landed in a puddle, and his feet slid under him. He found himself on his rump, being yelled at by the hound, Kai.

"Get up! Get up now!" Kai called. By this time, Kabol didn't care about the words coming out of his mouth, and he put effort into zoning them out. Kabol stood up and ran back in line for the monkey bars. Kai grabbed him by the tail and pointed toward the start of the course. "Do it again! And do it right!"

Kabol obeyed. How could he not? He'd seen what Kai had done to Ben, what Kai did to people who did not follow his orders. It was in his best interests to listen to what he was told or else he would suffer a case of "Intense Training."

Kabol got to the first obstacle, a simple wooden waist-high wall. After climbing over it, he was required to ascend a much higher wall, almost ten meters high, with a knotless rope. Kabol got halfway to the top before his hands began to slip and his arms started to burn.

It was too much, and Kabol fell. There was no one in line behind him. He was going to be the last one on the obstacle course. Kabol grabbed the rope to try again.

"Get up there!" Kai yelled, making Kabol jump.

"It's too slippery," Kabol rasped. He felt his tail being tugged hard, pulling him off the wall. He landed on his back in a puddle of mud.

Kai loomed over him. "Pathetic. Do you even have the strength to stop me from drowning you in the mud? Get up!" He grabbed Kabol and pulled him to his feet. Kai stood at least a foot above the cat. His breath turned to fog every time he exhaled. "Do you want me to hit you, Maggot? Go to the next obstacle!"

Kabol obeyed. He dashed, as fast as he could, to the next one. It was a single bar that hung two meters off the ground. Ten chin-ups, dead-arm hang for a second between each. It was harder than it sounded. After the third pull up, adrenaline bit into his mind. He remembered what Seraphs could do to civilians. The thought of Dinred and Isabelle waiting for him to come home boosted his flagging motivation. He felt like his body was dying. He knew this was its way of telling him it was burning out.

He didn't allow himself to give up, but by the tenth pull up his muscles refused to work. Through sheer will, he pulled his chin above the bar. He let go and landed on his feet. His arms were bent, even when limp.

Kai kept his mouth shut as Kabol ran to the next set, wires that had been strung half a foot above the ground, making square blocks of free space, in a long row. Kabol ran fast enough to clear it in seconds. Kai still yelled at him to do it faster.

Finally, the monkey bars. A few cadets were still slipping off them. Officers had started to pull a few of the recruits off to the side and make them hold a push-up position for a full minute. The lines were short and, in what felt like no time, it was Kabol's turn. He wished this weren't so. The more time he spent not using his arms, the better they felt, and they might become more productive.

He grabbed the first bar. It was colder than he remembered, and just as slippery. Blood rushed to his hands. With every movement, he seemed to be calculating a dozen things at once: speed, too fast and he would slip; momentum, too slow and he would fall; motor skills, one finger out of place and he would start over; arms, if one lost strength, he would begin again.

He trusted his instincts and body to calculate all this. All he could think about now was what he was about to fight for, who he was fighting against. He was thinking about what he needed to prevent and what he was going to do. What pain he would endure.

He didn't even realize he had made it to the other side. He instinctively ran to the next setting. Tire swings hung above a pit. Child's play. Then he crawled under barbed wire. This was followed by carrying two ammo crates full of rocks and dirt down a five-meter patch of mud and back three times.

By now, he was lightheaded, unable to recall how it had felt to complete each objective. His body felt numb, and alive. He only concentrated on breathing, running, and staying on his feet.

Finally, the last stretch; Kabol had to run at full sprint and climb over a small dirt cliff. He thought about the fight with the Seraph, the aura of fear and death. He ran past a few cadets on his way to the wall. He dug his feet in, feeling mud crawl between his fur and socks. He crawled as fast as he could until he got to the top. The first thing he did was drop to the ground and lie in physical agony. His skin and fur itched against soft blades of grass, and his nostrils were filled with the scent of dew. His heart was pounding hard in his chest. He closed his eyes and breathed while he could. He tried his best to regulate the flow of air into his lungs.

Kabol stood up and tried walking. Lying stagnant on the ground after a hard workout would have unwanted consequences. After a few steps, his legs gave out.

"Get up," Kai barked behind him. The Sergeant lifted him off the ground by his arms. "Are you alive?"

Kabol was silent save for his panting.

"I'm impressed." Kai dropped Kabol back on the ground and pushed him on his back with his foot, making the rain spit on the cat's face. Kai clapped his hands slowly. "Not bad, was almost even good. Vargas!"

Hayden ran to Kai's side and saluted with his fingers on his brow and his throat bare.

"Corporal Vargas, Private Anton here will be your battle buddy. When he screws up, you screw up. Likewise, so on, so forth, and so be it. Do you accept this man as your lawfully wedded battle buddy?"

"Sir, I do, Sir!"

"Glad to hear it, Cadet. Anton…" Kai's voice turned more powerful. "Get up!"

Hayden helped Kabol to his feet. Kabol's muscles ached and all he wanted to do now was sleep. He could barely stand, but right now he feared Kai more than death. Hard to conceive that Kai wasn't throbbing with joy at the pitiful sight Kabol made.

"Vargas, make sure he doesn't die on you. Anton…" Kai smirked and pointed to the start of the obstacle course. "Do it again."

Kabol obeyed.

11

Ziyad shifted his body into a more comfortable position.

The sounds of propellers were muffled in the metal carriage. He was staring at a screen with his helmet off. It was a live feed of the pilot of the Raptor T-VTOL, a helicopter with twin jet-propelled wings that could land and take off vertically. He was on a troop transport, unlike the Raptor A-VTOL choppers made for assaults that bore cannons and heavy tank-killing machine guns.

He was proud of his race for being the first and only to develop the kind of technology that could turn a helicopter into a jet fighter in a matter of mere moments, all of it able to be controlled by a single pilot.

"We're arriving on drop point," the pilot called. "Estimated time of arrival: three minutes. Get your gear ready and make sure you don't hit your head jumping out because we're going in a little hot."

Ziyad swiped a finger across the screen in front of him, minimizing the live feed on a tab. Another screen opened, showing a map and briefing. Ziyad swiped it again. A bunch of civilian loyalists were fighting back against an occupation in a city surrounded by enemy forces far more advanced than they were. The forces were so small the *Basilicus* didn't have time for it.

It was such a small problem, the Father thought they would only need one Seraph suitable for the job and that the nine new recruits should jump in too. *This skirmish is so small that it's just another day of training.* Ziyad didn't need information; he knew his orders, his one true mission.

Ziyad put on the helmet and turned it on with the switch on the side. The spectacles found his eyes, and he could see the briefing and live feed, on his Heads-Up Display, in the upper corner of his vision. He held out his hand in front of his eyes, waiting a second for the software to recognize him; then he swiped a few more times to make sure his actions had been registered.

A loud beep almost made him jump. He had an incoming call. He clicked on a green button on the screen to accept it, lowering the briefing's volume, creating another live feed of Cypher.

"Ziyad! Buddy!" The fox put on a happy face.

Ziyad clicked the red button in the bottom right corner, closing the call and video. He crossed his arms, listening to the audio of the mission. He heard another beep, and he answered the call with a sigh.

Cypher didn't look too impressed either. "What's the big deal?"

"I'm sorry." Ziyad held his voice at such a professional, emotionless level that even the most automated of computer systems would be proud of him. "This channel is for military use only. Please hang up to try again, never."

A huff of air left the fox's nostrils. "Don't talk like that. You're sounding a lot like your ex-wife. How come I never see her anymore?"

Ziyad clenched his fists. *You know well what happened to her!*

"Oh, that's right! She… Right, right." Cypher tried to play it off as an innocent mistake, which only made Ziyad furious. "Let's change the subject. The reason I called is because I wanted to let you know I won't be on the *Basilicus* for a while."

"My prayers have been answered," Ziyad muttered. It was not like they enjoyed seeing each other that much anyway.

"That makes two of us. Anyway, they're sending me on a wild goose chase. Some of our historians insist the royal bloodline isn't fully severed. So, with them thinking they may have another child, they sent me to hunt down a possible heir to the mighty throne of this disoriented country. I'm a little excited."

This piqued Ziyad's interest. He was happy that Cypher couldn't see behind the mask; he didn't want to give him the satisfaction of a reaction. The new Godsend, Maria, had assassinated the royals with a bomb large enough to obliterate the palace. The whole place had collapsed on itself. No one, not even Maria, could have made it out alive.

"Why would they send an honor guard to go snooping about?" Ziyad pointed out.

"I volunteered," Cypher said almost proudly. "It's extremely rare that a foxen becomes a Godsend. It hasn't been done for more than a century. I get to be a part of proving history. Call it a personal honor, if you will."

"How about I call it a waste of time? So if that's all, I think I'll be going now. I have to fight a skirmish in a couple of minutes."

"What? No kiss good—?"

Ziyad cut the transmission and hummed in relief. Cypher always managed to find a way under his skin. Ever since the academy back on the *Basilicus*, he'd been faster, smarter and, in some cases, more athletic. If it weren't for that mangy fox making him look bad, he may already have become a Godsend.

Ziyad rested his head and tried to relax. One day, he'd surpass his rival. Cypher didn't fool him. He was in it for the prestige, so he could outrank the bird. But it wouldn't matter if Cypher found the heir if Ziyad could bring back a hundred claimed wolfen. Assuming he could find any here.

He touched his armored shoulder to make sure his knife was

sharp enough to remove ears and trembled in anger. That damnable red-eyed cat had it. Ziyad would curse him if he knew his name, but he would always remember the face. Gray fur, brown hair, a white triangle of fur from chin to brow. Ziyad clenched his scarred hand in hopes that one day he would squeeze the life out of him with whatever dexterity he had left in it. He prayed he would meet him again. The only word going through his mind was "hate." He had put so much effort into thinking about how much he hated someone he'd known for mere moments.

Ziyad promised himself that one day he would have Red Eye's ears.

A loud beep made him snap back into reality. The briefing was over, and the pilot pressed a few buttons showing all the occupants on the same screen. Nine foxen in small square boxes spread across the screen. Their armor was quite similar to Ziyad's, but their helmets and boots were different.

The helmet's beak was a snout, customized specifically to each foxen. The ears were covered by oval pointed plates. They hadn't earned any feathers, but if and when they did, they would be just behind the ears and oval protectors. For now, the backs of their heads were exposed and their hair was a poor substitute.

Their plantigrade feet were far different than his talon-toed boots. Their tails were exposed, for the most part, but they lived their entire lives avoiding getting them shot off so they must be good at protecting them by now.

Each of the foxes was also distinguished by colors and designs, parallel to the purpose of Ziyad's yellow stripe.

None of them truly mattered to Ziyad; they weren't truly Seraph material. One of the three women, Alexis— the one with two vertical purple stripes down her face—had burned down a bunch of houses in the name of Avon. It was laughable that she would think she deserved his title.

Ziyad didn't even want to think about the male who had wept in the sanctuary, Renatus, the one with white ovals around the eyes and the white line that went straight down his forehead and split into two on the sides of his muzzle. He understood that his sister had died, but for a worthy cause. He should be proud. The sanctuary was a place of solace, hope. Someone striving for the title of Seraph shouldn't be crying in sorrow in the holiest of places.

Faith came first.

"All right." Ziyad caught everyone's attention. "In less than two minutes we will be over a drop zone. We will be under direct fire from small arms, nothing too serious. The VTOL will hover over the ground at an altitude of about six meters. Trust your suit to take the damage from the fall. Be sure to land on your feet; you already give me enough to laugh at.

"The objective is to hunt down and kill or capture all personnel that are not Avon; wolfen are top priority. If they bear guns, they are dead men. If not, they are to be captured to be brought to the *Basilicus*. If there are any questions, ask now."

Renatus was the first to speak. "What happens to them there?"

"Atash—none of your concern. Are there any other questions?"

Alexis spoke up next. "Why aren't we carrying firearms?"

Ziyad turned his gaze to her camera feed. His dumbfounded face was hidden behind the mask. *Does she know so little about becoming a Seraph?* For a moment he didn't want to answer. "The role of the Seraph is to hunt stealthily and brutally. Strike fear into the hearts of all grunts. The true purpose of Seraphs is to have utter faith in Avon's designs in the line of duty. We need no gun, only faith backed by blades."

Alexis chuckled a bit. "Gee, Commander, keep going. Preach! Why don't you tell us your maiden name while you're at it?"

"Insolence," Ziyad murmured as a few of the cadets laughed. *You also cannot claim kills from gunfire.* But Ziyad refused to tell them this. *They'll find out. They'll get what's coming to them too.* He looked at the clock. Estimated time of arrival: thirty seconds. The VTOL switched from jet mode into a hovering position as it found a place to land. "If you're all done we have a fight to win. ETA is—" Several snapping and crackling sounds were heard as bullets scratched off the armor of the VTOL's wings, and the pilot forced the hatch in front of him to open. "Right the hell now! Go!"

Ziyad jumped from the aircraft. Bullets whizzed past him, striking and even piercing the hull of the aircraft. His feet hit the ground with a thud. He could feel the impact. It would have mortally wounded a normal man, but the armor was conditioned with this purpose in mind. The entire hovercraft was debussed in a single second.

Ziyad scrambled for cover. A four-barreled anti-aircraft turret hid in a building down the street, posing as an anti-infantry turret. The shells fired out of that weapon pierced the hull and exploded with a pressure-activated trigger.

The aircraft lit ablaze and spun out of control. If it had been a normal chopper, all occupants would have been killed by the first volley.

Ziyad ran as fast as he could to the closest thing he could consider cover: a nearby house made of bricks.

A single wall wouldn't stop those shells. He hid deep inside the house until he was sure the shells would explode in another room and that he wasn't targeted. Either would do nicely. He took a moment to take in his surroundings.

The intel had been wrong. The term "light resistance" didn't include a turret that could pierce through armored vehicles. The turret was down the street about thirty meters. It was stationed at a turn that must've led to an open plaza, perhaps to take convoys or infantry by surprise.

The street was a kill box, and it was entirely bad luck that, out of all the roads the pilot could have flown over, he had picked this one.

Ziyad was in what appeared to be the kitchen of a café. The turret was still firing, even after the pilot's "Mayday" ceased in an inferno on top of a connected building. A glance out a shattered window revealed shells being shot, at street level, at a house across the street.

"Status report!" Ziyad chatted on the radio. "Is there anyone still alive?"

"This is Alexis." Ziyad was able to hear the feminine voice of the foxen over a loud chain of thuds and crumbling brick. "I'm pinned down across the street! There are shells tearing apart the room next to me!"

"Find cover! Everyone fan out. Watch for any more turrets!" Ziyad ordered as he set his vision to the "omnipotent" setting. The fragments the shells spewed out should be blocked by the armor. The force, equivalent to a grenade, should also be nullified by the armor's conditioned effects. But nothing could protect him from a direct hit. If a fragmentation bullet was stuck inside the armor with him inside it…

He ignored the thought. The omnipotent setting's orange glow shimmered on the ground like soft waves of water in a still pond. Someone was coming. He turned to his left to see five leonas, as amber three-dimensional figures, just a few rooms away. The images of their bodies weren't entirely accurate, and their faces were going to look a bit like sludge even up close. But the vision had already scanned their weaponry telling him, on his HUD, he will be safe from their primary weapons.

They may have come from the turret to flush him out. They must've never seen a Seraph before, or else they'd be trembling in their boots. But Ziyad wasn't going to underestimate a leona again. He had learned his lesson.

The buildings were connected to each other. Ziyad hid by a door until they were just a few rooms away. His forearms twitched hard enough that the suit registered the motion and the blades jutted out. Long, thin swords, double edged, diamond tipped like an estoc. The only thing more durable was tank armor.

He waited, poised to strike. *The first one through that door is going to be missing a head.* He was almost spot on with that assumption. The door burst open. Ziyad responded with a lunge and a swipe.

One. He counted his first kill.

The closest soldier wasn't fast enough to dodge his next swipe. Ziyad kept with his current of motion and swiped again. The blade grazed the cat's armor. One swipe was never enough to take someone down unless it was deep or in a vital area, but a good stab did the job easily. He jabbed with his other hand.

Two.

The other soldiers weren't close to the door. They fanned out, guns pointed toward the Seraph. Ziyad's blade was stuck inside the wailing cat. The gears in the arms allowed him to easily lift the body, and he charged toward another soldier, who was hesitant to shoot his ally.

Ziyad heard a sickening wail, accompanied by gasps for air, as he hit a wall.

Three.

"Take the shot!" a surviving soldier called.

Ziyad's eardrums were riddled with the pinging of small bullets bouncing off his helmet. He turned his head and pulled off two bodies from his blade with a sweep of his other hand. He charged at the remaining bodies.

The fourth soldier ran out of ammo from his submachine gun and pulled out a large pistol; its caliber might have been high enough to dent his armor. Ziyad registered this in time to dive and swing his arm, satisfied when he saw a severed hand on the ground. He swung a leg and placed his talons on the leona's chest. With a hard squeeze and help from the suit's motors, he shoved the cat into the ground. The cat's armor cracked.

Ziyad heard a satisfying series of snaps and yells. *Four.*

The fifth one was out of ammunition. He abandoned it and pulled out a knife. The under-suit was designed to withstand pressure and impact but offered little in the way of repelling something sharp.

The soldier placed the knife in a reverse grip, with the blade pointed down, and attempted to retreat without turning tail. Ziyad lunged and swiped, careful not to lose his balance. The cat jumped back, not wasting time reaching for his sidearm, which bore a smaller caliber to the others.

Ziyad kept up the charged jabs and swipes, not giving his enemy a chance to take in his surroundings but not putting himself at the same disadvantage. It worked perfectly according to Ziyad's plan. His enemy tripped over a fallen statuette.

Ziyad jumped, lowering his heavy boot into the cat's body, making him wail in pain. He lifted his leg and decapitated his adversary with a kick.

Five.

In less than a minute, Ziyad accomplished more than a whole Avon squad could in thrice the time. He put away his blades and turned off the omnipotent vision. Adrenaline pumped through his veins. It was silent save for the grinding of gears. It wasn't his suit.

The wall facing the street in front of his building was completely missing. He turned to see he was in clear view of the turret turning its sights on him.

12

Ziyad ran as fast as he could to another room.

The area behind him lit up, its air distorted and shattered by the shrapnel that bounced off his armor. The explosions followed Ziyad as he ran through the building. He ran up a staircase, relieved that the gunfire didn't follow him. The turret must've been shooting blindly.

Downstairs was completely destroyed. The bannisters of the stairs were gone for the most part, the floor was littered with metallic shreds, and something Ziyad presumed used to resemble a couch was spread across the ground.

He could feel his shoulder and arms bleed. Searing pain seeped into his muscles every time he moved. Some of the shrapnel must have found its way between the armor and under-suit and burrowed its way into his skin due to Ziyad's constant movement.

The sound of explosive shells stopped. Ziyad half expected the building to be standing on lone, bare columns. He headed toward the closest window to glance at the turret. The crew was visible, scanning the buildings. A soldier pointed at him directly and the barrels turned to follow him.

Ziyad hid and prepared to run, but the rooms in front of him began to fill with explosive rounds as they penetrated the walls and continued to burst in air. He started to retreat until he saw, on his peripheral vision, a white reflection.

Alexis was darting through the lower floors of the buildings across the street. The stream of blasts stopped. Ziyad could only presume they were going to point the guns at the fox. He turned back and ran, as fast as he could, through the rooms that had been under fire.

His presumption was right. The turret was taking aim at his comrade. The weapon was only six meters away. He charged into the room next to him, blades still unsheathed. The door had been completely blown off the hinges from the detonations. As Ziyad passed what was left of the arch, something heavy hopped onto his back.

Keeping his footing, he pushed his body against a wall, breaking the plywood. He threw the person on his back in front of him. It was a filthy mutt, in gray power armor with thick plates, a metal helmet covering his entire head, and a sharp stiletto. Ziyad was about to crush his head in, but he wasn't fast enough.

A *Demon-class trooper!* The bulky cur had little maneuverability compared to Ziyad, but much more strength. Ziyad attacked, swipe after swipe, stab after stab, but the golem was unaffected. With a sickening laugh, the mutt punched Ziyad's chest, flinging him into a wall.

Ziyad had to kill him, but how? The mutt's joints were also well armored with several plates and rings covering each other. Ziyad would break through them eventually, but it would take time he didn't have. He got to his feet. His armor took a dent but saved him from a liquefied ribcage.

The mutt jabbed, with his knife, at Ziyad who, in turn, retreated from the room. Ziyad thought of a strategy, one he had learned from the red-eyed cat. The appeal of weakness. He had only one chance. Ziyad jumped back from another stab, grabbed the stiletto, and used his added strength to bend the blade.

Ziyad felt a hard thud as the mutt slammed his skull into his head. He landed on his behind and scurried backward. The towering demon stepped forward, perhaps grinning under his mask. He grabbed Ziyad's leg and pulled him under himself. A punch to the gut was added. Ziyad felt its pressure but no pain.

The Avian curled up as if he was mortally wounded. The mutt snickered at his reaction and grabbed Ziyad's head. The mutt turned, looking for the stiletto, and crouched to reach for it. Ziyad saw this as the golden opportunity he needed for survival.

The Seraph grabbed the demon's wrists, wrapped his legs around its arm, and went for its neck with his talons. The mutt screamed in surprise and pain as Ziyad bent his body forward, causing its arm and elbow to snap backward.

The hand was no longer able to grab him, and he bit his talon down on the creature's neck before twisting his body and allowing his other foot to touch the ground. Able to stand up and with the mutt on its knees, Ziyad let go of its neck and stabbed hard at the throat with his blades.

Even with blood spewing out, the mutt got up and took a swipe with the dagger, acting as if it were the hook of a sickle. Ziyad ducked out of the way and stabbed the left eye glass of the helmet. The mutt lay silently and its heavy body went limp.

Again, Ziyad's muscles flared with pain and blood. He didn't take a breather, though he felt like he needed one. He turned and dashed as fast as he could. He was a story above the turret, and the crew either wasn't paying attention or couldn't see him. Perhaps they thought he was dead.

He saw an opening that provided a clear view of the emplacement, a rotating turret with a single gunner behind some sandbags. The turret was firing at the other side of the street, toward the residence that Alexis was in.

He ran and jumped, through the large opening, toward the gunner and swung his blade as he landed next to it. Satisfied with a decapitation, Ziyad turned his weapons on the surrounding troops.

One was pointing his submachine gun at Ziyad, and the other immediately dropped their weapon. Ziyad grabbed the machine gun from the soldier and inspected it after kicking the trooper across the room. The gun looked pitiful. An old design, decades old; it had a long barrel, a light disgraceful stock, and a magazine of exposed bullets, which were fed from the side like a typewriter.

Ziyad wondered about its effectiveness as he pointed the gun at the surrendering soldier. The soldier tore off the face wrap, revealing a feminine facial structure. At first Ziyad thought it was a young man, but her slim figure changed his mind. Did she think she could get off that easily? Unfortunately for her, Ziyad believed in equality; all cats were alike. He aimed down the iron sights.

Suddenly she dropped to the ground after a loud smack on the back of her shoulder. Above her stood Renatus, who gestured toward the gun. "I thought we didn't use firearms."

Ziyad growled at his disrespect, but stopped when he realized how correct his statement appeared to be. "Where were you? Why didn't you report in?"

"I thought instead of fighting it from the front, where it could see us, I would go around the back. Less likely to get shot, yes? I didn't report in because I was sneaking about. Did you see me right next to you in the café?"

Ziyad didn't believe the fox. He would have seen him if he was there.

Renatus turned to the woman. "That armor… She's a conscript."

Ziyad didn't think twice about the armor. It was primitive. A metal breastplate with a faded New Albion flag in the top right corner, it had shoulder pads belted to the plate, along with a satchel and harness for the canteen and ammo. The helmet, if he could call it a helmet, was flat brimmed like a saucer. The woman also had a large amount of cloth around her neck. She had used it, earlier, to cover her face for added warmth.

"How do you know?" he asked the foxen.

"They wouldn't waste time or money making actual armor for them." Renatus checked the pulse on the woman's neck and then moved the soldier who had been kicked. After confirming that they were both alive, he turned back to Ziyad. "There should be a big guy around here."

"I got him." Ziyad smirked at his accomplishment. "You'd think if they wanted to protect this emplacement, they'd have more of those demons around."

"He wasn't here to protect them." Renatus dragged the bodies next to each other and began removing the ammo and weapons.

"Hell of a job, Commander," Alexis called as she was halfway across the street. "Saw you take on that huge guy. Was it part of your plan to be manhandled?"

"Yes it was," Ziyad snapped, turning around to see Alexis lightly toss a metal object at him. He threw a hand up and snatched it out of the air. It was a silver pistol with elegant engravings. The caliber was average, larger than the submachine gun. Ziyad's arms hurt holding the gun. The shrapnel stung deeply.

"Found it on a guy back there. He won't need it anymore." She leaned close to Ziyad, who stood a head taller than she did. "Thought you might like it."

A loud whistle came from a nearby building. Ziyad headed to the room Renatus had come from to see several civilians walk out of a building across the street.

"Commander…" One of the foxen called over the radio, as he exited behind them. "Guess what we found."

He was followed by several Avian and foxen soldiers in lightweight, white-plated armored suits without helmets. They carried much more sophisticated weapons: automatic shotguns with chains of shells, machine guns that would fire at a rate so fast each one required three rotating barrels, and even pistols that held up to two dozen bullets.

One of them was pulling a little gray-furred girl by the ear, making her whimper in pain.

"Halt!" Renatus called to the soldier.

Ziyad paid little mind, focusing more on the gun Alexis had given him. He checked the amount of ammo, and found nine bullets.

"You're hurting her. I said halt!" Renatus pointed to the Avian soldier. "Stop right there!"

"Both of you halt!" Ziyad pulled a needle full of a painkiller from his belt. He took off the top part of his helmet and put it around his neck. He welcomed the respite and placed the syringe back into his belt.

He turned to face Renatus and the Avian soldier. He didn't care for rank; he was superior to them both. The Avian was hiding the girl behind him; Renatus was attempting to grab her before Ziyad ordered him to be still.

Ziyad pointed to the girl and motioned the soldier to show him her. The Avian was reluctant but he obeyed.

She was a wolfen juvenile in a pretty yellow dress that her mommy and daddy must have bought her. She was frightened by the Seraph's presence and curled herself at the feet of the once-intimidating soldier. The tip of one of her ears appeared to have been cut, making her more difficult to be counted as a confirmed kill. Now she was just another refugee.

"Good catch, Renatus." He nodded to the fox before turning to the bird. "Soldier, you have your orders?"

"Yes, Sir." He swallowed and saluted.

"I have mine as well. Be on your way. Leave her here."

The soldier nodded and continued with removing the refugees from the combat zone. Ziyad stepped toward the girl. She curled up behind her fluffy tail, closing her big blue eyes.

"It's all right." Ziyad knelt and patted her on the head. He pulled out a small chocolate bar from his rations belt and offered it to her.

She turned away from the big scary monster.

Ziyad poked her with it. "Have you ever tried it before? I don't mean chocolate in general. I mean this kind of chocolate. From the mainland? Take it. It will help make all the pain go away."

The girl was hesitant at first, but she took the chocolate tentatively and started unwrapping it, whimpering a "thank you."

Ziyad stood up and, without looking away, asked Alexis, "Where are the other Seraphs?"

"Out and about, Sir."

"They needed to see this," he muttered, mostly to himself. He waited patiently for the wolf to finish eating the chocolate bar. In the meantime, he checked his pistol. Its silvery surface reflected his mask. The mask he had earned through undying faith, the mask that insolent foxen wore around him. Foxen that didn't deserve it, foxen that questioned his faith. The faith that had raised him and fathered him, the very faith that loved him. He was Avon's will.

The girl finished eating and looked up to see Ziyad holding his gun to her forehead.

13

Kabol was frozen stiff.

"Where am I?" he asked aloud. He was in a brown room with the windows blown out. Glass was scattered about on the wooden floor. Kabol's heart begin to pound when he noticed the only door in the room had no knob.

He felt like air, while at the same time too heavy to run. He could sense the pressure on his arms whenever he pinched, but he could not feel it.

Kabol remembered how to walk. He looked out the closest window. The sky was brown, save for the dark black smoke shrouding the cloudy atmosphere. It was quiet enough that he could hear the distant cry of a motherless baby. Outside he could see a monument, the Arc De Triomphe. He was in Gaul. Kabol shook his head, wishing he could forget his mission.

The door opened and in came Hayden. "Kabol, where is he?"

Kabol looked around; somehow he knew who Hayden was talking about. Kabol pointed to a foxen in the corner. He was tied and gagged. A high-priority target, name and rank unknown, but Kabol knew it was him.

"Good." Hayden exhaled with relief and smiled, a sight Kabol hadn't seen in a while. "Then with any luck they won't follow us." Hayden motioned for Kabol to follow as he headed downstairs.

Kabol ran after his friend, gun in hand. At first Hayden walked down the steps, one by one, in a leisurely fashion. Kabol followed, realizing something was off. Hayden began to move faster. The wooden steps became stone. He walked down the stairway for an entire minute before he was sure.

Hayden started running.

Kabol raced after him, but Hayden continued to pick up momentum. The hallway was dark. Kabol couldn't see Hayden anymore. He was unable to see past an outstretched arm. Soon he heard planes fly, and their engines echoed loudly throughout the stone corridor.

Then there was light, and he was able to see a turn at the base of the stairs. As he turned the corner, he was in a tunnel containing a row of subway cars. He was in the metro. His armor was scratched up. He was bleeding from a cut on the side of his face that he remembered fondly from a minute earlier.

An air siren started blaring and several loud crashes were heard above the surface. The tiles on the columns began to crumble. A loud grinding noise came into earshot as a fiery subway car crashed and derailed.

Kabol fled from the tumbling train and hid in the crevice between the rails and the platform.

He heard cries. Not ones you'd hear from a child or the dying on a battlefield. From the tunnels came a dozen foxen soldiers. Ten of them were carrying shields and SMGs, one carried a flame thrower, and the last carried a grenade launcher.

Gunfire erupted above the platform. Several mutts tried desperately to shoot at the shielded men. The soldiers armed with flame throwers and grenade launchers shot at them while taking cover behind a shield wall.

Kabol hid and let his fellow soldiers die at the hands of the Romans. Guilt and fear stabbed at his heart, and horror seeped throughout his body as if it had replaced the very blood in his veins.

The shooting stopped and he heard pounding steps as heavily armored golems marched toward the stairs. Someone ordered them to fan out. Footsteps marched in every direction, including his.

It wasn't long until a foxen jumped down in front of him, one with a shield. He drew a cigarette from his breast pocket and lit it with a match, unaware of Kabol's presence.

Kabol drew his knife and leaped toward the man. His terrified blue eyes pierced into Kabol as he plunged the knife into his neck. Kabol was stunned, almost heartbroken. The fox shook his head as he grabbed his neck and coughed blood, reduced to whimpering.

Kabol jolted back as the foxen stumbled, legs kicking in agony. Its eyes were fixed on Kabol before rolling to the back of its head. Kabol wanted to apologize. He wanted so badly to say he was sorry. He wished he'd done it some other way. He wished he'd never done it at all!

The other foxen called for their friend on a radio he'd taken from the newly dead body. Kabol covered his ears and ran, refusing to learn the name of the life he had just taken. He ran down the tunnels, and even with his ears covered he could hear them calling, wailing the name of their brother, father, and son.

He found a door to stairs that led down to darkness. Bullets whizzed past and bounced off the stone walls beside him. He sprinted down the stairs.

Soon, there was no light. Kabol closed his eyes and opened them. It made no difference, so he left them closed. He heard crying, and a hand tugged hard on the fur on his chest.

His armor was gone. His limbs were heavy with fatigue. He opened his eyes. In his arms was a dying foxen, his smooth golden fur visible only from the light of a burning helicopter.

The fox was young; he couldn't have experienced his life to its second decade. Tears streamed down Kabol's face, and he cried out in agony. Kabol noticed several bullet wounds in places his armor had failed to protect.

For the first time in what felt like a long time, he didn't know what to do.

The fox trembled, begging for his mother. Kabol called for a medic, but he knew there wasn't one within miles. The boy sniveled that he was cold. Kabol hugged him and begged him to stay with him.

The boy died in his arms.

Kabol felt a tear drop from his own face, landing in the blood of his former enemy. He looked up to see Hayden. His face looked different than he remembered it, dead, as if he could no longer smile. His cold eyes were shifting between Kabol and a new figure.

A white leona covered in blood, with a helmet and a Cheshire cat-like smile, sat next to him.

A blink later, and he was somewhere else. All his worries and fear and hate were gone. He was holding hands with a white cat, a different one. Dinred. He felt… happy, full of sincere joy. She smiled as he lifted her hands to his lips and kissed them. He knelt and she gasped at the sight of Kabol pulling a small box from his coat pocket.

He saw a blinding flash behind the cat. Kabol blinked rapidly. His eyes were sore, and he could see a horizon of fire and chaos. Streams of bullets ripped through the air in a skyline of crumbled buildings. All sense of familiarity was lost. He could feel it in his bones; he was in an earthly hell.

He was on a stone street with a fenced river to his side, sandwiched by another street. Cars, houses, and choppers were all on fire. The smell of sulfur was in the air. The stream ran rapid with scarlet blood. Kabol turned around, looking for anything, anyone. He saw, through the fire and death, the Seraph. Yellow-striped beak, armor stained, with red blades drawn.

Kabol was armed with a knife in his trembling hand.

The Seraph charged down the stone path. Kabol turned and ran, but he couldn't get far. Every time he looked back, he saw the Seraph standing patiently just a few feet behind him.

Kabol gripped his knife with the blade pointed down, turned, and stabbed at the Seraph's neck. The Seraph casually lifted an arm and smashed it into Kabol's wrist so the knife was dropped. Kabol stared in fear as the dagger vanished. As it passed the Seraph's waist, the Avian jabbed a long blade straight through Kabol's breastplate and into his heart.

Kabol could feel every ounce of immeasurable pain.

His body was lifted into the air, hanging off the Seraph's blade. The creature lifted his other arm over his chest and swiped at Kabol, slitting his throat.

Kabol's vision began to fade as he found himself on the ground. He wanted to curl up and die. He heard crying once again and looked up. He saw a man in New Albion uniform, with a bleeding medic's cross on the back of the breastplate, gray fur, and brown hair, grieving over an unrecognizable body.

Kabol feared what he was seeing. The man continued to grieve, and it was as if Kabol had heard those cries all his life. The weeping man turned his head and faced Kabol with red eyes. Kabol knew it was his doppelganger, but no matter how hard he tried, he couldn't recognize the creature.

Kabol noticed the bodies that lay behind him, impaled, decapitated, mutilated, disemboweled, bent in unnatural ways. Then there was him. He was no longer crying. His doppelganger stared at him, his eyes filled with anger and sorrow, and madness and death, putrid regret from an honest man that shook him to the bone.

Fire blazed behind the true Kabol. It burned like hell. Kabol reached out a hand to himself. He tried screaming for help, but his lungs had no air in them and his tongue flailed wildly without making a sound.

Kabol felt his feet burn; he saw his other's feet burn with him. He tried to scream as the pain seared his flesh, ignited his fur, and crawled up his legs. The other Kabol turned away and began to drag a faceless corpse that clung to his arm. With every step he took, he was more and more engulfed in flame.

Kabol could feel his back on fire, then his neck and chin. The pain was inexpressible; he began to see the bones in his outstretched hands as they disintegrated in front of his eyes.

⁂

Kabol woke up with a gasp and nearly hit his head on the bunk. He was sweating and breathing heavily. He was back in the barracks. Back to reality.

The beam of a flashlight shone on his face. "It's me, Buttons. Yer awake?" the barrack's fire watch asked. He was a silver-furred leona with gray hair. Kabol could hear him chewing on some sort of plastic.

Kabol took a second to get back into reality and nodded. "It was a night terror."

"I could tell…" He lowered the flashlight. "From all that shuffling you must've 'ad a terrible fantasy, Lad. Get back to sleep; it was only a dream."

The guard walked off.

It was only a dream, Kabol told himself. Most of it was.

"It was only a dream." A familiar voice whispered from under Kabol's bed.

Kabol's heart and body almost jumped from such a nightmarish encounter, until he recognized the voice. "Ben? Is that you?" Kabol whispered. "You scared me. What are you doing down there?"

"Something happened in my barracks."

"What kind of something?"

It took a moment for Ben to reply. "I don't know."

Kabol knew he wasn't going to get an answer. He asked a more important question. "Are you daft? How did you get in here? How did you get past the fire watch?"

"I know. Crazy, right?" Ben answered. Kabol imagined him with a wide smile. "Just go back to sleep."

Kabol was hesitant, but he was also tired. He humbly agreed to what his friend asked.

14

Kabol didn't sleep well after the nightmare.

The Sergeant went through the morning routine: yelling "lights" as the white bulbs popped on and running down the aisle like a hungry madman after a delicious-looking feral dog. Within a few minutes everyone was in ranks outside.

The sun glared into Kabol's eyes. By now Kabol was used to the warm glow.

Kai inspected the ranks quickly before standing in front of it all. Beside Kai, Ben and a few others stood at attention.

"Ladies and gentleman…" Kai nodded to Hayden. "You have completed the first course of training. Your bodies now look more like soldiers and less like you've never lifted something over a kilogram in your lifetime. We will be moving to my favorite part, showing you the guns, how they work, and how to use them to properly to murder the wits out of your enemy.

"Alas…" He paced in a line in front of the cadets. "I regret to inform you that there will be more of you pissants for me to deal with. The rodents you see standing in front of you will be your cheerleaders and playmates for the rest of training. What's the reason why? That's under investigation."

Kabol looked at Ben, who was the only one in front with a crooked smile like a kid who had gotten away with something. Kabol impatiently asked, as quietly as he could, "Ben, how did you get up there? Weren't you under my bunk last night?"

"I don't know what you're talking about," he answered with his eyes shut.

Kabol almost leaped in surprise when he saw Kai march into view. "Headbutt!" Kai slammed his head against Ben's skull and pushed him down. The mutt placed his boot on Ben's gut. "Inaan, you pathetic excuse for walking meat, you do not talk while I talk or so help me I will raise the world's average IQ by having you starve to death in the brig."

Ben didn't salute. "Yes, Sir," he said in a groggy voice.

Kai turned his devilish sights on Kabol. "And you, Maggot." He stepped forward and stood directly in front of him. Kabol kept his poise, but he could feel sweat on the back of his neck. Kai was an entire foot taller than he was, and he blocked the sun's glow and warmth.

Kai grabbed Kabol by the sides of his head and lifted the cat to eye level with natural strength. Kabol still stood at ease, even as his feet dangled. His head started to hurt in the mutt's grasp, and his neck was stressed as it carried his entire weight. "Now you listen well. If I ever catch you out of line again, I'll make sure you will never see your precious home."

Kai set Kabol down gently and pushed his head to the side hard enough it almost knocked him over.

The Sergeant scanned the ranks. "If any of you have the bright idea of reporting me to a superior, go right ahead. I write down everything I do on a daily basis in my diary anyways. Command knows all about how I run things; that's why I'm here. And Command also can't find anyone with enough courage to tell me to my face that I am relieved of duty. All those who are brave enough are in the front lines one hundred and twenty kilometers in that direction."

One hundred and twenty? Kabol thought with concern.

"Now then, we will report to the armory. Your equipment just came in, and I'm going to walk you through it before you jog with it. I'm sure half of you still fumble with buttons, and the other half will get your fur caught in the zippers. Inaan! Get up, Buttercup; we're leaving."

Kai made them jog a few more laps around the pit, this time in ranks. He made sure that Ben and Kabol were in the back. It hadn't rained in a few days, which had turned the dirt and dust into a cloud of debris Kabol had to inhale. By the third and final lap, he had never been so upset to see the sun out.

Soon the Sergeant led them away to the armory. Kabol didn't feel well, but he noticed Ben smile, with grit on his teeth, no matter how many times he spat on the ground.

When they'd arrived outside the armory, Kai showed them the weapons and armor they would utilize, all the while calling them hussies and meatsacks. In Kai's hand was a small-caliber machine gun. "All of you maggots and walking grease-pikes, ears to me. This is what most of you will be using." He held up a submachine gun-type weapon. Its stock was two thin bars and a padded wooden block at the end connected to the weapon. The barrel was long, and it reminded Kabol of the pipes at the bottom of his sink. The handle and the trigger, along with the rest of the body, were the only parts that looked like an actual gun. The exception was that the ammo from the magazine fed the barrel horizontally rather than vertically, like a typewriter.

Kai continued, "This, you pathetic snot-wads, is the Callum SMG. It is inaccurate when in full auto, spews like someone who tastes urine in their soup, and jams like horrible music. Good news is it can be unjammed easily when banged hard enough against your enemy's skull, and it can clear a room full of do-gooders within moments."

Kabol wished Kai were joking when he described the weapon's faults. Unfortunately, the similes were spot on. The weapon was terrible, and it was cheap. However, it was underestimated and could still kill. Kabol remembered seeing Hayden, a few years back, hit scores of enemies with it.

He managed to get a few shots in from a medium range. *Just don't let the muzzle spit out all thirty bullets, and anyone can become a deadly foe with it.*

"Next is your armor. Take a seat," Kai ordered.

There were no chairs, so the cadets did the obvious and sat on the ground. It was still early, and the cool pavement sent shivers up Kabol's spine.

Kabol waited for all the sets and pieces to be passed out. He was one of the last to be handed one. It was a green-tinted piece of metal that didn't weigh much and, on the upper left corner, it had the Union Jack, the flag of the New Albion kingdoms.

Kabol flicked his knuckles against the plate. It rang in his ears exactly the way he'd thought it would. He put it on, and the breastplate stopped soon after his sternum. He began to adjust some of the straps over his shoulder as the mutts tossed a helmet at him. The helmet was a dome with a wide rim circling the outside. It, too, was thin and, when Kabol tightened the strap around the bottom of his head, he could barely feel the helmet. He only noticed its effects when the rim shielded his eyes from the sun.

The entirety of the armor weighed less than three kilograms, or almost six pounds. Kabol had been away from the imperial measurement system long enough that the metrics the Germans used were starting to grow on him.

Kai explained while pacing around the cadets, "This will be your standard issue armor. It isn't bulletproof. In fact, assume that no armor you wear is bulletproof; you'll live longer. If my pet dog knew that, he'd still be here, may he rest in pieces. But the armor isn't completely useless. It's one of the lightest pieces in your arsenal; you can even swim in it."

As Kai was talking, Kabol finished hooking and attaching all of his armor, before he even got grieves for his boots. Ben was right behind him, along with Hayden and a few others.

"Anton!" Kai barked. "You already got it on? Wonderful, you can dress yourself. I'm legitimately impressed. Stand up."

As Kabol stood straight up, Kai pulled out a stiletto and slashed across his armor. The force knocked Kabol onto Ben. The yellow cat gave Kabol a Cheshire cat's surprised look that Kabol did his best to ignore completely. He was dumbfounded, however, that he wasn't bleeding. The dagger hadn't cut through the plate. Kai ordered Kabol to stand again, which he did.

The Sergeant pointed to the gashed insignia on Kabol's chest. "The armor will stop knives from cutting, ricochets from piercing your flesh, and stray bullets from ruining your precious fur. Maybe it could stop a hollow-point bullet showing your sternum and organs its sweet motherly love. But it will not stop an attack with more than fifty kilos of force behind it."

He shot a glance at Kabol and then at Ben. "It would also do very little against machine gun emplacements. Charging one of those head on would be like throwing a kitten into a blender. And no matter how many times you do it, it doesn't get any less messy—trust me. This armor doesn't allow you to do stupid things. I'm not going to name any names but I'm sure some of you, like Inaan here, would find a way to get yourself killed relying on this pathetic excuse for protection."

Kabol felt anger seep into his neck and head. Kai's constant attempts to pick on Ben and him were getting under his skin. At that point, he'd done it so much that the novelty had turned petty, and his jokes are just simple insults a child would make.

He also felt that Kai's tolerance for Hayden was little more than favoritism based on race. For a moment Kabol thought the Avon were killing the wrong people, but he refused to dwell on such a thought. He didn't want anyone to die, ever, but Kai was testing that conviction.

Kai continued, "Now that all of you are dressed and ready, let's go for a jog. Corporal Vargas! Front and center, squad leader."

Hayden ran next to Kai and saluted before calling everyone to attention.

Kai stood next to Kabol and cleared his throat. "Back of the ranks, Maggot."

It was hell. Kabol ran through kicked-up dirt and dust, following the troop. Everyone had been given a face mask, an extra cloth scarf hidden under the armor to help retain the warmth of their breath and keep debris from their face and nostrils. Everyone had one but Kabol.

As they were running to the pit, Kai had grabbed the scarf from Kabol's armor and cut it off. Now the troop had been jogging in the circle enough that there was no more dust to kick up. That's when Kai ordered that they march in a smaller radius, closer to the middle of the pit, where there was much more debris.

All the troops ran until their armor was a disgusting tint of brown. *Just breathe through the nose...* Kabol tried to remember what he'd learned in the university. *The body will handle the rest.*

Wishful thinking did little to help.

Kabol found himself collapsing an hour in. His lungs had trouble expanding. "Anton, what happened?" Kai asked in a cheery tone. "Vargas, get everyone to the laundry and get them to clean their gear, then go the mess hall, and off to the shooting range. Anton will be with you soon."

Kai grabbed Kabol's arms and pulled him away from the pit. "Blessed be those who care. Those who teach, and consider. Those who see the world as a marble slate they could chisel into beauty." Kai dragged him several meters away, to a corner of the base behind the barracks, and dropped him with a thud. Kabol's chest hurt from the fall, and he began coughing frequently, his breath kicking up debris. Kai pulled out his canteen and gave Kabol a drink, letting his throat become less sore.

"Cursed be those who hurt," Kai continued as he pulled away the canteen before Kabol could be sated. "Those who breed ignorance, filth, and horror. Those who see the world as their own and not the wrong they cause."

Kai ordered his subordinate to stand up. Kabol, as beaten and battered as his organs were, did so. He could barely keep his spine straight.

"But those who are apathetic…" Kai started to speak through his teeth. "Those who see the wrong, the ignorant, the sick, the dying, and the cursed and do nothing. Those who watch the world boil in its own blood without ever so much as a care. It is you whom I hate the most." Kai stepped in front of Kabol. "Do you know who said that?"

Kabol shook his head, throat torn and unable to speak.

"It was me. Just now, Moron!" Kai kneed the cat in his gut as he had done the day they met. "I hate you, Kabol. I hate you and your country and your people. And I hate your people almost as much as I hate your country, and I hate your country almost as much as I hate you.

"Your people probably didn't even know there was a war going on. I bet they didn't know the front line was a sea away. They were too busy eating and gawking and couldn't go to bed hungry a day in their life. And your country, they knew there was a war. They knew people were dying, were being murdered in the name of a religion. They. Did. Nothing."

Kai placed his foot on Kabol's back, keeping him on the ground, and with every other word he said, his foot dug deeper into his back. Kabol could feel the hatred radiate from his commanding officer. The only difference between Kai and the Seraph he had met in New Albion was that the Seraph was heavier.

"Then there are you, the aristocrats that knew everything and did nothing and only watched. Hell, I bet you refused to watch. Was that helpful? Maybe to you? I bet you've been fed every day with a silver spoon. You're only going back to see if your stuff is still there. You make me sick. That hat you had when you arrived here, that fedora, that expensive fedora. I've checked. You could have fed a poor family for a week, and you bought a hat. That is why I hate you."

Kabol tried to spit out dirt, and his head flared in anger, but that's exactly what Kai wanted to see. He wouldn't let that happen. Kai was right. Kabol had never cared about the war until it was at home. He had never known how close it had gotten. And the government wanted nothing to do with the Avon.

But Kai was wrong about one thing. Kabol had never had a silver spoon. He wasn't an aristocrat. And he was almost happy when he remembered the house and all its responsibilities had burned down.

Cursed be those who are ignorant. Kabol was happy, for once, that Kai had actually taught him something. "You're wrong. You see… the hat was a gift."

Kai, unamused by the retort, kicked Kabol hard in the side of his body, satisfied only when blood was coughed on the ground.

15

Dinred was on edge.

Ever since that day Isabelle had told her secret, ever since she had said she was the only inheritor to the throne alive and it would only be a matter of time before she was hunted down, Dinred had been on full alert. It was hard for her to sleep at night, or even eat in the presence of Avon soldiers.

She had been speechless when she heard that her mutt, the servant, would inherit the kingdom. Isabelle almost hadn't believed it herself until she told her story and predicted what the Avon would be looking for.

The royals had kept her a secret; she was, to put it bluntly, a bastard. She had been unwanted and hidden at first, but now she was an unfortunately lucky dog who would receive a kingdom if she wasn't skinned alive first.

Dinred couldn't believe it, but there had been stories about how the bloodline hadn't been severed. A birth certificate had been hidden in the palace vault, revealing the queen's affairs. Maybe the Avons' media was less corrupted than New Albion's, or maybe they sought to demoralize the populace and show them their beloved queen's foolish nature. For whatever reason, it had been printed and passed out as both propaganda and a wanted poster, but her real name hadn't been announced.

The description of the queen matched that of Isabelle.

The cat feared what would happen to her servant, her queen, if they found out who she was. Until then, she had to spend her days and nights in a cramped old room, a refugee.

Dinred had already had enough stress. She mourned for her husband. Isabelle had told Dinred that the last time she'd seen Kabol was back at the house when it was alight. Kabol had told her to go and make sure she was safe.

She knew Kabol could take care of himself. Maybe he'd gotten onto a transport? He could be waiting for her right now in Gaul.

Hope was meaningless. Kabol had been unarmed against the armor-clad soldiers. Against a Seraph, no less. She'd had a hint of what it was like behind the mask, Kabol was gone. Dinred shook her head, banishing those thoughts from her mind. She had mourned him with Isabelle, away from prying eyes.

She loved Kabol. She thought back and cherished every moment she had danced and joked with him and his stubborn hide. All those little snipes he'd throw at her, his scarlet eyes and sultry voice. His nature had always been the opposite of hers. He was everything she was missing, and likewise. She'd miss him.

Now though, she had a duty. When eyes were on her, she must keep her head high. Her life had changed in the past several weeks. She'd been widowed and stricken of her wealth and status, and now she wore what she used to consider rags.

The nurses, with much help from the behavior of the soldiers, had agreed to harbor her mutt and her without questions, so long as she helped with simple labor and helped deal with the stubborn armed men.

She was on her way back to a fellow nurse's room with bandages and empty syringes. She wanted to stop by and see how Isabelle was doing. The last time she had checked up on her had been an hour ago.

As she entered the room, she was stunned. On the bed was a white feathered Avon in a Seraph's black under-suit: Ziyad. He was more scarred than the day they'd met. His shoulders and arms were covered in bandages.

Dinred was both shocked and worried. Where was Isabelle?

A female doctor was blocking the television. "I told you, you're not supposed to be in this room. You have your own."

"Mutt," he grunted, painting a puzzle cube. "As far as I am concerned, as of this moment, this room is empty. Save for me. It's mine for the time being. Get out."

His words made Dinred anxious. What had he done with her? She had to be around here somewhere!

The doctor sighed. There was nothing she could do; by this time she was used to none of the soldiers listening to her.

Ziyad turned his beaked head toward the door and noticed Dinred. He smiled. "Ah, Mary, get in here."

"She's helping my nurses," the mutt said.

"No she isn't." Ziyad's eyes darted to the doctor. "*You're* helping the nurses. She's staying with me. Now get out."

The mutt looked upset, but she had little choice and obeyed. She took the supplies out of Dinred's hands and stormed away.

"Mary, what a pleasure to see you." Ziyad started painting the final side of the cube a different color from the rest.

"That makes one of us." Dinred scoffed, angry that she was being held in this room almost against her will. "I don't recall saying I wanted to stay with you."

"I don't recall asking you." Ziyad gestured for her to sit. "You're the only company here that I enjoy, so I intend to enjoy it. If you don't want to make the most of it, that's your decision."

Dinred sighed; she was going to be here for a while.

She took off her coat, no longer needing it to traverse the cool halls if she was going to be here in a warm room. "You're not supposed to be in this room?" Dinred asked as she headed toward the closet.

As she opened the closet, she nearly jumped. Inside was a golden retriever mutt sitting with her legs to her chest and her tail curled around her. Isabelle! Her eyes shot to Dinred in terror. As soon as she recognized the cat, she knew she was in danger. She quickly put a finger to her lips, begging for Dinred not to make any sudden moves.

"Apparently not," Ziyad said. Dinred threw her coat onto Isabelle as Ziyad continued. "They said it was someone else's. Now it's mine. Funny how that works, hmm? I wanted to stay here, because I figured that the best place to find you was where I last saw you."

"You were looking for me?" Something about that made Dinred worry.

"I never got your last name."

Dinred glanced at the closet. It lasted for only a fraction of a second, but she was able to see Isabelle shake her head with a finger to her lips. "You didn't ask politely," Dinred said, trying to buy time to think of a name.

Ziyad put down the puzzle cube and paintbrush. One side was drenched in yellow, and the other sides were a mix of other colors in small squares. He stood up; he was slightly taller than Kabol.

The Avian cleared his throat. "Do we have a rat in here?"

Before Dinred could stop him, he grabbed the knob of the door.

Dinred held her breath as Ziyad yanked it open. Isabelle looked surprised and held her palms in the air. Ziyad stood in silence; his glare was indecipherable.

"Why is there a mutt in my room?" he murmured.

Before Dinred could talk, Isabelle shrugged. "Oh, I'm sorry. I was here first, saw you, then figured 'hey maybe he wouldn't like seeing me in here' so I hid and did my best to stay out of your way. Is that a problem?"

Ziyad continued to glare at the mutt before confessing, "You have a point," and slamming the door shut. He turned. "Don't ever hide things from me. Ever. Surname?"

"Scaston." Dinred muttered her maiden name, suppressing the urge to swallow.

Ziyad said nothing about her name. It seemed he already knew most cats ended their last names with an "on" sound. "Marineet Scaston. I'd never have guessed that was your name if I was given a century."

He went back to his bed and stayed silent, picking up his brush and painting without a care in the world.

Dinred felt respite flow through her. She no longer had to worry about the mongrel in the closet. Dinred wanted to praise Isabelle for her quick thinking. Certainly if her name was asked she'd find a way to wiggle out of the question. She almost envied that gift.

"Why did you want to know my name?" Dinred raised an eyebrow.

"So I know who you are, obviously." Ziyad reached in his under-suit and pulled out a necklace with a silver ring on it, before tucking it back in.

Dinred grazed her ring finger. She felt comforted when she touched the tang of a metal band. The symbol of her bond to Kabol.

She remembered what he had said to her when he proposed with a stainless steel ring. *They say love is blind. If that is true, the moment this ring is no longer beautiful, I am no longer loved.*

He was right. The ring was beautiful, but only to her. Her adoration of him was the only thing that made such an insignificant object worth everything in the world. Its underwhelming value had also made it one of the few trinkets she could keep without making refugees loathe her.

Ziyad finished painting the cube and placed it next to a children's brush pallet. Every side had its own color. "Finished," he remarked with what seemed like pride in his voice.

"Congrats, you cheated," Dinred scoffed.

Ziyad smiled. "I, at least, solved the problem, the puzzled that belittled my day." He tossed the cube to her. "It's an Avon proverb. It's to show that no matter how troubling the problem is, there will always be a way to overcome it."

"So instead of solving the problem like you're supposed to, you deface it until it looks right?"

Ziyad's smile grew wider. "My solution may seem unethical to you. The way I see it? My life has one less problem. Hence it is all the better."

Dinred narrowed her eyes. "What are you getting at?" Why would the Avon need such a philosophy? If it's unethical, why do it when unnecessary?

Ziyad shook his head and lay back on his bed. "You cats will never understand. Your mindset is different from ours. Tell me one thing you think needs to happen to make the world a better place. You'll be wrong."

Dinred paused, puzzled that a soldier occupying her country had asked her such a question. His audacity made her too angry, and she refused to answer for a moment. She finally added, "How about we get rid of the troublemakers?"

Ziyad grunted. Dinred couldn't tell if he was agreeing or entertained by her remark. "Well," he said, "I guess you might understand us after all."

Dinred didn't know what he meant. Something about the bird was off. It occurred to her that Ziyad may be talking about another matter entirely. She raised an eyebrow and her tone was more inquisitive. "This isn't about a simple puzzle, is it?"

He smiled. Before he could answer someone thudded on the open door. It was an orange foxen with brown hair and blue eyes, wearing the same under-suit as Ziyad. He looked furious.

The fox stepped toward the Avian. Fury radiated from him like an aura that turned the air as rough as sandpaper. He kept his voice down and spoke through his teeth. "Commander, may I speak freely, Sir?"

Ziyad shook his head. "No, Renatus, you may not. I've told you to return to the *Basilicus*. I will not have you test my patience like you test my faith. Your absence would be much appreciated."

"Sir—"

"Leave!" Ziyad nearly screamed.

Dinred was frightened, and something told her legs to flee.

The fox turned and stalked off. Ziyad gazed at the door before taking a deep breath and sighing. He didn't turn his eyes from the television in front of him, but spoke with almost clouded eyes. "I'm sorry, Mary. I never wanted you to see me like this. In your language I believe they say 'It's rude.'"

The way he said 'it's rude' tugged at Dinred's heart. It was Kabol's favorite saying. Hearing it made her think about all the times he'd used it against her, as if it were a perfect reason not to have fun. She'd always give him a terrible gift just to rub it in his face that he couldn't decline it because "it's rude." She took a moment of silence to remember a time she had used the comment to trick him into wearing a blouse.

"Are you all right?" Ziyad asked.

"It's nothing." Dinred shook her hand as if she were scrubbing the thought from the air. "Just nostalgia being a sore." She sat back and perked an ear, and her tone of voice was no longer soft. "What did you do to tick him off?"

Ziyad didn't answer.

Dinred heard footsteps come toward the door. They were much heavier than the foxen's. They sounded like metal on stone. A Seraph stood in the doorway.

It was another foxen. This time she had a redder tint of fur and short black hair. Dinred could only tell that by looking at her exposed face, the only part that wasn't armored. The foxen's dull brown eyes shifted around the room until it landed on Ziyad. "Commander, was that you screaming? Ouch, and I thought I get on your nerves."

"What do you want, Alexis?" Ziyad sounded less than thrilled.

Alexis ignored her commander and stared inquisitively at Dinred. She took a few steps and narrowed her eyes as she pointed rudely at her. "Wait, haven't I seen you before?"

Dinred shook her head. She had rarely seen a foxen. If she had known one, she'd remember it.

Still under the illusion that she had met Dinred, Alexis nodded her head. "I'm pretty sure you look familiar. I try not to forget faces. Ugh, this is going to bite at me all day."

Ziyad threw his hands irritably in the air. The foxen had walked directly in front of the television set. Ziyad gestured to Dinred and rolled his eyes. "She's a white cat with black hair in the middle of New Albion. What a rare sight such a thing is! Seriously though, Alexis, I saw three others just like her on my way to the hospital."

"Yes, Ziyad, I have been here longer than you. Just you try and tell me something I don't know." Alexis continued to inspect Dinred. "I'm certain of it. It's starting to upset me. She looks like someone I should have knocked some sense into long ago."

Dinred's eyes widened and her heart began to beat rapidly. What had Dinred ever done to deserve a threat like that? She didn't mean that, did she?

"You will not harm her," Ziyad said, letting his temper get to him, and pointed to the closet. "There's a mutt in there if you need to release some steam. Just get out of my room."

"What?" Dinred jumped from her chair. "No!"

Her heart sank as the foxen growled, putting on her mask. She opened the closet door. A terrified Isabelle tried to get farther back in the closet, but the foxen wasn't prepared to show mercy. She grabbed the mutt and, with the help of her power armor, easily dragged the poor creature to the hallway by her hair.

Dinred chased her, only for the Seraph to push her into the room and onto her back.

Ziyad made an angry comment that Dinred didn't catch. Adrenaline was pumping through her blood and, as far as she was concerned, the only thing in this world was her, the mutt, and the fox.

Isabelle cried in pain as the foxen punched her hard in the gut, demanding to know why she was hiding. Dinred cringed at the yelps her friend made with every blow. How could Ziyad suggest she do this? Dinred screamed at the fox to stop, her courageous anger triumphant over her fear.

Her command fell on deaf ears.

Dinred couldn't do anything other than yell. A feeling of helplessness crept into her as her anger began to be replaced by fright. Isabelle lost all strength to resist. She was, at this point, a carcass that could barely mutter sounds. Even if she wanted to, she couldn't tell the soldier her reason for hiding.

Alexis threw Isabelle into the wall before her arm twitched and a long sleek blade jutted out of the gauntlet. She was tired of the mutt's silence and had decided blood was a good enough answer.

"Stop now!" Dinred gathered the courage to scream. She grabbed the wrist the blade was attached to and hung on to it, putting her entire weight on the arm.

Alexis shot a glare at Dinred and smacked her face with the other hand. With a thud, Dinred hit the ground. Her ears rang, and she could smell the blood dripping from her nostrils.

The foxen stood over her, but not in a stance that asserted dominance; she was afraid.

Dinred looked over her shoulder. Her ears still rang from the blow to her head. She saw Ziyad at the door frame. If she hadn't been out of her wits, she would have tried to strangle him.

Ziyad looked livid. His knuckles twitched in anger, and his voice was ear-piercingly loud. "What did I tell you?"

Everything was silent. The world hushed at the bird's voice.

"What did I tell you?" he repeated, marching toward Alexis. The fox looked stunned, scared, and speechless. Dinred could tell she was frightened enough to curl into a ball. "I ordered you not to touch Mary. Remove your helmet."

The fox removed her mask. Ziyad swiped it from her and smacked her forehead hard enough to make her mouth bleed.

"Go to the *Basilicus*. You're relieved of your post." Ziyad stepped back and looked around. An audience had gathered, full of nurses, patients, soldiers and bystanders. All eyes watched the foxen who had been shamefully and insultingly beaten for her negligence.

Alexis didn't look back at her superior. She left without a salute, leaving the mask behind.

Ziyad dispersed the crowd while Dinred rushed to Isabelle, who looked strangely different. Her hair had been ruggedly cut shorter since she was in the closet and, beneath all her pain, Isabelle still smiled like she had gotten away with her life intact. She kept whispering thanks, to whatever god was listening, that she hadn't been recognized.

"Why would she recognize you?" Dinred asked under her breath.

Ziyad told one of the onlooking soldiers to find Alexis's post and to replace her with someone more competent before he turned to Dinred. "Mary, what is she to you? The mutt? A friend?"

Isabelle nodded, but Dinred was the one who spoke. "She's been a close friend for years."

Ziyad's eyes shifted between the two. "I'm sorry I unleashed Alexis on her. If I had known she was worth something to anyone, I would have thought otherwise. Get inside. I'll tolerate the mutt sitting in the corner. Just make sure she doesn't talk."

Dinred followed his command, but she bit back a bitter remark.

How could Ziyad possibly suggest that the soldier beat Isabelle? But she wanted to at least thank him for punishing Alexis. Dinred shuddered at what would have happened if he hadn't stopped her.

16

Kabol let out a sharp gasp of pain.

Never in his life had his body suffered through such physical torment. His knees shook with burning pain, his eyes stung from sprayed pepper, and his chest bled from lashes of whips and knives.

The taste of the blood bore into his mouth like bile. Soon he became desensitized to the taste, and it seemed just like drool coming out of his mouth.

Tied to a chair and unable to move, Kabol felt another smack from the rod wielded by Kai. It had only been a few hours since Kai's confession, but it felt like hours. The first thing Kai had done after that was drag the cat's unconscious body to a small hot shed and announce it was time to train for interrogation.

"Say it, Maggot," Kai growled. "Say, 'The cats don't deserve Albion.'"

Every inch of Kabol's being was telling him to say it, trying to convince him that it would stop the pain. Kabol knew better. He knew what would happen if he broke.

It was hard for him to breathe, and the simple act of staying conscious was a chore, a job that Kabol could barely accomplish in his current state. The cuts on his arms and the stinging sensation in his lungs after every breath begged him to give in to what Kai wanted to hear. His body nearly shut down with relief when Kai said he was done for the day. He clenched his teeth when Kai said he'd be back tomorrow.

This wasn't training; this was actual torture.

On the other side of the room, Ben hung on a pipe, limp, dangling, and half-dead. He had passed out after mocking Kai's futile attempts to get him to talk, spouting at Kai that he could hit his own family harder than anything the hound could dish out. Kai made sure that he didn't do permanent damage to his own cadets, careful not to make them more useless then they already were. But he'd made sure they wouldn't forget their time in his care. Kabol cherished that very thought, but it disappointed Ben.

"Kabol…" Ben whispered his name when the hounds were absent. "It's about time to wake up, Kabol."

Kabol managed to open his eyes, a challenge with his mind twisted out of reality. He just wanted to go home.

In front of him sat Ben, his tinted fur still an unnatural color, alas, stained with patches of white and a new dye of bleeding red. His white eyes, which were both near- and far-sighted, were as wide as his horrible smile.

"There we go, up and at 'em," Ben shook his hands, rattling his chains. He inspected the cuffs and links, shaking his head. "There's a way out of these cuffs. This'll be fun."

Kabol was too tired to question what he meant by that. The unasked inquiry was soon answered. Ben grunted as he began to force his hands out of his restraints. Kabol winced at the cracking of bones moving beneath his friend's skin.

Ben, however, laughed. He laughed maniacally, insanely, as if this were a thrill to live for. Ben closed his eyes as his own blood dripped onto his head from his suspended limbs overhead. The laughter masked the noisy snaps and pops of bone as he forcefully pulled one of his hands through a cuff.

Fur and blood dripped through the air as his thumb was mangled out of place and the restraints slipped over the bar. Ben landed on his feet, quickly snapping his thumb, wrists, and fingers into place. He looked at Kabol, whose fortitude was reinvigorated by fear and horror.

Kabol wished he were unconscious, in a state where pain didn't constantly crawl through his veins, in a reality where he wasn't tied to a chair with a man who had willingly mutilated himself to escape like an animal in a hunter's trap.

Ben looked at a nearby table with knives, whips, and hard objects that they'd both been acquainted with. Kabol was unsure what Ben was thinking when he saw them. He had reason to fear for his life.

Ben grabbed the knife, went behind Kabol, and cut through the ropes that bound him. "It's all right, Kabol. As much as I like it here, me and you need to get to the hospital. So don't you worry one bit. I got you."

Ben cut Kabol from his bindings and slung his friend's arm around his shoulder. Kabol limped, leaning on Ben, heading toward the exit.

Kabol was tired and physically scarred, and all he wanted to do was sleep. He didn't know what would have happened to him if he had sat and waited for Kai to return.

He made it a few steps outside and was confronted by guards. They were surprised, not at the condition the two cadets had been found in, but rather that they'd escaped.

For the next week, before returning to his own bed, he dropped in and out of his wits in a hospital room. When word got around about Kai's actions, Kabol received flowers and balloons with a note on it:

"Don't try to impress me."

⁂

Kabol almost jumped from his bed at the sound of his barracks door slamming open. "Gas!" A loud voice broke the silence in the slumbering room, followed by a metal cylinder sliding across the floor with white smoke spewing out of it. "Get up now, you are being gassed!"

Every figure in the room went from quiet sleep to hellish panic as they leaped from their bunks and searched under their beds for their gas masks.

Kabol pulled his from under the bed and quickly strapped it on. Something was missing though. He felt the side of his mask and found out that the air filter was missing. He could see Hayden, whose mask was untampered with, search through his bags for a spare filter, before he decided to do the same.

"Halt!" Kai's familiar voice resonated, ending the panic in the room.

Kabol stopped, unable to find his filter.

The hound entered through the thick, harmless mist. Every step seemed heavy with disappointment as he peered down at the cadets. He was wearing a black mask that covered the entirety of his head, contrary to Kabol's mask, which covered the face and snout, leaving the ears exposed.

"Ten seconds," Kai did little to hide his dissatisfaction. "Ten seconds and all you had to do was put a mask on, and now every one of you maggots are dead. You're a letdown to the ones who have the mask on."

Kabol looked around to see that no other cadet besides Hayden and him had their mask on properly or at all.

"All of you maggots would be squirming on the ground like a dying fish if the gas had any intentions to kill you. Keep your masks in arm's reach at all times! Move out to the pits. We have a few training exercises to go over, and I shudder at the thought of what you will be capable of by the end of the month."

Kai removed himself from the room, ordering that the windows and doors stay open for the gas to escape.

When Kabol was ready, he, Hayden, and Ben left the barracks together. Kabol turned his head when he heard some distant yelling. A nearby building started to erupt in smoke. The same white gas that had escaped his own quarters was in several buildings.

Kabol forgot how long he had been here but, evidently, Command had noticed they were short on time.

Dressed in his armor, Kabol dug into the dirt beneath him with his shovel in hand. The entirety of Baker Company had to dig ditches and foxholes in the woods outside of camp, turning them into channels and trenches that would later connect them.

The air was chilly with cool dew, and the wind gusting through the trees helped him relax, something his body needed. Ever since his escape, whenever Kabol thought of the hound, he felt anger. This was a nice change.

What's the point of training? Kabol reminded himself. *To learn to suppress rage, and place it somewhere else.* Kabol had seen soldiers lose their heads. If you couldn't handle a man yelling at you, or physical abuse, you didn't belong in war.

But that didn't mean he had to like Kai.

Kai was absent from the group. He had left right after telling the recruits they looked as cute as toddlers in a beauty pageant held in the worst of slums.

⁂

Hayden had been left in charge, walking around to see if someone was slacking. Every once in a while he would trade off with others, grabbing their shovels and giving them a break.

Ben was digging holes, not trenches, his Cheshire cat-like smile never fading. His gear looked as if he had rolled around in the dirt to get a good feel for it. He said it helped him dig.

Kabol's hands ached and bled from the previous hour of target practice. His shoulders were no better, feeling almost numb with pain, at times, from the kick back from the poorly made gun. The weapon was as inaccurate as he had remembered. Anything farther than several meters and he'd be lucky to hit what he was looking at.

"Hey Anton," a brown leona called his name. "I've been wondering, what happened to you? Why is Kai out to get you?"

Kabol let a short-tempered breath out of his nostrils. "He didn't like my hat." Kabol felt glad that he wasn't the only one who had noticed Kai's distaste for his existence. Then again, Kai wasn't very keen on hiding it.

"There has to be more than that," another cadet called.

Kabol, realizing he should remember names more often, answered, "He thinks we all live care free. A daft assumption, but I'm not one to judge."

"Is it true you were an aristocrat?" This time, Kabol remembered the name of this silver-furred, black-haired cadet. Everyone called him "Buttons" because he chewed on them when anxious.

"No, I was a doctor." Kabol put his shovel down. "I *married* an aristocrat. Kai thinks I've been spoon fed, but he doesn't know I worked the coal mines most of my youth. When you get the chance, tell him to stop spreading rumors."

"How did a miner become a doctor?" Buttons pried.

Kabol stopped shoveling and sneezed on some dust while thinking of a way to answer as simply as possible to avoid small talk. A shadow fell on his face. He looked up to see Hayden standing over him with a spade.

"War," Hayden answered. "This isn't the first time Romans and Avon thought Europa belonged to them. Kabol here thought it'd be better to die with a gun than a pick. I should know. He was under my command for most of the time. Kai's rank too."

Buttons turned his head. A plastic pebble clicked between his teeth, being chewed like gum. "Wait, Kabol, you were a Sergeant? Why are you here then?"

"I was in a different army." He wiped the sweat from his brow and picked his shovel back up. "Besides, Hayden left out the part where I came here to Deutschland to get my credentials. It was cheaper by an arm and a leg."

"Inaan!" Hayden turned his attention away. "Dig trenches, not holes."

"You're just jealous you can't dig as deep!" Ben's voice sounded faint and distant.

Hayden rolled his eyes and jumped into the ditch next to Kabol. "I never did ask." Hayden nudged Kabol and intentionally raised his voice so others could hear. "What were you thinking fighting a Seraph unarmed?"

Those words perked a few cadets' ears and drew some eyes.

"Kabol, you fought a Seraph?" Buttons asked.

"He was winning too," Hayden answered before Kabol could reply. "Dodged a swing, grabbed the knife, and went for the neck. Almost killed him too."

Shoulder! He wanted to correct. Kabol felt flustered with the admiring attention of so many people burning into his back. He wasn't supporting his actions. The mere thought of the metal Avian gave him angst. He had been so close to death. His heart stomped hard in his chest, and he felt like he had a lump in his throat. He cleared his throat, attempting to rid himself of his trouble. "You forgot to mention the part where you swooped in and saved me."

"Still, you're a laudable inspiration to us all. Kai didn't even teach us how to fight Seraphs yet. I guess he doesn't think it would make a difference." Hayden snapped his fingers, diverting the attention of the troops from Kabol. "No breaks yet. Get back to digging."

They dug together, matching the rhythm of Buttons's clacking teeth and humming. Kabol's ears perked at a familiar tune. It started with a gentle melody. He'd heard it before. He looked at Buttons, who seemed unaware of his peer's curiosity.

"Where did you hear that song?" Kabol asked.

Buttons hummed as his gaze met Kabol's scarlet eyes. "I heard it on the radio the other day. They kept playing it."

"Kabol, hand me those binoculars." Hayden pointed to a set of binoculars on a closed wooden box of rations at the bottom of the trench.

"What was it called?" Kabol asked Buttons as he grabbed the binoculars and handed them to Hayden.

"Hmm…" Buttons tried to remember.

"Tanks," Hayden murmured as he peered through the binoculars.

Kabol shrugged, waiting for Buttons's answer. "Don't mention it."

Hayden shot Kabol a glance. "No, enemy tanks! On the horizon!"

Hayden handed Kabol the binoculars and he peered through them. Across the open field, behind a border of trees, was a light tank of Roman design, camouflaged green and with branches strung on it. It was smaller than most tanks, essentially just an armored box on wheels and a comfy machine gun turret. He could see the machine about a hundred yards away, just big enough to fit a single soldier and a couple hundred small bullets for the weapon.

There weren't any other tanks for as far as he could see. However, he could be wrong. They moved silently, and he would have never have noticed this one if it weren't for Hayden's keen eyes.

"I can see only one. Is it a scout?" Kabol tried to stay calm, but already his heart was throbbing and the blood was leaving his hands.

"Don't be stupid. Of course it's a scout." Kabol looked up to see Kai, whose shadow blocked the sun, the amber glow in his eyes changing to scarlet. The hound was writing in a red heart-shaped diary that possessed his full attention. "A Gromatici drone to be exact and he's just here to take a peek. Command and the officers are aware of Roman movements. They're so sure of beating our front lines that they're scouting ahead."

Kai closed his book, shooting a glance at Ben's hole and sighing.

"Barker Company's awaiting orders, Sir." Hayden saluted. The company followed his example.

"At ease." Kai gave a mocking salute before continuing. "If you can remember one lesson from me, a single soldier behind enemy lines is worth a dozen in front of it. They're dangerous, and there's one right there. Command doesn't have any means of taking out that one. So I hope you don't mind me volunteering everyone under my control to take care of the problem. By everyone I actually mean you."

A few gasps were heard. Kabol noticed the faces of the men: some were afraid, a few were angry, but most were in disbelief. Kabol was angry. He spat, "You're sending us to our deaths."

"Don't be silly. I have full faith in you people and your abilities." Kai scoffed.

"We don't even have weapons!" Kabol raised his voice. The cadets began to realize Kai wasn't joking. "You said we were here to learn how to dig trenches and foxholes, not fight a tank!"

Kai looked at the troops below him, their faces now terrified. Kai's ears and tail ascended sharply to mimic surprise. "Whoops! Or I would say 'whoops' if I didn't already tell you this was a training exercise? Did you not notice the explosives?"

Kai gestured with his foot toward the box of rations at the bottom of the trench.

Kabol opened the lid to the case, revealing several sticks of explosives. "We're actually going through with it," Kabol said in disbelief.

The soldiers stirred, making a commotion.

"The tank's going to kill us!"

"No way is that going to happen. He's lying, just trying to scare us."

"We don't stand a chance."

"Enough!" Kai growled loudly enough to silence the men. "It's an unmanned, automated rover. It's not going to move unless told to. Now if you can all shut up and calm down…" Kai turned to Hayden. "Vargas, the men trust you, or so I hope. I want you to take charge and flank that vehicle."

Hayden nodded. "Rules of engagement, Sir?"

"Go nuts, but do your best not to burn the forest down. You guys are also the clean-up crew."

Kabol's muscles grew tense at the thought of battle. It was a simple machine, but a machine nonetheless. If it had any intentions of killing him, he had little to say about it. He could be targeted and shot at. He would have to be lucky every time bullet missed, while the bullets only had to be lucky once.

Hayden looked at Kabol, reminding him he wasn't alone, that there was hope and strength in numbers and strategy.

Kabol nodded to Hayden. The mutt smirked and looked up at Kai. "Orders are clear, Sir. Give us ten minutes."

⁂

Kabol was hidden behind a thick tree, a stick grenade in trembling hands. He forced his breathing to be calm and ignored the quiver in his legs. *I have grenades. If I miss, I'll just throw another one.*

He was alone, save for Hayden. His friend was on the other side of the machine, with grenades of his own. They had left the troops to continue to dig and make it look as if nothing was unusual. Kabol and Hayden had his favorite, and most deadly, advantage over his opponent: surprise.

Kabol leaned over the trunk and got a glimpse of the rover. It was four or five yards away; its engine was barely audible when it sat dormant. Up closer, he could see that the armor was slanted from the front toward the back. It looked like several small trapezoids were pointing toward the front of the tank. If it was shot from the bow, a bullet would merely grind off it. If it was attacked from the back, however, there was little protection other than an inch of steel.

The turret stared into the distance toward the trenches, recording what live feed it could and storing as much video as possible. Hayden poked his head out from behind a tree and locked eyes with Kabol.

He pointed to himself, then to the enemy, placed his palm to his nose, and moved his head as if it were a turret. Then he pointed to Kabol, placed one hand on top of the other, and twisted before pretending to lob an object. Hayden topped it off by using his hands to arrange a makeshift explosion and using his lips to form a silent boom.

Hayden's enthusiasm made Kabol forget about danger as his actions began to make sense. The mutt would distract and the cat would go in for the kill. Kabol responded with his own gesture: a single thumb pointed up.

Hayden nodded and began a high-pitched whistle.

The turret made a short beep and turned, at a break neck speed, toward the noise. It stopped for a fraction of a second to scan the area and determine whether it was wildlife or foe before opening fire. The weapon was heavily silenced, making it as loud as a normal conversation among three people.

The bark from the tree behind which Hayden hid was being chipped away. Kabol took this opportunity to dash to a nearby tree, careful not to step on any twigs. As he got behind a trunk, he heard a snap under his feet.

Kabol heard a beep as the turret spun to face him. After its scan was unsuccessful in finding a life form, a second later, it returned to firing at Hayden. If the Gromatici knew there was another opponent, it would perform combat maneuvers. However, they were normally smart enough to initiate that protocol once its prey had hidden. Why did it not flank its opponent when they were stuck behind cover?

Unless… Kabol realized a terrible truth.

He pulled the pin on the grenade and gently tossed it onto the box. The turret's camera scanned the grenade and recognized the lifeless stick. Its self-preservation protocol forced it to drive away. It was unable to escape the explosive, causing it to ignite and turn into a ball of fire.

Kabol dashed to Hayden, who was leaving cover and beginning to celebrate with a hug. "Too easy, huh?"

"Get down!" Kabol yelled as he tackled Hayden behind a large rock.

With a pop a bullet whizzed past right where Hayden's skull would have been if he were standing.

"There's another one!" Kabol called over the sound of bullets snapping off the boulder. "One held you pinned down, another flanked. That's why it didn't try to chase you."

"Smart." Hayden pulled out a small mirror from a pocket and looked over to the side. "This one is directly behind us. Five meters. He's painted like the forest floor." Hayden's fur bristled on his neck. "He's standing still! You said I was pinned down? You mean like how we're pinned down now?"

Kabol's eyes widened and his tail stiffened with a gasp. *There's a third one!*

He could hear it now, an engine in the distance flaring up as the machine kicked into overdrive.

"Split up!" Hayden called. "Stay here and we're dead."

Hayden ran to the closest tree. A bullet sailed by, tearing off a shred of cloth from his waist. Kabol heard the machine switching between targets. One shot for Hayden, one for him. He sought the closest tree and waited for a bullet to redirect off the builder. When he heard a loud one, he dived for the tree.

This action made the machine pause in confusion over which target to shoot, firing off another shot at Kabol a second too late. Hayden took this time to find a slope to hide behind; if the tank attempted to crawl to it, it would most likely fall over.

Unfortunately, the tank knew this. Hence, there was only one plausible target. With a single beep of communication, the Gromatici charged for Kabol. The leona was prepared for this and tossed a live grenade in the path of the vehicle.

The machine stopped and went into full reverse to escape the explosive effects before turning into a ball of flame from behind the turret.

Hayden revealed himself from behind another bush and shouted, "Where's the last one?"

A soft beep was heard from far away. Shots were fired, and metal rebounded off the bark of several trees. Hayden and Kabol both took cover, not knowing which direction this assailant is coming from.

Something was off though. It was hitting several trees that were nowhere near the two of them. Light shone in Kabol's eyes as Hayden looked through his mirror. "Inaan?"

Kabol looked in the direction Hayden was gazing.

On top of a dirt-covered Gromatici was a pickaxe-wielding Ben with his leg toward the side of the camera's turret. The tank turned slowly, attempting to get accurate shots at a being that wasn't there.

Hope surged within Kabol. He had never been so happy to see Ben in his life. It warmed his heart to see the tank panic. This bugged program would only work if there was no ally to kill the enemy on the Gromatici's turret. That meant this was the only one left.

Ben swung the pickaxe over his shoulder and slammed the tip into the camera, shattering it in sparks. He repeated this motion until the turret shut down completely, emitting smoke from its fried circuits.

Hayden had the same look as Kabol must have had: shocked, impressed and confused.

Ben, on the contrary, had his usual smug smile before sitting down on the turret. He gestured with a finger switching between Kabol and Hayden. "Kai told me to tell you to stop messing around. It only takes one grenade to kill a rover; learn to throw. As well as, is it really that hard to take out a single unmanned tank? And something about me staying behind until nature claims me. Sorry, I zoned out during his last part. Why are you guys breathing so hard?"

"We almost died," Hayden answered.

"Ben…" Kabol was flabbergasted at Ben's carelessness and pointed to the burning carcasses of the tanks. "Do you see this? Do you not recognize this?" After Ben had been silent for a moment, he continued, "Rome is going to be here within the week. We're dead if we don't get out of here."

Ben shook his head. "Do I look like I care?"

Such a reply silenced Kabol. What did he mean by that?

Ben asked again, narrowing his white eyes. "Do I look like I care? Like I care about this place? Like I care about them? I don't want to give that impression. There are many things I don't want, but that one is at the top of my list. Did I ever tell you—?"

"Inaan," Hayden interrupted in a fatigued growl. "Now is not the time. You're going to die one day. One day soon if you keep acting like this. Just shut up, and act normal for once!"

Ben laughed scornfully, standing up and swinging his pickaxe on his shoulder. "I'm going to die? Kabol, Hayden, my friends… I just stabbed a tank to death with a pickaxe. I *am* death."

He hopped off the tank and treaded toward the trenches, whistling a tune he had made up.

Hayden followed, holding the part of his back where the bullet had grazed him. Kabol grabbed Hayden by the shoulder and pulled him back. "What was that all about?"

The mutt's blue eyes glared at him. They were cloudy with thoughts and trouble, fatigue and nostalgia. It was obvious that whatever was bothering him, he just wanted it to end. He didn't say anything. He just looked at Kabol, as if he couldn't find the words.

He smacked Kabol's hand off his shoulder. "If I am no longer able…" His voice sounded rough, as if he were awoken in the middle of slumber. "If I'm not here to keep him in check, promise me you will take care of him."

"What are you talking about?"

"Promise me. That you will. Take care of him."

Kabol was quiet for a moment. He'd never seen Hayden like this. What had happened to cause the strongest man he knew to confess something like this?

Kabol nodded. "I promise."

"That's good." Hayden swallowed and cleared his throat. "That's good," he repeated, showing little fear or trouble. "Thank you. We should get back to the trenches. Before Inaan starts telling fish tales."

With a pat on Kabol's chest, he walked away.

Kabol slung his bag of grenades over his shoulder. *This isn't over, Hayden.*

He cleared his mind of everything but being a soldier. He could practically hear the snipes Kai would think of when he returned.

Worry still hung in Kabol's mind. Soon those trenches would be used to fight enemies Kabol had once washed his hands of. Soon these forests would be in flames and would make names forgotten. Soon, after all was settled, those trenches would be graves, and this forest would be flat.

His thought repeated in his mind. *This isn't over, Hayden.*

17

"You look irritated."

Dinred heard Ziyad's observation and was not amused. She hadn't decided whether to forgive him for his audacity in letting that woman attack Isabelle. She found herself content to just sit back and cross her arms to brood.

Isabelle was taking this much better, not making a big deal out of it to the point she didn't even act like it had happened. She was facing out a window, against her will for the most part, but she entertained herself by doodling people she found in a nearby newspaper. Ziyad hadn't questioned why she had cut her own hair. Dinred thought he had paid so little attention to her, he hadn't noticed.

The Avian lowered the volume on his television and calmly asked, "Mary, are you ignoring me?"

Dinred kept her silent glare away from Ziyad. She couldn't look at him without getting angry.

Ziyad sat up. "I said I was sorry."

"I know."

"I meant it too."

"I don't believe you," Dinred answered, creating silence. She clenched her fists and looked at Ziyad. She narrowed her eyes and spoke softly as if being in public were the only force that had convinced her not to yell. "Why are you even here? Why can't you leave me alone? Haven't you done enough?"

Dinred didn't understand why he was so fascinated with her. The only thing she'd done was to try to show as little interest in him as possible.

"You don't like me," Ziyad concluded as if he had known the answer since the first day. "I didn't mean to hurt you. What will it take for you to forgive me?"

"It's not that I don't like you. I don't even know you. But what I do know, I don't like." Dinred stood up and walked in front of the television. "Why do you keep bothering me? My life was fine until you and your friends showed up and wrecked the place!"

"There are many ways to argue with a Seraph. None of them are a good idea." Ziyad waved his hand as if tossing out the statement. "Besides, friends? They are my family. They have fought and bled by my side. To call them 'friends' would be insulting."

"Oh! What a difference that makes! You still ruined everything. My life was wonderful before you came along. I had a house, a husband, and friends—"

"So you're mad at me?" Ziyad was surprisingly calm. "What did I, specifically, do?"

Dinred felt her fur start to bristle on her neck. "You almost got my best friend killed because she was a mutt."

"I said I was sorry. I have asked what I may do to prove it. What more could you possibly want?"

Dinred bit her tongue. He hadn't done anything else to her. He hadn't taken away her house or her husband, he had no intent to harm her, and he had shown at least some compassion for Isabelle after he nearly got her killed. She had no reason to be mad at him.

"All right." Ziyad's legs slid off the bed and he sat up. "Let's start over, a clean slate. Would that make it better?"

"Would it?" Dinred crossed her arms mockingly.

"It would." Isabelle answered for both of them, not looking away from her doodles. "I wouldn't mind if we go ahead and start over." Isabelle stood up and strolled over to the Avian. She held out an outstretched arm. "Name's Lisa."

Ziyad looked at the mutt's hand, then at her eyes. For a long moment he was silent. Dinred wondered what was going through his mind. To her surprise, he shook Isabelle's hand. "I guess it's time I finally got your name. As you know, I am Ziyad."

The Avian turned to Dinred. She figured if Isabelle could forgive him, so could she. She shook his hand. "Fine, we'll start over. But only if we are completely honest with each other, and no more mistreating Lisa because she's a mutt."

Ziyad smiled. "I'll start with being honest." He turned his gaze toward the mutt and cleared his throat. Isabelle nodded and went back to her chair to draw.

"Rude," Dinred said plainly. "OK, so you're being completely honest? Why are you here? What do you want from me?"

"You are one of the few people who know their place. Though you act out of line, you are respectful. You do what you're told. It's a horrible shame how few times I have said that." Ziyad sat on his bed. "Now it's my turn to ask you something. You say you had a lot of things, a life as well. What were you?"

Dinred tried to think of something to say. She had no reason to lie to him now though. "I was an aristocrat. I had money and knew people. Does that make you think less of me?"

Ziyad shook his head and leaned toward her with interest. "What was it like?"

Dinred noticed how much ambition was in his voice. She shrugged. "It had its problems, but it was mostly wonderful. I really enjoyed it all, contrary to my husband. He didn't like money, thought it was a dirty word too. But at least he made up for it giving away what he made."

"Your husband sounds like a good man." Ziyad sounded sincere. "You speak in past tense. Did something happen to him?"

Dinred nodded and pointed to Ziyad's armor in a nearby chair. "A bunch of jerks who dressed an awful lot like that killed him."

Ziyad took a shallow breath and frowned. "I see. I'm sorry for your loss."

"You didn't answer why you are here?" Dinred asked, eyes clouded with emotions she wished not to express. "I mean, the Avon in general. We left your war alone. Why did you invade?"

Ziyad looked from Isabelle to Dinred. "Hmm… There is no easy way to explain it. Not in a way you'd understand. Not with your words." He stood up. "Come. Follow me." He whistled to Isabelle. "You too, mutt. Erm… Lisa."

"Where are we going?" Dinred said.

"On a field trip."

⁂

The moon reflected off the glimmering fountains of the palace gardens. Dinred's heart lunged at the sight of the once beautiful palace, that had shimmered in gold and silver, now turned into rubble and a few isolated columns.

All of the plants that had hugged the walls of the palace had been burned to ashy remnants that defaced their leafy predecessors to an unjust degree. The shrubbery connected to them had suffered the same fate. However, many of the other flowers and bushes at the fence had survived, untouched by flame.

The once dim lights that had created an inebriating atmosphere had been replaced with military grade floodlights inside and outside the gates. The speakers still played recorded music.

The Avon soldiers had created a perimeter around this heavenly scene, allowing few to enter that were not of their kind. Every once and a while, the cat would see a soldier walking around with their family, telling stories of old about statues that bore significance in the garden.

Many of the statues and busts had been burned, destroyed, or stolen. The Avon claimed they had not taken such prizes, but who else would?

Dinred got in with the help of Ziyad and his status. He allowed Isabelle to tag along so long as she stayed meters behind him. He was here to answer all of Dinred's questions in true solitude.

"Such wasted beauty," Ziyad began as he traversed the grounds, by Dinred's side, leading her to the plaza.

"You should have seen it before it blew up," Dinred answered with her mind somewhere else. She slowly began to realize where she truly was. This was the last place she had danced with Kabol.

The lamps had been shattered and destroyed, benches were mangled and melted, and the once charming pavement had been scarred black by napalm. When she had danced that day, she had never thought the wonderful world she'd lived in would look like this.

"This, Mary, is why we're here." Ziyad stood in front of the fountain in the middle of the court.

Dinred looked at the statue in the center of the fountain. A wolfen sat among a throne of bone, thorns, and death. Cerberus. The masked, armored man, with his head and shoulders in the form of a wolf, sat staring at Dinred and Ziyad with bloodied ruby eyes.

A melted and burned plaque lay, unintelligible, at the base of the fountain. The statue was completely untouched. The looters may have been unable to reach the precious stones due to the thorny iron vines that coated the monstrosity.

Dinred held her arm out toward the masterpiece. "We drove twenty minutes in silence just to look at a statue?" She was grateful for being here and out of the hospital, but this is overly dramatic for her tastes.

"What was he to you?" Ziyad asked, ignoring the question and watching the scarlet eyes sparkle in the floodlights.

"Emperor Cerberus? Hmm… Well…He created social order, respectable classes, and he united all of Europa; technology and economy flourished under his reign. He was also respectful enough that our ancestors even called him our savior. He's done some good. I hear he's also done terrible things, but haven't we all?"

Ziyad stepped forward and faced Dinred. "Terrible things. That's an understatement." He raised his arms as he paced. "He was a brute, a tyrant, a demon. He turned us Avian races against each other. He caused mass panic, united countries by conquering them, placing them under his banner." Ziyad growled as he turned back toward the fountain. "He burned down Europa, enslaved every mutt along with anyone who refused to bow. Every achievement you described was built on the broken backs and corpses of millions."

Dinred had heard much of this before, but without the intensity of a preacher. But he hadn't answered her question. "What does this have to do with New Albion?"

"Wolfen." He faced the fountain. "Brutish, tyrannical demons.

We cannot allow another Cerberus to be born."

"That's what this is about?" Dinred felt as upset as she had in the hospital. Her husband had died for some superstition? "You don't like a dead guy so you're going to invade all his territory and make people suffer?"

"Wolfen are not people like us." Ziyad's voice sounded surprisingly calm.

Dinred's mouth dropped open. "How can you say that?"

"Mary, have you ever seen one?"

"No," she admitted, fury building in her spine, "I haven't."

"I have," Ziyad snapped and walked toward Dinred. His voice croaked out his next few words. "I saw one wrap his hand around my wife's neck. I saw him tear her throat out just because she was in his way."

Dinred froze. Her anger was dissipating in silence.

Ziyad continued, a little choked up on his words. "She wasn't even armed. None of us were. I saw them kill my entire family. I saw them murder and slaughter my people. I saw them train their children for war, using them as well. Have you ever wondered what you might do if you had to shoot a child? It's a terrible feeling, worse when you realize you're used to it. They are brutish, tyrannical demons."

"What are you going to do with them?" Dinred's words dripped from her mouth as her throat became scratchy. "What are you going to do with the wolfen you find that didn't kill your family?"

"Mass exodus; they will not be harmed." Ziyad cleared his throat. "If they do not fire at us, they will be sent to the *Basilicus*. We are not the bad guys. We are here to gather them, put them in their own lands. There it will be easier to keep an eye on them."

Dinred felt her heart scamper, and she placed a hand on her chest. "My husband died because you don't like people?"

Ziyad was silent for a moment. "Your husband's death was surely unintentional."

"No!" Dinred yelled, feeling her eyes begin to tear up. "A Seraph murdered him the day you showed up. It was completely intentional. He was unarmed, and all he wanted to do was help people, and your friends murdered him. How can you say…? Why…?" Her breathing became noticeably heavier.

Ziyad stepped toward her and hugged her tightly.

She tried to push him off, but he held on. Then, feeling pathetic, she closed her eyes. For a moment she felt like she truly was in Kabol's embrace. She stopped struggling and laid her head on Ziyad's shoulder.

"I miss him so much. Why did they have to take him?"

Ziyad was quiet. Nothing needed to be said.

To Dinred, this was a comforting hell. She had stopped holding her feelings in after so long, but she only had a foe to confess it to at the moment. She held her breath and refused to open her eyes, lest the moment of embrace would go to ruin.

She caught herself swaying from side to side, attempting to get him to dance.

She wrapped her arms around his body and returned the hug, allowing the moment to slowly slip away respectfully. She caught her breath back and opened her eyes. "I'm sorry." She cleared her throat, silently cursed herself for succumbing to the intoxication of the night. "I normally don't allow myself to mourn around people."

"I understand," he answered calmly, "I have done the same."

She released her grasp and stepped back. "Were…" Her throat was still dry. She wanted to ask a question, one whose importance was nearly immeasurable. She worried what the answer might be. "Is there a chance…? Were you the one who killed my husband?"

Ziyad shook his head. "On that day, I hadn't killed a soul."

Dinred nodded and smiled. "I believe you."

Isabelle walked behind them with her hands to her snout. She removed them and stuck her tongue out, revealing a pair of googly eyes over her own peepers. "Check it out, I found these behind one of the statues. Someone has a bad sense of humor."

Dinred found her intrusion in her hour of need entertaining. Ziyad, however, did not.

"Take those things off." His voice was stern, like a disappointed father. "Now is not a suitable time to goof."

"Lighten up, will you?" Dinred scoffed playfully. Isabelle's antics were always at the right time to cheer her up.

Isabelle apologized to the Seraph and began to head back to the predetermined distance she must stay away from him.

Dinred nudged Ziyad in his shoulder with a fist. "Be nice. Thanks, by the way, for getting the fox off of her. If you truly were terrible, you'd have let her die." They began to walk back to the truck that had driven them here. For the first time since the Avon had come, she was calm, nay, even happy.

She disagreed with Ziyad's motivations and plans. She understood his zealous claims about Cerberus and the wolfen, but not his solution to the problem. Still though, if he fixed his attitude, he might become a loyal friend. That was something she hadn't had in the life of politics.

She only wished her husband were alive to see this.

Ziyad nudged Dinred the same way she had done to him. "Don't worry, dear Mary. As long as I am alive, neither of you are in danger from her."

18

Kabol felt a knuckle grind against his chin.

"Too slow!" Hayden, his sparring partner, called as he jumped back a step out of Kabol's reach.

It was hard for the cat to concentrate. All around him was the rigorous scrapping of leonas and mutts sparring together. Their once rough and uncalculated movements had now been retrained into grapples and untelegraphed jabs.

Kabol clenched his rubber knife in his hand, shaking off the pain in his jaw. He circled Hayden, who cautiously watched his every move. He threw a jab without his dagger. Hayden backed out of it just as Kabol made a stab with the wobbly blade. It would have connected with his shoulder if he hadn't moved.

Hayden tackled Kabol, not hard enough to knock him off his feet, but enough to get a grip on Kabol's hands. His grasp on the knife loosened as Hayden dug his fingers into Kabol's wrists, almost enough to break the skin and draw blood.

Hayden turned his hand hard. Kabol couldn't hold the knife anymore. As the knife dropped, Hayden quickly twisted the cat's arm over his shoulder, forcing Kabol to painfully turn until their backs were touching. All attempts to struggle were futile as Hayden pressed down, using his body as a torque and wedge, flinging Kabol's light body over his shoulder.

Hayden made a fist and it shot toward Kabol's neck before stopping short. "Dead," Hayden grunted. It had only taken two seconds for the mutt to kill him in a combat situation where he had the advantage.

"You can't kill an equal with a knife, Maggot?" Kai was walking by, inspecting the troops. "How about you learn how to use that thing? And why are you not using Ju-Jutsu Verband like all the others?"

Hayden stood up and saluted before holding out a hand and helping Kabol up. "Sergeant Kai, Sir! Private Anton and I have extensive knowledge in—"

"Some sort of advanced pugilism," Kai interrupted. "A mixture of the cat-like reflexes of Carthage's finest, prettiest, fanciest martial arts, along with the mutt's power and practicality of Olde Albion. A hard thing to learn, but can make you completely unpredictable in battle. Almost clever. I forget the name, what was it again?"

"We call it 'advanced pugilism,' Sir."

"You're both stupid for using it." Kai grunted, looking between the two. "You honestly think the Avon invaded you without knowing what you can do?"

Kabol was going to speak up to tell Kai he had managed to stab a Seraph, but he kept quiet when he remembered that the Seraph didn't know he was an ex-soldier. Kai may be right. If Kabol fought the yellow-striped Seraph again, the Avon will surely win.

"They invented Taka'rin in response. I'll show you what they'll do. Give me the knife."

"With due respect," Hayden began, "it isn't necessary, Sir. We can do—"

"Give me the knife now, Maggot. Two of you, on me."

Kabol handed the toy to Kai, who backed up a pace. "Sir, that's not necessary."

Kai charged without warning. Hayden was the first to put his hands up, but Kai was already on top of him. The hound placed his leg behind the knee of one of Hayden's spread legs, quickly kicked it, and leaned forward. Hayden landed on his back with a hard thud and a knife across his throat. Kai rolled out of the way before Kabol could take advantage of the grounded cur.

Kai then turned his attention toward Kabol, preparing his knife for a thrust. The hound lunged at Kabol, fast enough Kabol had to dodge him and hard enough that the flaccid knife would have cut the skin.

Kabol saw Kai's exposed flank, but refused to act on it with the knife swinging toward him. He jumped back, missing the blade that Kai swiped with, and returned to a position to defend. The hound didn't let up. He lunged again.

This time Kabol wasn't fast enough, and Kai managed to get a grip on his right ear. Kabol kicked at the hound's kneecaps, but it ultimately did nothing. Kai forcefully bowed Kabol's head, exposing the back of his neck and stabbing it with ease.

Even though Kabol was already dead as far as sparring was concerned, Kai kneed him in the gut. "For old time's sake. Here is another for good luck." Kai kept to his word and kicked again.

This time, however, Kabol grabbed onto his knee. He used his shoulder to press against the dog and knock him off balance. With Kai's back to the ground, Kabol folded his hand into a fist and pounded on his snout.

This wasn't sparring.

Kai wormed a leg toward Kabol's collar bone and kicked him hard enough to dislodge his pin. Kabol was on his feet, preparing himself for another attack, but was pulled away. Hayden was drawing him back. Kabol tried to wiggle free, and the idea of harming Hayden to help loosen his grip crossed his mind.

He'd been constantly insulted, mentally harassed, and flat out tortured without saying a word. He'd had enough, and Kai would somehow pay if he could help it. He wanted to see how well the hound would stand against his "intense training."

"Kabol, stop!" Hayden commanded. "This isn't you."

He didn't listen. "Let go of me."

"Think about what you're trying to do." Hayden lowered his voice. "Would Dinred want this?"

Hayden's words burned into Kabol. *Dinred.* Kabol began to loathe himself. In the midst of his anger, he had forgotten what motivated him to go back. He had forgotten what mattered most. Dinred, Isabelle, home.

Kabol calmed down. His chest felt heavy as he recalled his brutish action: assaulting an officer.

Kai, now on his feet, glared at Kabol. "Vargas, let him go."

Hayden released the cat. He felt exposed and unsafe with Kai getting in his face.

"Are you mad?" Kai taunted. "You should learn how to control yourself. What were you planning on doing if you got on top of me? You think I'd let you do anything?" Kai grabbed Kabol's hair and pulled it back. "Tell me what you think about me. I dare you."

Kabol shook his pain-filled head. "I don't think about you."

Kai smacked Kabol's chin with the back of his hand. "Don't lie to me, Maggot. You hate me, don't you? I can see it in your eyes."

Kabol spoke through his teeth. "I fought a war for you."

"With me, Maggot, you fought a war *with* me. And now here we are. What help have you been?" He pulled back farther. "What do you think about me, Maggot?"

Kabol bit hard, holding back insults. He remembered the first thing Kai had taught him. "A good soldier doesn't think."

For the first time Kabol saw Kai with an almost sincere smile. "What do you know, Private Anton?"

A *good soldier acts.* Kabol slid a leg between Kai's knees and dug his sharp claws into his wrist. He put a shoulder unto Kai's groin and lifted him up over his shoulder and then smashed him back on the ground. "I know that you're a rotten, pathetic, flea-bitten fetcher."

Kai got up and growled. The hound clenched his fists and bared his teeth. He thought Kai was going to charge at him, but that wasn't the case. Instead, the Deutschlander steadied his pose. "You are looking to die today?"

"Seeing as how you are an enlisted soldier, I sincerely hope you did not expect the enemy to warn you of an attack." Kabol mimicked the old man's words.

Kai puffed a breath of air. "You are right. But there's a time and place for everything. And right now, if you choose to talk like an enemy, if you choose to act like an enemy, then I shall treat you like my enemy."

Kabol swallowed a lump that had appeared in his throat. What had he gotten himself into? Isn't this what Kai had wanted from him?

The hound reached into his trench coat and pulled out his stiletto. He crouched down and stabbed it the ground before backing off. After a few paces he stopped and pointed at it. "Whatever you do, do *not* let me get that knife."

He left the consequences unsaid as he marched casually to the blade.

Kabol didn't know what to do, what Kai might do. As the hound reached for the knife, Kabol brought his elbow down. Kai reacted quickly, using his other fist in an uppercut. Kabol felt it barely graze his skin.

Kai reached for the knife and pulled it out of the ground. "Dead." He charged.

Kabol braced himself, not for the knife but for the force of a collision. He paced backward, preparing himself to grab the hand with the stiletto, but careful not to telegraph that to Kai. The hound was close enough to plunge the dagger into him, but Kabol slapped his hand away. Kai's momentum made him release the dagger as it dug through thin air without stopping.

It was once again on the ground. Kabol took this opportunity to grab the knife and charge, but Kai was prepared for this.

Kabol used the stiletto to stab down with far less force, as his other hand swung a fist to the hound's side. Kai grabbed both hands before they connected and held them above his head.

The hound smirked and shook his head in disappointment as he started to turn Kabol's wrists and the knife started tilting down. Kabol could feel the tip of the blade on the skin of his arm. Pain seared through his arm as the blade broke the skin and cut his flesh, and warm blood oozed down his fur.

Kabol screamed and used the strength in his legs to kick the ground and propel his head forward into Kia's chin and neck. Kabol took the opportunity, when his opponent staggered, and hopped onto him.

Kabol's weight and momentum weren't enough to bring him down. He quickly acted on a risky decision and climbed over the hound's shoulder with an arm around his neck. Now Kabol had the cur's throat in his elbow and began to rip the knife out of his hand.

Kai abandoned the knife entirely, focusing all his efforts into elbowing Kabol into his stomach.

The insurmountable pain stunned Kabol as Kai loosened the grip around his neck and hurled Kabol away, using his arm as leverage.

Kabol immediately got to his feet. His chest was heavy, his breaths were deep, and his hand throbbed in agony. None of it compared to his anger and will to punish Kai.

"You don't look so good." Kai cleared his throat, attempting to get his breath back. "You look like a tired old man."

Kabol clenched the dagger near his feet. Kai was right once again. Kabol smirked at what was possibly the worst insult Kai had ever given him. "You look worse for wear. Maggot."

Kai's brow lowered in anger. He held out his arms, showing his chest completely, and pointed to his heart. "Try me."

Hayden yelled. "Kabol, don't!"

He didn't listen.

Kabol held the dagger in a position to thrust it into Kai's heart. He didn't plan on killing him. He knew Kai was playing him for a fool. He'd stab at the heart, but Kai would block his hand and knock the dagger out of the way. Kabol wouldn't let that happen.

He charged his enemy and stabbed quickly toward the center of the chest. Kai braced his left hand to grab and moved it toward the cat's arm.

Perfect! Kabol thought. Without stopping the flow of movement, Kabol twirled the blade from facing up to facing down and twisted his arm to stab Kai in the shoulder. As his knife was about the find its target, his arm stopped abruptly and the dagger fell out of his hands.

Kai had blocked Kabol's arm, which was stabbing with so much force he lost his grip on the dagger. He could see it, the blade gliding past Kai's chest. A black-gloved hand snatched it from the air.

"Dead!" Kai yelled as he stepped forward and stabbed the triceps of Kabol's outstretched arm.

A sharp sting rushed up his arm, making him cringe, and a yell of agony escaped his mouth. He couldn't control his whimpers and wheezes.

With a smug smile Kai twisted the blade.

Kabol couldn't take it anymore. He hated this feeling. He hated this place. He hated Kai.

The cat punched the hound in the neck and jumped on him. Kabol didn't know what he was doing. He only knew he was on top of Kai. His instincts took over and he began to repeatedly punch him in the face. All these weeks of insults, torture, and taunts was enough motivation to kill a man. He struck his mentor relentlessly. The man was already still and almost lifeless.

Kabol removed the knife from his arm and prepared to stab the mongrel in the chest.

An arm crawled between his neck and chin, and a hand stopped the blade from plunging. "That's enough!" Hayden screamed and dragged the cat back.

Kabol was out of his wits, but his head started to cool as he came back to his senses. The other cadets had long since stopped sparring. As he was dragged away, he could see and feel the looks of a hundred men burn into him.

❧ ❧

Kabol was alone now. His arm was bandaged up, and the bleeding had stopped. His muscles still felt terribly hurt, but not as bad as his chest. His heart felt weak and embarrassed. The feeling you get when you've made a big deal over nothing, the feeling of regret.

He could barely remember anything that had happened. One moment he'd had a knife in his arm, and then he'd had it in his hand. He didn't even remember if he'd planned where or if he was going to stab.

The only thing he knew was that he wished he had not insulted Kai in front of all the cadets. Kabol chuckled sorely at himself. *Yeah, that might have been where I went wrong.*

He heard the barracks door open. In came Hayden the mutt with a cross attitude. "What were you thinking?"

"I wasn't," Kabol answered as if it were a good excuse, moving his right arm and getting a feel for it. Kai hadn't stabbed deeply, and the stiletto's blade hadn't caused permanent damage when he tore it from his arm. It still hurt, though there were medicines for that.

Hayden wasn't as casual. "I'm disappointed in you." He was pacing around, tossing his hands in the air, trying to put his frustration into words. "He's going to have your head. This isn't you! How could you do this?"

Kabol felt disheartened when he heard his friend admit he had failed to meet expectations. "The worst thing he could do is complain. I'm in a different army, remember?"

Hayden tried to calm himself and sat next to Kabol on the bed. "You're ridiculous. And you're using Ben's logic, which is terrifying."

He let out a sigh, then spoke with some hope, as if he were convincing himself there was no problem at all. "The officers are questioning what was going on. Eyewitnesses claim the Sergeant started it. Saying he spouted threats and provoked you. However, they also say you tried to kill Kai when he was no longer a threat."

Kabol frowned and nodded his head. "Attempted murder."

"You've made quite the spectacle." Hayden glared unnervingly. "Consider how he treats you in public. What's Kai going to do when he wakes up?"

Kabol slouched. "Nothing he hasn't done already."

19

"Where is he?" Kai's voice boomed throughout the barracks.

Kabol's ears perked at the booming voice. He was both afraid and calm at the same time. Calm because he was surrounded by peers, but afraid because it might not matter to Kai. The day had just ended, and the twilight hours could have an unpredictable effect on the ill minded.

Kabol was also not in a position to deal with Kai. His right arm clinked with cuffs hooked to the end of the bed. He had been put under house arrest for his actions and made to sleep on the floor, giving him bad posture.

The barracks, which had been preparing to sleep a moment ago, was now up and spooked. They were ready for a show of dimwitted cleverness from a smart-mouth with nothing to say, or a fistful of frenzy from an insulted maniac.

A few more voices called Kai's name, yelling at him to come back. Kabol yanked his chain again; the cuffs were on tight with only enough room to rub his sore wrists. But the wooden bar was loose. He thought if he pulled hard, he might have a chance of it breaking.

Someone fiddled with the front door at the other end of the room before kicking it down, completely destroying the deadbolt and chain, along with the hinges.

There at the door stood Kai. His coat was missing, and his arms and neck were exposed. With his fur bristling and his fists clenched, he pointed at Kabol. "You pig-dogged mouser!"

Kabol placed his foot at the end of the bed and, with much effort, tore the wooden frame. With his arms free, he grabbed the splintered stick, the only weapon he could find.

Kai marched toward Kabol, as he spouted unspeakable insults and threats in his native tongue.

Kabol swung the bar and struck Kai as hard as he could beneath his ribcage. It had little effect as Kai ignored it and wrapped his hands around Kabol's neck. "You pig-priest! This is entirely your fault! You did this to me!" He spoke in his own language once again, pulling Kabol's head until his snout was in the hound's ear, and whispered, "I will see you die in ways you cannot imagine."

Another voice was heard. "Stand down!"

Kabol was thrown to the ground and quickly got back to his feet as Kai marched toward the door. There stood Hayden, fully armed and armored, with several guards.

"I said, stand down," he repeated.

The shepherd hound pointed to the mutt and muttered another phrase foreign to English.

Hayden looked over Kai's shoulder and locked eyes with Kabol. "Translation, please?"

"I'd rather not," Kabol answered honestly.

Kai turned around and said nothing. To the cat's surprise, he placed his hands behind his head and knelt down, muttering, "I'll eat your corpse, mouser."

Kabol ignored that comment.

The hound's hands were cuffed by officers he had once called subordinates. He stared, with a sickening smile, at Kabol. His glare was broken by the guards as they escorted him out of there.

Hayden marched toward the center of the room and stood at ease. He waited for the cadets to stop talking among themselves. His muzzle curled into a smirk and he nodded to Kabol whispering, "I got your back."

Kabol felt flustered, only for a moment, before Hayden straightened up. He noticed Hayden's armor had a brand new rank on the shoulder and breastplate. Not one that belonged to a Corporal, but one that symbolized an officer.

"Cadets! You may be wondering what has happened to Kai. Fret not. Command felt insulted that one of their finest officers had been beaten in combat by a cadet. His reign of terror is over. Command has found someone brave enough to relieve him of his duties. Me. From now on, you may refer to me as Lieutenant Vargas, or just LT. Company, attention!"

The entire group of cadets clicked their heels together and straightened their arms and back.

Hayden broke his pose and strode up the aisles. "You, men, have suffered the strains of some of the hardest military training, with your mentality being pushed as hard as your body. You've made your mothers proud. Now place your hand over your heart. Prepare to recite your oath."

After all of the men had placed their hands on their hearts, Hayden continued. "Repeat after me. I, state your name, swear by all accounts…"

The men repeated it properly.

"That I will defend the helpless; that I shall stand when all else lies; that I will not turn tail at a sign of danger; that I will not leave another man behind; that I, state your name, shall be patient and merciful and kindhearted, but follow orders to the letter. And that if I, state your name, were to break this oath, I will burn."

The men finished repeating the oath. Hayden saluted. "Congratulations, chaps. From this day on, you are now soldiers of New Albion. Behave yourselves. Alas, there is no celebration. We are short on time. You have a few moments to thank, or to pray to, whatever god you believe in before you are required to pack. We're leaving."

Kabol tossed his luggage onto a nearby chair. His eardrums rang with the sounds of train tracks jittering under him. He had yet to obtain sea legs worthy to stand on. He wasn't upset about it at all; but rather a little excited to be rid of those barracks.

He spent most of his time preparing by looking for the hat Kai had stolen. He had given up his search to catch the last train out of there. Hayden and Ben were waiting for him. He still needed to thank them for their patience.

He was surprised at the sight of the train. It wasn't a rickety one like the one he had left Gaul in. This one was more appropriate for carrying people instead of cargo. His room had pictures, windows, and even a carpet. It was the only train they had left after sending troops by the thousands. It had been made specifically for officers traveling in times of peace, but Kabol wasn't complaining.

He fancied himself at the minibar in the middle cabin of the train. The fact that its grand variety of alcohol was the first thing he'd noticed worried Kabol. He had never cared for whiskey, but if there was ever a time, it was now.

He helped himself, seeing as he couldn't find the bartender.

He couldn't sleep with all the shaking. It was too loud. He was so used to sleeping in silent nights in the warm barracks. It was the only thing he missed about that dreadful place. He was glad Hayden had gotten them out of there before he had to go back to the pit.

He rested his head on the counter with the longing for sleep aching behind his eyes.

The door shut lightly; someone had the obvious intention not to wake Kabol. The footsteps were as silent as a sneaky micen's, even on the obvious wooden panels beneath the carpet he could barely hear them. They grew heavier as they got close to the bare floor near the bar.

"You're drinking this watered-down sod?"

Kabol's eyes shot open and glared at the man named Buttons. He had been so close to drifting off to sleep. To wake him now removed what appreciation he had been given.

The leona started fiddling with the bottle in Kabol's hand. "Aye, this isn't even fit for a bottle." Buttons placed a flask on the bar. It was a large bottle with the rim encrusted with gold paint. The label was a mutt drinking from a feral's skull with a banner under it, "Stray Dog's whiskey." Buttons read aloud, "This'll knock you on your post."

Kabol looked at the bottle's proof and contents. He found the number, 151 ABV, too high for his liking. He was almost completely sure that if he took more than a single shot, he'd be lethally poisoned. "I'm trying to find something to make me drowsier, not something that will make me fall off the train."

"Nay, lad." Buttons scoffed. "You'd be drinking whiskey the wrong way. This is happy juice that borrows joy from tomorrow; drink it right, it makes you feel alive. It'll teach you to learn to find new things to love and vice versa. If you sleep it off, you'll only learn to live to regret it."

Kabol ignored him and took another shot of the weaker drink. After some silence and another swig, he determined that he wasn't going to sleep at all that night with the racket and shaking. A large thump that spilled his drink confirmed his suspicion. He asked,

"Where's Lieutenant Vargas?"

Buttons pointed to the ceiling. "He said he needed some time alone and climbed out the window onto the train."

Kabol rested his head on the bar; his buzzed mind didn't know how to comprehend the situation. He pricked an ear in surprise. "Wait, what?"

The mutt Kabol knew would never climb on top of a moving train; that was something someone who wanted to have fun would do. The last time Hayden had acted out of the ordinary had been years ago, and that was when something had been bothering him excruciatingly.

Kabol got up from his chair and felt lightheaded. He was unable to tell if he had gotten up too fast or if the swill was starting to take effect. He held onto the bar, hearing one of Buttons's petty snipes. "Where do you think you're going? Not far, I'll assume."

Kabol waited until he got his footing and headed toward the door that exited the cabin. "Sod off."

"Wait, are you going to climb the train? You can't even stand up straight."

Kabol ignored him and slid open the door. The thundering noise of the wheel and rails spooked him immediately, and the rails beneath him disoriented him, speeding by faster than Kabol could comprehend where the wooden planks were.

He noticed a ladder on the side leading to the top of the train car and turned around and smirked, purposely slurring his speech. "Nonsense, I drive better drunk."

"Wait, what—"

Kabol slammed the door, let go, and allowed the momentum to drag him to his right. He fell over the railing but gripped it tightly before he could fall farther. He crawled over to the ladder on the side. He climbed it as fast as he could and lay on the roof.

He heard the door open, and he poked his head up to see Buttons call his name and look over the side of the railing, calling his name once more. Buttons muttered a few indistinguishable words, in horror, and looked around for anyone before rushing back inside.

Kabol waited for the door to shut before bursting out with laughter. The one thing he missed from working in the coal mines was messing with people who thought he had fallen off the carts and trains. He almost felt nostalgic.

Kabol finished his fit of laughter before standing up. The train wasn't moving fast enough to blow him off his feet, but it was moving at a pace that made it obvious it had a schedule. Unlike in the cars, Kabol felt like it was easy to walk up here. He had more experience on trains than in them.

He took a gander around. Trees and forests surrounded the tracks under the full moon and starry sky. He took notice of the far end of the train. On the caboose a figure stared at the tracks.

Hayden, Kabol presumed.

He jumped from car to car, a task that turned out to be harder and riskier to perform than he remembered. It only took a few jumps before Hayden turned around and saw his old friend, but by that time Kabol was only a boxcar away.

He turned away, facing the passing tracks as Kabol hopped on. The mutt asked, "What are you doing up here?"

"I came to see you." Kabol strutted until he was next to Hayden and began to sit with his legs dangling off.

"Well, you saw me." The mutt sounded hoarse. "Now what?"

"Now I talk. Something is bothering you."

"Is it that obvious?"

"If it were any subtler, I'd assume you were happy. What's wrong?"

Hayden lay on his back with a hum. "Your actions are unacceptable. If I wanted to talk about what bothers me, I'd have talked about it."

"I know you better than that."

"Fair enough." Hayden waved his hands in the air above his chest, giving Kabol the impression that he didn't care about it. He then paused, seeming uncertain what to say. "It's a personal dilemma. I'll get over it."

Kabol rested his body next to Hayden, and their shoulders connected. He stared at the stars and mid-sky moon. "I can tell when you're lying, Hayden. You never hesitate when you speak honestly."

"I 'spose so." Hayden's blue eyes looked about from star to star. The moving plethora of dots looked like mysterious sparkling black granite. "Have you ever fought a religious person before?"

Kabol nodded his head. "Only once."

Hayden narrowed his eyes. "Then you know what they do. The tenacity that faith can give. Some people laugh at the religious. Find them funny. But in battle? I do not find them something to be mocked. I find them something to be feared. Especially when they get it in their heads that their gods don't like you. I've seen their faith build marvelous towers that touched the sky. And I've seen others' faiths bring those towers down." He fell silent before asking, "Are you religious, Kabol?"

Kabol always hated that question. He hated the looks he got and the assumptions made. It always got under his skin when someone said, "You never meet an Atheist in a foxhole." It was war that made him ask questions. He shook his head. "If there were someone looking out for us, he's gone now."

"Aye." Hayden smiled. "Then you are at a disadvantage. They do not fear death. Death is like a metaphor to them. The Avon, Kabol, believe in reincarnation. Their death will only make them into stronger beings. And when trained properly, there cannot be a better soldier."

Kabol was quiet. He didn't remember the last time Hayden had spoken so many sentences that didn't concern orders. "Hayden, I didn't know you were the philosophical type."

"I was for the longest time. Gets boring when you realize they all say the same thing."

Kabol blinked, trying to think of something to say. He was intrigued by his friend's argument, but was that his real problem?

"Wild guess, you're concerned about the safety of the men?"

"How many men do you think are going to die by next week?"

Kabol took a deep breath and nodded. "That sounds like something we shouldn't think about."

"These men now have their lives depending on my every word, against an enemy that I have not fought before and I am scared of." Hayden sounded like his old serious self. "I wanted Kai gone. But I didn't want this. Not again."

"Then why did you take it?" Kabol asked sincerely. "If you didn't like it, then why do it? Surely there was an easier way?"

"It was something about myself I had to sacrifice. Sometimes you have to forget yourself to do the greater good. Sometimes a man will do things he couldn't imagine he'd do with cool blood."

Kabol jested, "That sounds like something Ben would say."

Hayden glared silently at Kabol. Had he said something wrong?

Hayden's brow lowered. "Don't compare me to Ben. He's—"

"Why?" Kabol interrupted, changing his larking tone to an inquisitive one. "You never do answer that question." Before Hayden could respond, Kabol stood up. Perhaps it was the buzz of the whiskey or the night's unforgettable presence; fear or rage took hold of him and pushed his will far more than the breeze could. "You never did explain why he is like this. What was he talking about in the forest?"

Hayden sat up and stared at Kabol before averting his gaze as he thought of the proper words. He closed his eyes and the look on his face was not of aggravation or ire, but sorrow. His ears drooped to the sides. "Ben is… different. Sit down. This'll take a while."

Kabol obeyed and sat attentively.

Hayden continued. "He and I were friends since grammar school. He was a good boy, loved to help people. We would feed stray cats part of our lunch and name them silly names. But then some bullies came along and one just, well, broke the cats' necks.

"I was very cross and unhappy, but Ben? He was fascinated. I went to get a teacher or the principal, and when I got back, Ben was missing and the bullies…" Hayden cleared his throat and shook his head. "I found Ben under a bridge. He was crying, saying he needed to be put down. He was afraid of something that, back then, I didn't understand. I should have seen the signs. He's no longer afraid, Kabol. In fact, he's happy. Now he sees death as a way to end suffering. Says he's never seen a dead man cry.

"Then war came. A mortar fell right on top of his house. Killed his family. I had to dig him out. He still hasn't shed a tear over it. And now, every time I leave him alone for too long, he gets into trouble. I left him alone now. I did. But first I knocked him out and threw him into a footlocker."

Kabol no longer had anger running through his blood, but rather concern and curiosity. Hayden had to go to such lengths as to incapacitate his childhood friend to make him behave himself. He wasn't sure if that was loyal or villainous.

Kabol started thinking out loud and putting the pieces together. "That's why you made me promise to take care of him. You think you're going to die and he's going to be alone."

Hayden nodded. "You're afraid?"

Kabol was still. His mind was racing. Then it dawned on him. What if he were to die? If he were to be missed? Dinred had Isabelle, but the thought of leaving her behind brought him anguish. He shook the thought from his head, trying to get back on track. "The way Ben rushes into danger, I wouldn't be concerned about it myself." Kabol attempted to joke. He was never really good at this humor thing, which might be why Dinred enjoyed Isabelle's company.

Hayden was unamused, giving Kabol a disappointed look.

Kabol rubbed the itch on the back of his head. "Sorry."

"I don't like that answer. But you're right." Hayden got up and faced Kabol before wrapping his arms around him and hugging him gently. Kabol did the same, realizing this had never happened before. "Good talk. Get back inside. I'll follow you shortly, but the stars are noticeably more beautiful tonight."

Kabol broke into a smile. "Try not to fall off the train."

"Don't tell me what to do." He smirked, releasing the cat. "Oh, one more thing. There was something I wanted to give you." Hayden pulled out a dagger from one of his pockets. Its edges were lined with reinforced diamond, and everything from the tip to tang was thin titanium. It was the Seraph's blade! "I found it on the ground when you were done fighting the Seraph. Thought you might like it."

"Thanks." Kabol twirled it and tossed it from hand to hand as he backed away. "I'll put it to good use."

Kabol stepped into the cart with the bar. The atmosphere had changed completely from how he remembered it.

Troops found their way into the cabin, singing drunken lyrics in slurred voices. One was playing a violin, well enough that it was obvious he'd stayed sober. The drunkards all sang to the tune completely off key. Buttons was behind the counter, looking very relieved to see Kabol's not-so-dead body.

On the end next to Kabol, three guys were playing cards and telling jokes. All around the room was laughter and music. And then there was Ben, who seemed to have escaped from the footlocker.

He didn't seem cross at all, even smiling as if maybe he thought the whole thing was a joke. He was also shirtless. The white cat's fur was a light yellow now, thanks to a highlighter he had found and taken the time to color his fur with. Nothing could be done about his purple hair turning gray though.

Kabol sat next him. "That can come off really easily."

Ben only smiled.

Buttons pulled up a bottle next to Kabol. "You bloody scared me with that trick of yours. Heart was pounding until I saw you hopping back. Thought they were going to blame me for sure."

"This isn't the first time I've been off to war. I can hold my liquor." Kabol smirked, reaching for another glass of the weakest spirit and pulling out the knife. "Take a look at this."

He handed it to Buttons, who whistled at its beauty. "T'is a fine catch. Hayden wasn't lying when he told us you killed a Seraph, eh?"

"I wouldn't say I killed him."

"I hear the mortality rate against them would be like head buttin' a brick wall until yer skull caves in." Buttons handed back the dagger. "Assuming the wall also hit back." Buttons lifted up the bottle of Stray Dog's and chugged a swig before placing it back on the shelf. "I oughta get to sleep before I keel over."

"I'll see you tomorrow, Buttons." Kabol watched Buttons head to the back of the train. A soldier from the card game asked to take a gander at the knife as well, and Kabol gently tossed it, hilt first, on their table.

He looked around the room. The air itself felt in good cheer with laughter and jokes and stories being told by bards. Ben behaving himself was icing on the cake. Kabol grinned, feeling a breeze through an open window.

He felt nostalgic once again, remembering the days when he'd stand on his balcony with Dinred and watch the shining palace on a rare sunny day. *I'm coming home, Love.* He started to think of romantic metaphors to tell her.

"Guys!" Ben stood up, his fur bristled on end. His eyes were wide and his ears were twitching. "Shut up! Everyone shut up!"

The entire room went dead, turning their gaze toward Ben.

Ben looked at Kabol with a finger to his lips. "You hear that?"

Kabol listened. From one of the open windows, a slight whistle was heard, a familiar one, too familiar, coming closer, and closer.

"No!" Ben screamed and grabbed Kabol's arm, dragging him toward the caboose, "Run! Everyone run!"

The cabin next to theirs burst into a massive inferno. The bar's whiskey and ale spilled as the entire room flipped on its side as the boxcar derailed.

<h1 style="text-align:center">20</h1>

Ziyad held the silver pistol firmly.

He didn't like the use of projectile weaponry. He saw the value, but if he refused to kill a man without looking into his eyes, or in some way he could not defend with equal skill, then that was the worst kind of murder.

He did not devalue the advantage a bullet would bring, but he despised taking life with a pull of a trigger. If you were going to take a life, make it mean something.

The teachings of Avon state that Seraphs shall only claim kills slain in the truest of forms. Bullets create the illusion of safety for those who use them. *When your enemy realizes his only means of killing you is useless, he shall bare the face of true horror as you, my angel of death, shall claim his soul.* He reminded himself of his creed. *That you who slay in my name shall strike terror in the hearts of many. So much so that they shall set aside their guns, kneel, and thus be spared.*

That's what it meant to be a Seraph, to carry His will when words failed, to kill their men and morale. He was to become horror incarnate and create chaos, and have the very sight of him be a death sentence.

Yet they still fought.

The leona, the mutts, the wolfen. Why?

Around him, a new city burned to ash with yet another rebellion quelled. More lives wasted in pitiful attempts at unrest. Why? What did they fight for? Under what name did they throw away their lives? What country? What king or god or man?

Their numbers dwindled with every battle, but no matter how

many were routed, scattered or killed, they fought as if they remained constant, or even growing.

The answer remained a mystery as their blood dripped from his gauntlets.

In front of him a prisoner was on his knees, feline tail and body without armor. His face was covered by a black sack and his hands were constrained by wire.

The mere smell of the animal made the Seraph's left hand twitch with pain and fury. Ziyad growled through his mask. "Cat, tell me. Why do you fight? Do you not fear?"

The prisoner was quiet, with nothing to say.

The Seraph placed the pistol on the forehead of the being. "Death calls for you. He told me to make it quick, precise, horrific. Then you submitted. I now shall only do two of those things. Answer me if you want it to be quick."

The prisoner was quiet.

This struck a nerve with the Avian. The audacity this being must have to ignore a Seraph, an angel of death, in the position he was in was insurmountable. If he wanted to look in the eyes of his killer, then his wish would be granted.

He removed his mask. The crisp, amber air burned at his eyes. He pinched the sack and tore it off the prisoner's head.

The cat in front of him gazed with anger through dark blue eyes. Unfathomable and irrefutable loathing that suppressed the part of the mind that should hold fear.

Hate.

Ziyad felt silent ridicule until he realized the lesson behind his prisoner's nerve. This man had nothing.

No. Ziyad corrected himself. He still had two things. One was hope. Hope that the Seraph would surely die. Hope that the followers of Avon would be driven from his home. Hope that one day this would all be over.

It was something that the fear Ziyad brought could not take no matter how much he tried.

The second thing this man had, however, Ziyad could take. He placed the gun against the man's head, between the eyes. He would forget the man's face; he might even forget how he had killed him. But he would not forget the lesson.

⚊⚊⚊

Kabol wheezed air through his nostrils. His back was in terrible pain. His neck felt knotted, and his limbs throbbed in agony.

The cheerful songs and voices that he remembered felt so distant now. The air was chilling to the bones. Where was he?

He opened his eyes to see that he was still in the room. It was dark. The lights had been blown out and shattered by the force of the impact. The room was deathly silent, save for an eerie creaking noise.

Kabol came to reality. He was lying on his back against a wall. In front of him was the other end of the car with its door blown off. Outside was the dark and cloudy sky. The boxcar was hanging off a ledge!

Kabol sat up quickly, feeling a sharp stabbing pain in his back. It was dire enough that he was involuntarily forced to lie back down, and he almost cried out in agony. He rolled onto his stomach, realizing the hell he had gotten himself into.

Corpses of his comrades cluttered the space around him. Their bodies had scorch marks along with visible bruises and limbs and other parts twisted out of proportion. At his feet, Kabol could see a head resting on him, dripping the crimson ooze.

The silver fur was unremarkable, even when it was drenched in blood. At his neck Kabol's knife protruded with the blade gouged in deeply. Kabol's heart sank in sorrow. He hadn't known the man very well, but to hear a colleague's laugh before their untimely death was sickening.

Kabol was tempted to say a silent prayer, for old time's sake, but decided against it. He was dead, so it would have done no good. Kabol looked around. Wet blood was everywhere. Some stains looked as if he had been dragged or rolled, as if the fall hadn't killed him.

Kabol stood up much more slowly than last time. This time he was without crippling pain when he got to his feet. He reached down and gently retrieved his knife from the corpse, closing the cat's dead eyes respectfully.

"Pst."

Kabol's ear twitched when he heard the whisper from above. Ben, who had stolen a shirt off the dead, was glaring down from behind the bar's counter.

"Hey, Kabol, are you alive?"

Kabol glared at him. He was silent, as if standing up was enough of an answer.

"Oh good, then I won't eat you." He climbed down from inside the bar, using the shelves behind the counter as a ladder. "Give me your hand and I'll help you up. Also, that man was like that when I woke up, except with less blood and a lot more screeches. Anyways, I need your help. I can't get out of here alone."

He held out a hand when he stood on what was left of the liquor shelf. Kabol wasn't too happy about Ben joking around about the dead, but he was right about one thing. That counter and the only exit off were too far from each other. They'd need to work together to get out.

He grabbed Ben's hand, carefully not stepping onto the shattered glass. "I did not appreciate that remark about—"

"Tough." Ben scoffed as he grabbed his hand and helped him onto the counter. Now that they were close together, Kabol noticed that Ben's fur was much more yellow. Had he really put on a new coat of marker?

Kabol decided to ask a different question that was on his mind. "How did you know where the mortars were going to hit?"

Ben climbed to the top of the counters, humming as he thought of an answer. "I've spent my entire young adult life hearing them." He jumped onto the edge of the counter closest to the exit, made a high-pitched whistle mimicking a mortar shell, and motioned with his hand as if it was falling from the sky. "Far."

He did it again, and this time the whistle became lower pitched as his hand got closer to the counter.

"Close."

Kabol climbed on top of the counter and cupped his hands next to Ben's feet. Ben placed his foot on the gray cat's palms. When the order was given, Kabol pushed Ben up and the yellow leona jumped high enough to grab hold of the ledge.

He quickly pulled himself up and leaned down to offer a hand. Kabol jumped and they gripped each other. Ben pulled hard and, without any real trouble, Kabol was out of the wagon.

He couldn't have prepared himself for the disaster that awaited them.

The train was separated and its tracks were completely obliterated. The power and impact of the mortar had been enough to bring the severed end and caboose to a halt, while the rest of the trail had derailed off the cliff side.

The cliff itself wasn't too high, maybe ten or twenty meters. Below the cliff was a forest, and spots of fire were seen, here and there, past the trees.

"Shh…" Ben perked his ears and pointed to the fires. "Listen."

Kabol did what he had been told. He could hear distant gunshots from afar.

"They're having fun." Ben smiled. "We better move away from the wreckage unless we want some fun of our own."

Where could they go? The train had wrecked and the cliff was too steep to climb down. It was not like the commanders had known they would be under attack.

When thinking about his commanding officer, Kabol was reminded of Hayden. "Ben," Kabol felt his fur bristle on end and his tail puff. "Hayden was at the caboose last I saw him. Do you think he made it?"

As the words left his mouth, he felt stupid for asking. How would Ben know? The yellow cat gave him the look Kabol would have given in a similar situation.

Kabol studied his surroundings further. On his left were the cliff and forest, and on his right another tree line led to woodland on a small hill. "Do you think he could be in there?"

Ben shook his head. "Me and you know Hayden. He's not afraid of danger." Ben held up a finger as if a brilliant thought had struck him.

"I know! How about we check where you left him. That tends to be where things are most of the time."

Before Kabol could respond, several shots were heard, close to them, inside the train.

Hayden!

Kabol looked at Ben for any ideas, but no words were needed. They both hopped onto the next car and ran toward the caboose. They were in a simple lounge with tables and love seats side by side in hopes of entertainment. There was also a TV shattered on the floor along with fragments of the table that had been dislodged or broken by the sudden stop.

Before they could get much farther, Kabol heard the propulsion of an engine. He ordered Ben to hide, and they both found knocked-over tables for cover. Kabol looked out his window, facing the hill.

As suspected, an Avonian V-TOL flew over some trees. It stopped and hovered over some tracks, opening its compartments. Out dropped a silvery figure. He made a lurid clang, when landing, as he crushed the metal roof.

This Avon looked different. His helmet was beakless, replaced by a snout. The feathers were missing from atop the head, replaced by ears. Out from his hip came the exposed tail of a fox.

The aircraft flew toward the fires below as the Seraph touched the side of his helmet. His black eyes turned red as he looked up and down the wreckage of the train.

What is he doing? Kabol thought. *He's just standing there, gawking at the wreckage.*

Kabol figured now might be a good time to move out while the Seraph was busy looking at the roof.

They moved in quietly, careful not to make a sound. After few seconds they left their cover before the Seraph made any sudden moves. The foxen began to run away from Kabol and Ben's position. For a moment, Kabol could have sworn the Seraph looked directly at him through all the debris as he jumped between the cars.

"I think he saw us," Kabol whispered.

"Don't be ridiculous," Ben said without lowering his voice, passing under an arch that belonged to an absent door.

More gunshots were heard, making Kabol increasingly aware of his situation, and he said, "Ben, do you have your gun?" Kabol felt uncomfortably naked without his weapon. All he had, in the middle of a war zone, was a knife.

Ben rolled his eyes. "Listen." Soon the gunfire stopped. "Do you think having a gun did them any good?" Ben pulled out a knife from his boot. It wasn't anything fancy or out of the ordinary. It was merely a sharply pointed blade on a hilt.

"Come on." Kabol still kept his voice low. "We need to get to Hayden. He's smart enough not to use a Callum, so I'm sure he's alive."

Kabol was the first to hop onto the next car, and Ben soon followed. Kabol slid the door open, hearing a loud bang as the car shook. It wasn't the door that had created that noise.

On the other end of the car was the Seraph. The fox swung his arm, knocking a familiar face into a wall, creating another thundering smash as his victim crashed into a box. It was Buttons. The Seraph's gaze darted toward the duo at the door, too late to see them.

Kabol held his breath. He and Ben had hidden beneath the windows the moment they saw the Seraph, but the element of surprise might be gone.

Numbers, Kabol. Think with numbers.

There was only one Seraph. Perhaps he was the clean-up crew. Kabol remembered the time he and Hayden had been pinned down. Numbers were useless when they were clumped together, and if he stayed pinned like this the Seraph would merely find a flank to attack from. Kabol refused to assume he was stupid enough to walk through a door that had just opened.

The ladder! Kabol didn't mention his plan to Ben. He looked at the outside of the train car and saw a ladder. He hopped on it and climbed to the other end as fast as he could. He whispered, "Ben, improvise!"

A window was shattered toward the end of the train car. The Seraph crawled out and lifted himself to the top of the train. Kabol instinctively pulled out his knife. The Seraph, on the other hand, kept his blades sheaved and calmly walked toward the leona.

The foxen pointed toward the ground, demanding, "Stand down."

Kabol focused on his enemy, spreading his legs at shoulder width and keeping his blade in front of him. He kept his focus on the Seraph. He was an orange foxen, or so his tail had him believe. White ovals surrounding his blue eyes, and an upside-down Y on his forehead.

The Seraph turned off the color of his eyes and stretched his arm with a wagging finger.

He speaks English? Kabol thought, slowly realizing that the Seraph had braced itself in a stance similar to Taka'rin, drawing his knife from his shoulder. *He's trained to kill Albion soldiers!*

The Seraph charged.

Kabol wasn't going to take a chance. He turned and jumped off the roof. He landed on the link between the cars and ran as fast and far away from the Seraph as possible. He was so preoccupied with trying to find the Seraph it didn't cross his mind to ask where Ben was. The Seraph hopped down, smashing the link between the cars.

The floor was yanked from under Kabol, making him trip. He wasn't sure if it was part of the Seraph's plan to break the link, but now the boxcar was being pulled gradually toward the cliff!

The Seraph simply stood at the doorway, holding his ground and preventing any escape.

Kabol considered his choices: fight the Seraph or fall off the cliff. No. *There has to be another way!*

"You have nowhere to run. Submit," the fox called. "Now!"

Kabol heard a bloodcurdling scream. Ben! From the roof of the other car, Ben leaped into the air. After he fell, he planted his feet in the sides of the Seraph's turning body. The powerful momentum Ben had built couldn't be stopped. It had knocked him and the Seraph on their backs.

The Seraph's knife slid toward Kabol. He picked it up, seeing that the Seraph's helmet had fallen off as well.

He didn't hesitate in getting up and jutting a single blade from his right arm.

Kabol figured using two knives was a silly idea. He'd have to split his strength and attention, and he was more effective focusing on one thing. The Seraph saw Ben get up but neglected him, focusing his efforts on the only cat with weapons, Kabol. This time, however, Kabol charged.

The Seraph hadn't expected this and parted his legs in preparation for the impact. It was a mistake.

Kabol slid his spare dagger under the Seraph's legs, allowing Ben to pick it up. The Seraph's attention was now divided. Ben made a stab for the neck, provoking the Seraph to focus on him and grab his arm.

Kabol took this golden opportunity to grab the bladed arm and dig his knife into the foxen's upper right ribcage in the exposed area below the shoulder.

His scream pierced the air as he fell to his knees. He still held Ben in his clutches, dragging him to the ground as he toppled over. He released him, placing his free hand on the oozing wound. Kabol had already removed the weapon and placed the tip of his dagger at the base of the foxen's skull. One single jab would end the Seraph's life.

Kabol closed his eyes; the only thing on his mind was the agonizing scream of his victim. The blade began to shake as Kabol's hands trembled. Just a simple stroke would end decades of experienced life and untold stories. He couldn't do it.

He released the Seraph, who fell on the ground, wailing in pain.

Kabol's instincts took over. He tore off his sleeve and placed it against the bleeding wound. "Hold still. I have to stop the bleeding!"

The Seraph's struggle was starting to ease. This worried Kabol. He was in too much pain not to yell, him being quiet now can only mean he was going into shock.

"Come on, stay with me!" He removed his enemy's hand and kept pressure on the wound. Then he saw what he feared. The Seraph's eyes were locked on him, staring at his killer before closing. Kabol called to Ben, "Get his armor off! Get him some air!"

Ben shook his head. "No."

"That's an order, Private!" he screamed.

Ben merely smirked as he crawled over to the mask and grasped it. "He's a dead man. And so are we if we stay here." Ben stood up and hopped out of the train.

Kabol recalled with horror. *The cliff!*

The train was steadily increasing its speed. The more weight was off the tracks, the faster it would fall. Kabol grabbed the Seraph and began to drag him. He was heavy, though barely budging. Kabol screamed obscenities as he pulled the arms as hard as he could.

With quick thinking, he unhooked what was left of the mask and unsealed the breastplate. It made the man much lighter, and Kabol was able to drag him much more easily as the armor continued to fall off. Adrenaline pumped through his veins. He found the strength to pull the man out of the train.

He hopped onto the ground and held the fox under the shoulders. The train started to slip under him and it quickly keeled over off the ledge, crushing trees, destroying rocks, and creating enough noise to pop Kabol's eardrums.

There was no time to celebrate the narrow escape. Kabol immediately went back to putting pressure on the wound. He cut off his sleeves and folded one into a square. He used the other one to tie the bandage down, wrapping it around the chest.

He checked the neck. No pulse.

Kabol placed his hands on the fox's chest and began to press down rhythmically. "Don't you dare die on me!"

Time started to become convoluted and bent. Every second felt like a lifetime. *Press down thirty times, check pulse, check breath, breathe in mouth, and repeat.*

He didn't know how long he'd been doing it. It felt like hours. Every moment was a chance for a life to be lost. He had never wanted to hurt the foxen. He had been scared. He should have surrendered!

His hands started to ache from the constant pressing. His throat became sore from trading his breath for the foxen's. His mind was tired from calculating the amount of pressure and air. Too little and he would suffocate. Too much and air would enter the stomach, causing vomit to enter the mouth or lungs.

The fox gasped in air.

Kabol felt relief flush over him as if a heavy weight on his chest had been lifted. "Thank you," Kabol repeated in whispers as he continued. Eventually the gasping stopped and was replaced by a regular breath. He stared at the breathing body, satisfied with how his ribcage grew and shrank with every lungful of air. The leona felt like he was being watched.

He turned his head to see several of his brethren watching him. There were so many that they'd crowded the track, almost blocking the train from view. Their faces ranged from impressed to sympathetic.

And in front of it all was Hayden. His face was neither impressed nor sympathetic; he had the face of a proud father. He walked up to Kabol and knelt down, placing a hand on his shoulder. "There's the Kabol I know. For a moment I thought Kai had killed you."

Kabol smiled. "He did try."

"So what are we going to do with the Avon?" Ben stood beside them. "We can't just leave him alive."

"And why not?" Hayden stood up.

"Because we can't take him with us." Ben closed his eyes, making him look drowsy, but he spoke without hesitation. "And if we could, what are we going to feed him? How are we going to make him walk?"

"You're suggesting we kill him?" Hayden growled. "An unarmed, defenseless man?"

Ben was silent before nodding. "Yes."

The soldiers were torn between the two. They realized that the Seraph had killed no one. The ones who had encountered the Avon, such as Buttons, had bruises and sore limbs, but nothing else. Although he was an Avon, among the people who had taken their homes and had slaughtered a trainful of people, they settled on trusting Kabol's judgment and couldn't bring themselves to end him.

Kabol's ears tuned into the sound of radio chatter. It was coming from the helmet that Ben had kept as a trophy. "We are not killing him." Kabol stood up. "Ben, give me the helmet."

Ben was uncertain, holding the helmet close to his heart like a baby before sighing and tossing it, underhanded, to Kabol.

There was a radio frequency and speaker in the left ear, as well as a button that allowed the wearer to reply. Kabol put on the helmet and heard an Avian voice over the radio. "Renatus, report this instant! What is the situation?"

Kabol cleared his throat. "This is Private Anton. Renatus is in dire health, and he needs medical evac. How copy?"

The operator was silent for a moment, long enough that Kabol thought he should repeat himself. In retrospect, he should have hidden his accent.

The operator continued, speaking with livid hate. "You."

The way the Avian said that made chills crawl up Kabol's spine. He felt a familiar presence and instinctively feared for his life. What did he mean by that? Where had he heard that voice before?

He took the helmet off and placed it next to the Seraph. "We need to move out."

Ben raised an eyebrow and opened an eye. "Did anyone else

notice Kabol just gave away our position?"

Hayden flicked his friend's ear. "They'd have been suspicious anyway if the Seraph didn't answer." The mutt raised his hand and gave the order to rally beside him, hushing any talk among the rabble. "There is a depot a few kilos down the track. If we leg it, we'll make it there long before the front lines." Hayden pointed at the train. "Everyone, go back and find a weapon. If you do not have a weapon, find someone who is willing to share their sidearm. We are moving out in two minutes."

Kabol finally estimated the number of troops and men. Out of the hundred or so that the train had carried, forty-two were left on the tracks. Considering the front line wasn't far off, and the front half of the train was off the side of the cliff, it was out of their hands to care for the missing.

The soldiers who had fired their guns reloaded their weapons and cartridges. Those without weapons ran back inside the train for anything they could scavenge.

Ben rubbed his fingers across his new knife. For a reason Kabol couldn't figure out, Ben tossed the knife on the ground with a disinterested look.

After Kabol got his own rifle, Hayden took point as he led all the troops away from the Seraph and train. He kept Kabol by his side. At one point he leaned over and whispered, "I'm proud of you."

2 I

For the first time since she could remember, Dinred felt at ease.

Albion had been different ever since the Avon arrived. There were fewer homes, for one thing. The hospital parking lot had been turned into a tent city during the three months she'd lived there. She was lucky to be allowed to help the nurses. It enabled her to have her own room, and she was permitted to help herself to some food three times a day.

She always shared half her food with Isabelle, who had started to hide less. Several Avon had seen her, and they didn't care. It seemed the publicity about finding the heir had died out. Dinred wasn't sure why, but she thought they'd figured out it only inspired morale when the leona heard that their monarch's bloodline was not gone forever. And when she really thought about it, the Avon would be stupid to think the leonas had left their only heir to the throne behind after having hidden her so well.

There was probably a plethora of reasons. Dinred figured that she could name them all if she truly took the time out of her day.

Dinred now spent her time washing blood off rags and bins and sterilizing tools. The past month she'd worked with her hands more than she had the previous year. Strangely, she didn't mind it. It felt like she was making a difference in her world, even if it was a small one.

She'd been trying to convince the doctors and nurses to allow Isabelle to help, but they pointed out she would only be turned away by the Avon. That was another reason Dinred was there: some of the doctors needed a leona's hands in non-life threatening situations.

She felt a rather bright glowing feeling inside her when she

187

thought about how much such a little thing made her day great.

Ziyad stopped by at least once every few days to say hello and see how she was doing. She'd had friends before, but they'd mostly leave a calling card or chat on the phone. They had almost never come by just to see her and talk.

She hadn't even heard from them since the invasion. Curious, but she knew better than to make daft assumptions.

Dinred felt a bit groggy when she awoke from a nap. Her shift was over for the day, but she still felt like she had time to burn. Unfortunately, all the good pubs were long gone.

She decided to do some studying at the library, one of the few places the Avon had left untouched. Whether it was out of respect, or simply for the sake of keeping a vast amount of knowledge intact, it had not been looted or bombed.

They'd kept it maintained, even if it meant removing all the refugees and ruffians. They'd staffed it with a few civilians who lived in the towering aircraft miles above, hidden behind the blanket of clouds.

It wasn't just any old library either; it was trimmed in bronze, silver and, in some places, gold carvings. The ceiling reached as high as age-old, steelless concrete would let it and was topped with a dome. A few statuettes of great poets and philosophers lined the circumference of the dome.

⁂

Dinred, however, wasn't there for sightseeing. She was curious and needed answers. As much as she trusted Ziyad, she felt as if his biased nature had gotten in the way of his convictions. What were the Avon after here? Surely not every Avon had seen their families murdered.

She searched through the aisles. Some shelves, with ladders and platforms, nearly reached the ceiling while others were built into a staircase to the next level. Dinred didn't know where to look, or even the name of the book she was looking for.

After asking an Avonian worker, she was pointed toward a nearby aisle. It was near a section of children's books. As Dinred passed, she could hear the distinct voice of an Avian, speaking clear English, telling a group of attentive children, a mix of cats, mutts and birds, the story of how Swift the Hunter feared not the eyes of calamity.

Soon, she stumbled on the book she was looking for in a small corner of its own. *The Recounting.* She pulled the book out and found a quiet place alone.

The volume was well translated and obviously written by a poetic historian's hand. It started with the story of Cerberus. He had altered the annals and his real name had been lost in the records of time. It told stories of the eight-foot, scarlet-eyed demon who rose from rot and ash in exile and incited rebellions that were small but effective.

Soon the eastern Asian countries, which at the time consisted mostly of Avian, grew to despise each other's people and beliefs. Cerberus brought them under one banner the only way he knew how, by eliminating all religions but his.

He did this without cruel intent. He chose a small sect of wolfen, who were the underclass in that society. He claimed that Mesopotamia had been run by both wolfen and Avian until most of the wolves explored other lands, leaving their bird-like brethren behind. The Avian were then vastly outnumbered and were conquered in their own lands.

Cerberus came into power at the right time. Sympathy among the Avian had grown after the wolfen protested they were people. Cerberus used this to his advantage. He made a pact: if the birds fought with the wolves, they would be by his side for eternity. At that time, he was a young commander, but a brilliant one. After the wolves saw him win skirmishes where the odds were stacked against him, and after they saw him singlehandedly take on three armored soldiers with knives, they were convinced that he was the demon of war, their savior.

He was named Cerberus, after the dog of death from his homeland's own mythology, by his foes and friends alike. He liked the name and decided to keep it. When his personal power armor was designed and created, he took pleasure in having a skull added to each shoulder.

"He"—spelled several times, in the book, with a capital "H"—singlehandedly developed the strategies that led him to conquer all the lands he deemed holy. Then the strategists of Russia and Greece sought his help.

He broke his exile and joined their ranks in the war against the Second Roman Empire.

By now, Dinred was bored and began to skim through the book.

She already knew how this story went. The Roman Empire collapsed, and Cerberus took charge of both Russia and Greece with a huge clique of followers. He showed his respect for the cunning skill of foxen and mutts by offering Rome as a vassal, and they accepted. Then came the mutts' rebellions, which worked out terribly. Then came the leona's suicidal war followed by the sacking of Albion and Carthage and blah, blah, blah.

She had learned all of this stuff in grade school. What she was trying to figure out was what they planned to do to punish a man who had been dead for ninety-eight years.

"Hello there." A proud voice spooked Dinred, and she jumped from her chair. She turned to see a dark green-feathered Avian with beautiful amber-like eyes.

"Oh, hello! You snuck up on me."

"Apologies." The Avian bowed his head. It wasn't long until Dinred realized the voice belonged to the man who had read to the children. He continued, "I was on my way to put a book back when I noticed you reading Avon's *The Recounting*. I must deduce you're interested in learning about us?"

"Yes," Dinred said. "I have questions, and I've heard this book has answers."

A smile crept onto the Avon's face. "I've read the book many times. If you have questions let us say, perchance, I might be of assistance."

Dinred shook her head, not wanting to be a bother. "You could say I've heard this before. I've heard a Seraph preach before."

"Tsk. Tsk." The bird wagged his pointed talon-like finger in the air. "It's not polite to assume I am among the commoners' zealous rabble."

"I'm sorry; I didn't mean to sound like I assumed anything."

"But you did." The Avian's words didn't hold ire. They seemed to be spoken in jest, gently mocking his own social stature. "However, you said 'sorry.' Your deeds are henceforth forgiven."

"Do most Avon act like you?" Dinred had the same playful tone of voice though, in hindsight, it was a valid question.

"Only the best!" the man said cheerfully, keeping his voice down for the library. He covered his beak. "Oh, I hope that wasn't too loud."

"Rules do not matter if you're important, Dear." Dinred gestured for him to sit. "I'm not one to talk religion and politics with friends, but you seem strange enough."

"I'll take that as a compliment." The bird sat down. "Seeing that you are sufficiently intrigued by His ideals to pick up *The Recounting*, I think you deserve them as well."

"I appreciate that." Dinred cleared her throat. "I've heard that Cerberus isn't popular, but the first chapters of this book seem to praise him."

"Indeed," Naseer said, "he's done some good and, without him, the teachings of Avon would be ignored. However, as you may know, beings of all statures are not always remembered for the good they've done. If a man could donate millions of his earnings only for a few bodies to be found in his basement, what would you think of him?"

Dinred could see that he was making a point. "So you were not fond of his slavery?"

"That's only the sin of all empires. There's more to it than that, but yes. We think all beings are equal," Naseer said with glee. "Slavery has its silver lining, but so does war. We learn to measure our consequences."

"Everyone is equal? What about the mutts?"

Naseer was calm and collected. "I, personally, see nothing is wrong with them. It's a shame they lack the gall to prove they should be treated as such. That how you can tell the commoner's birth apart from the aristocratic. The lesser never care what you look like, only how you act, and I commend them for it."

"Agreed." Dinred wanted to feel insulted by those words, but she shouldn't expose her history of being considered of such stature. She narrowed her eyes. "What about the wolfen?"

"What about the wolfen?" Naseer looked puzzled.

"One of the Seraphs preached about how the wolfen are a menace to society. He talked about getting rid of their kind in New Albion, so that no other demon could be born."

Naseer let out a chuckle. "That's silly." Then he narrowed his eyes and spoke more seriously. "Just wondering, what was the name of this Seraph?"

"Atasha, friend." Dinred crossed her arms. She wasn't going to rat out Ziyad to someone she didn't know.

"Touché," he said, before muttering and tapping the side of his skull. "That narrows it down."

"Is it true?" Dinred ignored his unimportant ramble and tried to focus on the subject. "Are you really evacuating all the wolfen?"

Naseer's eyes widened. Perhaps he was wondering how much she knew? He nodded. "It is true. The motive, no; the verb, yes. We are evacuating them, but that is so that they won't bother anyone here."

He expects me to believe that? Dinred continued to skim through the pages of the book, thinking of how to word her next sentences. "You should know, my husband was a doctor. He used to come home every evening and talk about age-old incantations and other horrors they used to call medicine. It was disgusting. He continued this for weeks, getting a kick out of my reactions, until I told him to stop, that I didn't want to know how a lobotomy worked. But one thing stuck out to me. For the longest time, people thought that blood was the reason for everything, be it illness, insanity, or just pure evil. One record stated a doctor used leeches to suck the unintelligent blood cells from a victim—I mean patient—so he would be normal. Do you know why we don't do that anymore?"

"They were wrong." Naseer smirked and gave her a friendly laugh. "You believe we think the wolfen are the bad blood of Albion, and we are the doctor and leech."

Dinred nodded. "You are not fixing any problems here."

Naseer smiled again and, this time, Dinred didn't know why. He motioned with his hands as if he were evangelizing. "The wolfen are not blood. They are like a limb: an arm. However, they are more beast than sentient, more thoughtless than careful, and more warmongering than philosophical. The arm has necrosis and maggots are eating at the flesh. Whose job is it to rid the body of Europa of this dire threat whence it is surrounded by enemies? The other arm, of course. And the other arm is the Avon. We merely wish to rid the body of the horrible limb, not destroy the arm itself. For even in its decrepit state, it still holds life, no matter how low we currently perceive it as being."

Dinred saw his argument, one less emotionally driven than Ziyad's. She understood now, but she did not agree. But what could she say? She couldn't just tell him he was wrong. Convincing a zealot the cups of their religion held little water was a task that could not be done overnight. Now she was wishing she had Isabelle there to give her insight on how to argue with this silver-tongued bird.

"What do your gods think of this?" Dinred felt like her mouth was dirty.

Naseer, to Dinred's surprise, didn't react irately. He carefully grabbed the book from across the table and flipped through the pages. He slowed down near some blueprints of armor, still turning pages. Dinred was able to see some designs for the Seraph armor and other similar things Avon and his followers had created.

He then placed a claw on a page written entirely in Avian script and said, "This page explains that all gods were once Avian. It was a common theme in the region Cerberus was banished to. All Avian were once foxen, and so on and so forth for every race. I say this for there are millions of gods, and many of their names matter not to most mere mortals. The only name and will that matters to all is Avon. And he would understand what we are doing."

"Who is Avon?" Dinred felt like she was going to regret that question and prepared herself for a speech.

"Avon was an Avian that grew up here in New Albion; at the time it was just Albion. He was a commanding officer at the front lines in a battle. He led his troops with an arming sword for morale purposes. Cerberus took an interest in him and stopped an entire battle to duel him with a sword and shield from a nearby museum. Avon fought bravely, even when his shield arm was broken. The demon was impressed and spared the entire army, and the bird. When the war was over, Avon was seated as his right hand man, even when our feathered friend despised him."

Dinred nearly zoned out but tried her best to pay attention. She had hoped her suspicions were wrong and she would get a short answer, not his life story. She wanted to learn about him, but now she remembered why she preferred bards over pastors. This is what she got for being caught with a holy book open.

"Avon hated how the emperor chose the class system. He hated how the demon had the final say in everything. And when Cerberus was old, and his chalice was poisoned, Avon sought his death via assassination. Even when weak, the demon killed a quarter of the twelve sent to end him. Avon was accused of treason and lynched by the upper class. Cerberus had no heir, and his vassals fell into madness. Every nation in his empire separated. Wake up!" Naseer slammed a hand down next to Dinred's resting head.

She jumped back into a sitting position and rubbed her eyes, "Sorry, sorry."

"Should I feel insulted that my speech was so dreary that you rested?" Even though Naseer's words sounded hurt, his tone was full of jest. "I shall presume you've heard this story plenty of times, so I will stop and say that he was once here and now he isn't."

"I'm sorry, again." She felt embarrassed. She hadn't dozed off during a lecture since grammar school. "I feel so humiliated."

"Nonsense," he whispered, leaning in and gesturing toward a concerned librarian looking over a shelf. "You aren't the one who yelled."

"It's getting late. I should really get back home."

Naseer stood up. "You're right. Where has the time gone?" He held out his hand. "It was a pleasure to meet you. I hope I said I was Naseer. Who might you be?"

"Dinred." She shook his hand, biting her tongue and wishing she had used a different name. What harm could it do though?

"Not the worst name I've come across." He smiled at his worst joke. "It was nice meeting you, Dinred."

⁂

Dinred arrived back at the hospital with questions answered and answers questioned. The next morning was a typical work day. Help sort the pills, play delivery girl, and help with anything that required a mutt to use their hands.

Her time with Naseer had not been not wasted. She had come to the conclusion that the Avon had not liked Cerberus since he had turned hypocritical, creating slaves and ruining his foundation and pact with the avians. At least that was when the rest of the world had stopped liking him as much as they used to. It had been a much better night of explanations than she'd had with Ziyad, moreover this one hadn't included an emotional breakdown, a plus in Dinred's mind.

It was almost just another day until her work was about done. As she was passing by a room, a familiar voice caught her ear. She thought nothing of it at first, just another doctor talking to a patient perhaps, until she remembered who the voice belonged to. Ziyad.

At first she thought it couldn't have been him. Normally he sought her out first. But peeking through the door she recognized his white feathers. He was sitting with his back facing the door, leaning forward with his hands on his knees.

On the bed was an orange foxen with beautiful eyes and tousled hair. He was bandaged with bindings and swabs to stop his bleeding, and he wore a muzzle that pumped oxygen to his snout.

He gave Ziyad a disapproving glare through a blackened eye.

"Excuse me, Miss."

Dinred turned around to see a red foxen in silvery armor and a leather cape over his left shoulder. She was sure she'd seen him before, and the Roman accent with the hint of Albion was familiar, but she could not guess his name.

"Sorry, I need to get through." The fox walked through the door. "Ziyad! Buddy."

Ziyad clutched his knees and looked away, muttering more words in Avian, before saying, "I was hoping it wasn't you at the door, Cypher."

"Ugh, you're so optimistic." Cypher shrugged. "Who's this guy? Wait, I never forget a face. He was… One of those foxes that—"

"Why are you here?" Ziyad asked impatiently.

"I was getting to that. So insensitive, I swear." Cypher pouted, stomping his foot on the ground with his lips quivering. "What is the new Seraph doing here?"

"He's not a Seraph yet. He has much to compensate for." Ziyad looked back at the injured foxen who held his gaze. "He is here because

I have questions that need answers."

Cypher was quiet. Ziyad turned toward him. He seemed to be wondering if the foxen's silence was due to his presence. The foxen had a finger on his chin. "Hold on, I forgot what I came in here for. Oh, right! Mission accomplished. We're done here. The Father has ordered all Seraphs to prepare to head southward for the last stronghold, and then we'll be going home."

"I'll stay behind with the soldiers," Ziyad said. "I'll help keep the occupation, along with my squad. They'll need some training anyway."

"Ziyad, do you know what fortress I'm talking about? The one down South?" Cypher, for once, started to sound concerned. "Your squad doesn't even have their titles yet, and you're suggesting they stay behind until… One moment."

Cypher's gaze turned toward Dinred, and he creased his forehead in frustration. Someone else called, "I got her."

Her arm was grabbed and twisted behind her. Dinred was pushed into the room.

"Alexis!" Ziyad said. "What have I told you about touching her?"

"She was spying on us," Alexis snapped back.

"Oh yes, she must be a professional! Just look how well she hid." The Avian folded his hands into fists. "You do not know her. She's not spying on us. She's waiting politely to say hello." Ziyad looked at the leona. "Isn't that right, Dear?"

"Hello!" she blurted out in an almost painful yelp. She tried her best to keep her composure.

"See? Now release her."

Alexis released Dinred and pushed her out the door.

“Gently!” Ziyad said. “Be respectful. She has more of a reason to be here than you do. Get out.”

Alexis followed Dinred out the door and stood guard.

She said a quiet thank you and apology, inside her head, to Ziyad. The last thing she heard as she walked away was Ziyad and Cypher talking.

“You said ‘mission accomplished.’ Whose? Yours or mine?”

“Both.”

22

Kabol's legs were tired.

He had been forced to march miles through day and night. It was either that or they would have fought a battle outnumbered and outgunned against an enemy they had not agreed to fight against. As if that weren't enough of a blow to morale, when they had reached the outpost they had been told that the three trains that were supposed to come for them hadn't arrived at all.

The troops had gathered around bonfires with their bags and cots, seeing as how there were no spare bunks. Their orders were to wait for trains to take them to their next destination: Gaul. It was one of the worst things a soldier could be told near the front lines.

When a soldier moves, his life is in his own hands. But if he is told to wait in one place, he starts getting ideas in his head that he is being watched. Getting thoughts that a single artillery round could get luckier than him.

Loud booms could be heard in the distance. It was their allies' joint artillery firing rounds, which would later be heard miles away. It was the only thing keeping the Romans at bay.

Kabol had heard talk among the conscripts about how the fronts only moved closer, how futile it was to stand up against the mechanized monsters, that one of their friends was now missing in action, and how the Nimbus class was unstoppable.

Hayden thought it best to stay away from the chatter. Kabol had found him, at one of the fires, far from the rest. He, Ben, and a few others gathered around the warm glow. Kabol figured the idea was a good one. He was disappointed to remember his materials were in his luggage at the bottom of a cliff. First it had been his hat, and now it was everything he needed to sleep well. At this rate, he thought, he'd lose his fur by tomorrow.

He glanced over his shoulder to see Hayden lying on his back, writing in a book he kept as a journal and using the fire as his only light. Ben had found a different way of entertaining himself. He was finding bugs and sticking them on the fire; spiders were his favorite. The two other soldiers were writing on pieces of paper that didn't belong to any book and were, most likely, their wills.

The gray leona was hungry. The train would come eventually, but he wasn't sure when. He'd had to choose between rest and food. He couldn't help thinking he'd made the wrong choice.

Kabol leaned over to see that Hayden was not writing, but drawing. It was a portrait of someone he couldn't identify right away but, on closer inspection, seemed a lot like Kai.

"Shame what happened to him. I didn't think he'd get court martialed." Kabol tried to speak the honest truth, but it came out as more of a cop out and a lie no matter how much he tried to mean it.

Hayden didn't react to Kabol's voice.

"Since when do you know how to draw?" Kabol felt uncomfortable, as if he were prying into his friend's personal space. He had thought he knew everything about Hayden.

"Since whenever," he muttered.

"You never do like to talk about yourself." Kabol was unsatisfied with having his question brushed off. "How come?"

"Don't like it. I'm not that interesting." Hayden sat up. He crawled over to Kabol and handed him the journal.

Kabol inspected the page, admiring the line art and shading. It was impressive, with years of training behind it. The lead had done little to match Kai's fur, but he could tell it was that devil.

"It looks good." Kabol's compliment was yet another cop out. "Better than I could do."

Hayden gently ripped out the page and tossed it into the fire.

Kabol gasped. "Why did you do that? It was good!"

"Didn't like it." Hayden stood up.

Kabol was aghast at his actions. He would have asked for the drawing if he had known what would happen to it. Kabol wondered why Hayden had gotten up until he saw a Deutsch soldier running from fire to fire. The soldier saw Hayden and headed toward him. The new blood saluted and handed the white mutt a parchment before running off. Hayden studied the letter, carefully tracing it with his finger.

"What does it say?" Ben asked, tossing another beetle into the flame, one big enough to create a pop in the fire.

Hayden left the fire and headed toward the center of the clearing without taking his eyes off the paper. Kabol, Ben, and other soldiers followed closely. He lowered the parchment and lifted his hand in the air, calling, "All soldiers under my command, rally to me."

Troops from all the fires stopped what they were doing and crowded around the mutt. Kabol felt claustrophobic being in the center of the mob, but he kept his poise in the cool dawn air.

Hayden cleared his throat and read aloud. "All New Albion commanders, rally your troops to the north of Gaul. Our eyes and ears have confirmed the Nimbus-class warship is preparing to leave New Albion skies on its voyage back to Swethin. We will cross the channel and regroup with our brethren who are at the Sea Wall, by the end of the week, and attempt to recover all occupied land and prepare its defenses. This will effectively and indefinitely eliminate the northern front for our allies. Inform all troops."

Talk started to stir up. Some of the men started complaining, others argued, and a few went back to their fires disinterested in the news. Then there were the men who looked worried, frightened even, to hear about the conflicts they would take part in. Very few, if any of them, seemed happy about leaving the camp.

"So we're forced to march again?" Ben growled, throwing his arms in the air. "We don't have any rations. None of us got to eat. We were sitting here wasting time waiting to get picked off by artillery, and now we don't even get to have an hour's sleep?"

The soldiers crowding around expressed the same weary anger.

"Enough." Hayden's voice sounded less friendly, and more like an order. "If I say you will march, you will march. Remember your training, and you'll live long enough not to see yourself cry to death."

The soldiers were quiet before Ben remarked, "Yes sir, Kai."

"Say that again." Hayden took a step toward Ben, keeping his chin up.

Ben brushed dust off his pants before looking Hayden in the eye. "If you insist—"

Kabol didn't want to know what would happen next. He jumped between them and separated them.

"Enough." He looked at the two of them and calmed his voice. "I know we're tired. We're all tired and hungry, and now we're just waiting for the next big thing to blow us over. I don't blame you for being brassed off. It's been a long night. But keep it together. Didn't you hear the good news? We're going home!"

Kabol wrapped his arms around Ben and Hayden's shoulders, pulling the mutt down to his height, and continued, "Home with all its glorious pubs and beautiful music. I don't know about you, but for me, every step I take closer to home is something I fancy with all my being." He let go of his friends and paced around them. "The songs, the jokes, the city streets and views. We're going back! I can't tell you how much I desire getting back to my wife and ridding myself of this cursed war."

As Kabol spoke, the troops began to change their mood. They seemed to have changed their disposition to the orders. Some seemed happy, others reminisced about the good old days, and a few just watched.

He continued with a few last words. "I don't know about you, but I don't mind the orders. On the contrary, I adore them. I don't care if I have to take another train or trolley, airplane, boat, or just a barrel and a paddle with a prayer. I will still be willing to start again, from boot camp, and march every step with a Cheshire cat grin if that means I'm going back to my wife. And may I be cursed if I'm not in the first wave."

He felt a hand on his shoulder and turned to see Hayden with a serious face but a soothing voice. "We get it."

Hayden's interruption did little to bring Kabol back to reality, but it managed to successfully shut him up. The cat felt amazing. He hadn't felt this excited since the coronation. Hearing the news and his own voice announce that he was going back made him struggle to stand without hopping like a giddy child. If it had been just Kabol and his friends, he would have let the urge take him.

When Kabol looked around at the troops, their expressions were elated, in complete contrast to moments before. They all had their own battles and names with faces to fight for.

Hayden held up his hand, gathering their attention. "All right thank you, Kabol, for that rousing speech. Remind me to make you my best man. I think that speech brought a tear to my eye. No, it didn't. Close. Not really. As for the rest of you, if you have any problems, let Kabol here charm you before you bother me." Hayden slapped Kabol on the back before walking off. "And get your gear, people. I can hear the train coming."

The troops went back to their gear, some motivated enough to run.

Ben was among them, motivated either by Kabol's words or something in his imagination; Kabol didn't really want to know what. Hayden gave Kabol another pat on the back before moving away.

The conscripts were heading toward the station as the train pulled up. It was an ancient locomotive pulling boxcars covered in rust and vandalism. Kabol, Hayden, and Ben were among the first at the loading platform when it stopped, eager for the next step in their journey.

"Pst." Hayden nudged Kabol with his right hand, holding out something in his left palm. He quickly clenched his fist, hiding it from view, but Kabol had seen enough of it to know it was candy. It was one of the chocolate bars that belonged to the Deutschland.

Ben tried to reach for it, clutching his buddy's shoulder. "Oh! Give me!"

Hayden wheeled his arm back when Kabol tried to snatch the sweet.

"Relax, both of you." Hayden's voice was soft, no longer having the lingering flame of a commander's control. He took off a piece and handed it to Ben, who cheered like a child at its delicious taste, and gave a bigger piece to Kabol.

It's been some time, Dinred, Kabol thought as he bit into the bar.

Don't worry, Love. I'm coming home.

23

The roar of four turbine engines engulfed the plane.

Kabol loaded his Callum and checked his other magazines. The exposed bullets made the argument that it could be considered a clip instead. Kabol didn't like it. He didn't care how much money or metal it saved if he couldn't fire his bullets well. Three magazines in total, bullets numbering up to ninety.

Considering how little thought had gone into the weapon, he was surprised that there wasn't any rust on his barrel or ammunition. He wished he'd signed up the day before he became a conscript, though they would have said he was too old. Still, in that case, he'd have gotten a gun capable of hitting a target.

He shook the thought from his mind, rubbing the stainless steel ring he called a wedding band. He was calm. The air and atmosphere were, for the most part, tranquil. He had managed to get some extra shut eye and a few picks of any rations while he was waiting.

Today was the big day. He was on his way across the channel. Through a window he could see other planes, similar to the one he was in, including one that carried weapons, rations, ammunition, and even an armored vehicle. The first wave consisted of many of these planes, numbering around a few hundred.

His was much smaller than others. The plane he was on was destined to land, while others were to carry troops and were substantially larger. Those were part of the second wave. They had been ordered to bring about twenty-four thousand soldiers to the Sea Wall where they would receive further orders, possibly attacking several Avon-held strongholds at the same time.

The third wave had been planned as the biggest invasion in history, bringing home a hundred thousand soldiers and their families. They would return to New Albion to be prepared to head to Swethin.

Kabol took pleasure in knowing he was in the first wave. Simple orders: land, drop supplies, scout around.

Deep down, he wished he could remember how to pray, even if he didn't need it. He dwelled on what Hayden had said on the train. The more he thought about it, the less comfortable he was realizing how true his words had been. He didn't even know if he could bring himself to kill a man.

He rubbed the ring once more and kissed it before clutching it tightly. He had to remind himself why he was going back.

He found himself judging the floor to be comfier than the cushion with springs sticking out that he had been assigned to. He had to curl his feet whenever another one of the air crew wanted to pass.

Ben paced from the front to the back multiple times, talking to himself about how he couldn't wait to get out of the plane. Hayden saw fit to whet the tip of his stiletto on a stone.

"Other than boot camp, I don't think I've seen you without that knife," Kabol pointed out.

"You haven't."

"There a story behind it?"

"My first kill. Nothing I want to share outside of that." He gestured with his dagger toward the radio behind Kabol.

Kabol got the message and went back to his station, "I don't know if this thing will work well when it is overcast."

"Worth a try."

Kabol put on the earphones and pulled the controller to his muzzle. "This is Private Anton of the New Albion forces. Sea Wall, what's your status? Over." He was soon greeted with static. He pulled the headset off. "See? Nothing."

"Are you sure it's because it's overcast?" Ben stood at the doorway to the cargo department. "I don't think it is. Is it on the right frequency?"

"I'm sure it's on the right frequency. It's written down here somewhere…" Kabol trailed off, looking around the radio for a piece of paper. He pulled a note from under a few sheets of paper. "Says it right here. And the numbers match. I don't know anything about radios. I'm a doctor. I cut people open and mess with their insides until they feel better."

"Where's your patch?" Hayden gestured with his knife to Kabol's shoulders.

Kabol looked at his shoulders, bearing only his rank's insignia with the medical patch missing completely. "I was never issued any."

"I'll get you one." Hayden stood up and placed his knife in its sheave. "There should be one in the back if you're lucky. If not, a substitute will do." Hayden looked Ben in the eyes. "Inaan, where are you supposed to be?"

Ben scratched the side of his head and pointed to the front. "Gunner or something." Hayden pointed in the same direction. Ben shook his head. "Buddy, you know light hurts my eyes. I'll fire that thing, then I'll get a headache." Hayden held his arm up, not saying a word. Ben only nodded and saluted before marching off toward his station. It was a ball turret on the bottom of the plane's floor that had a full view of the bottom hemisphere of the plane.

With Ben out of his way, Hayden headed into the cargo bay.

Kabol went back to repeating his message over the radio until he heard Ben's voice. "Kabol, get over here and look at this view. Quickly, before it gets covered by clouds."

Seeing as how his radio only relished in its static and unproductive nature, Kabol obeyed. He set his headset down and walked toward Ben's open hatch in the turret. Ben was standing next to it, whistling as he looked in it.

Kabol looked down to see there was a break in the clouds. Down below were several large warships. Battleships and destroyers were scattered about, all traveling east.

"Looks like Carthage sent her regards," Kabol announced. "The Royal Navy only has half that number of ships."

"They're probably going to chase the feathered folks back to Swethin," Ben said. "I think almost all of the north of Africa is in this war. They don't want the Romans to expand their territory again. Gods be with us if Asia gets involved."

Kabol shook his head. "We'd be calling the mainland Eurasia if that were the case." He backed up a few steps, prompting Ben to hop into the compartment and close the door. Kabol went back to his station, repeating the same phrase over and over again. He couldn't help but feel he was doing something wrong on his end.

After some time had passed, Kabol felt someone push on his back.

"Stay like that," Hayden said as he leaned Kabol forward. He had a dab of white paint on a brush and began to paint a circle on his back. "I guess they were saving this stuff for snow camouflage, but seeing as how they couldn't provide us with proper stickers or patches I'm surprised this isn't pink."

"We were not prepared for this whole army thing." Kabol admitted to one of his country's many faults. "Other than for ceremony, I don't even recall us having soldiers four months ago."

"You say 'soldiers,' but I wouldn't exactly say we have that even now." Hayden finished brushing a circle on the cat's back and began with his right shoulder. "An army? Sure. But soldiers? No." He began painting on the other shoulder.

Hayden closed the paint and placed it on the side of the walkway. He then started painting a cross with a red liquid.

"How much longer do you think this'll take?" Kabol said. "I mean how much longer are we going to be in this plane?"

"Don't worry about it. You're not the one who's claustrophobic." Hayden dipped his brush in the scarlet substitute and dabbed it on the shoulders.

Kabol looked at his right shoulder as soon as Hayden had finished marking it. The lumpy red texture looked very familiar. Kabol figured Hayden had found some berries and mashed them into a paste, but the more he tried to remember which rations had berries, the more he realized that berries were quite perishable. Were there even red berries that were used to dye?

"Hayden." Kabol sounded hesitant. "Where did you get the red paint?"

"I found it."

"Found red paint in military supplies?"

"Yes." Hayden finished painting the medical symbol and washed the brush off. "It came in a neat little package." He reached behind him and pulled out an almost full packet of blood and held in front of the leona. "From the med kit."

"What?" Kabol nearly jumped out of his chair at the sound of Hayden bursting into laughter. He stood up and faced the hysterical mutt who was laughing too hard at his practical joke. Kabol looked over his shoulder to see that Hayden had put a dab too much and some of the blood had trailed south.

Hayden was now clapping his hands and laughing. "It looks good on you."

Kabol wanted to be mad that his armor was now stained and ruined for his first day home. He wasn't sure if Hayden knew the blood would dry and turn brown. However, Kabol couldn't be mad. Hayden's laughter was contagious enough that the cat cracked a smile.

"Actually, you're right. I am chuffed about it." Kabol sat back in his chair, feeling a glow inside his chest. "Cheers, Mate." Hayden did the same, sitting across from him and putting the blood-filled pack aside. Kabol pricked his ears. "Hayden, I just noticed something. Where are you supposed to be stationed?"

"Hmm…" Hayden looked embarrassed. "In a different airplane. Don't look at me like that. I feel uncomfortable in these things, so I might as well be with the people I like."

Kabol didn't have much of a chance to smile. Ben walked between them, muttering to himself and rubbing his eyes as if he had been blinded.

Hayden snapped his fingers and got the cat's attention. "I thought I told you to stay at your station."

Ben didn't stop walking. "And I thought I told you that light hurts my eyes."

"You didn't fire the weapon, liar."

"True." Ben stepped into the cargo bay, smothering his hurt eyes. "But those spotlights did the trick just fine."

"Spotlights?" Kabol asked. Why would the navy need any

spotlights to see their own planes?

Kabol got off his cushion and ran in the direction Ben had come from. Hayden followed him to the open turret, and they both looked at the ocean. Kabol's fur bristled on his neck when he saw multiple tugboats and battleships, with spotlights, on fire.

The clouds covered their view for a moment, but another patch opened, showing a blockade of large gunships, each with artillery and anti-air batteries.

"Hayden," Kabol's words dripped from his lips in horror. "Those aren't our ships."

<h1 style="text-align:center">24</h1>

Kabol slammed on the door to the cockpit.

His heart was beating out of his chest in fear and worry. Whose ships were those? Surely not the Avons', but not their own either. Kabol called to the pilots through the door. "We have unidentified ships shining spotlights at us, looking for targets, and our own boats are burning. When do we panic?"

The door slid open, revealing Buttons in a flak jacket; Kabol could see the captain piloting the craft, so he must be the copilot. "We saw 'em. It's the Avon. The man on the scopes also says they're gunboats; they'll be firing with shells rather t'an Triple-As."

"What's that supposed to mean?"

"Doesn't matter; they'll be missin' a lot." The first officer closed the door, leaving Kabol with only the stranger's words.

Hayden hopped into the turret, only to be pulled on the shoulder by Kabol. "That's not going to do anything. Leave it to the destroyers."

Kabol continued to his station. He had to stay calm. He put the headphones on and repeated his call sign. "My name is Private Anton of the New Albion forces. Does anyone read me? Over."

He repeated this twice before jumping at a rattling sound. It sounded like light caliber bullets plinking off the floor of the plane. It seemed that the boats weren't equipped to take out large planes with heavier armor.

"Do you read me? We have a half a hundred planes full of supplies, and we're coming in hot. What is your status?" Kabol heard what sounded like a "hello" cut off midsentence. Hope surged through him. "Sea Wall? Do you copy?"

The plane shook at the sound of a loud boom. Then another. And another. Each time the sound went off, the plane shook almost violently. The door to the cockpit flew open and Buttons called, "They're firing ack-acks. Get yer flak jackets on or else the shrapnel will end ye."

"What are the odds of us touching down?" Hayden asked. "Should we prepare to ditch with the cargo?"

"Not unless ye plan to sink with it," the officer said. "We're a few miles off. Ye can parachute with the cargo 'en we're over land. But don't ye worry 'bout that. Flaks are there to hurt us crew and scare us out of our wits. Until we're on fire, stay calm."

Kabol could see past the officer and noticed a large black cloud in their path. A mortar must have gone off only a few meters in front of the plane before the door had been opened. Buttons was called back to the passenger seat and quickly closed the door.

"Ben!" Kabol called. "Get the jackets from back there."

"But they're heavy."

"Get them out here, now." Hayden said. "We'll need them sooner than we thought."

Ben carried two of them out: heavy jackets to protect every bone and organ that a man's torso loved from fragmentation. Ben already wore one, and Kabol and the mutt quickly strapped them on.

Ben was right, the weight of the object made Kabol uncomfortable. He was sure he'd thank himself later for wearing it, so he ignored the encumbrance and sat back at his radio.

Now he was even more uncomfortable. He was sitting in a metal monstrosity while under fire. He had the same feeling he'd had the other day, the terrible feeling that his life was no longer in his hands. This time he knew he was right about it. "This is Private Anton of the New Albion forces. Sea Wall, respond now! What is your status?"

The static was interrupted by a panicked voice yelling before being overwhelmed by the blaring noise once more.

"Come again?" Kabol said. "Sea Wall, respond!"

It was silent once again before the rattling sounds of bullets were heard and the voice spoke more clearly. "Abort! Get out of here!" Then it went dead quiet.

Chills ran up Kabol's spine. The Sea Wall was not only under attack, but breached. It had never happened before. No army had ever gotten near that wall. Its howitzers would shred any ship in sea, land, or air, no matter how big.

Kai had been right! The Avon were completely prepared for the occupation of the isle. Tactics that had conquered the capitol in a single night, insurgents that rooted out trains, soldiers taught specifically how to counter their unarmed techniques, ships placed to blockade a navy for quick docking, and now they had breached the strongest fortress New Albion had to offer.

A horrid thought reached the back of his mind. They were prepared for anything, but their shells, even their flaks, weren't strong enough to shoot a cargo plane down. Such an oversight seemed impossible.

"Get to the machine guns." Kabol stood up from his chair and turned around to see his friends didn't seem to share his fear. They hadn't figured out how soon they were going to die. "Get to the guns. Prepare for anything."

Kabol didn't wait for a reaction from them. He ran as fast as he could into a thin hall to the door of the cockpit. He knocked on it hard, almost rudely. "The Sea Wall has been breached. What are our options?"

The door slid open. For the first time, Buttons looked concerned. "It's under 'tack? We're expected to land 'ere. We don't 'ave enough fuel to make it back."

"It's not just under attack. It's been *breached!* They're capturing it."

The sound of the flak bursting in air went quiet. Kabol looked behind him. Hayden was at the radio, and Ben had disappeared into the cargo hold. The turret remained empty.

Kabol wasn't glad that the flak had stopped firing. He was horrified. The only reasons for artillery to stop firing were because they were out of ammo, their targets were presumed dead or—much worse, in this case—allied forces were in the kill zone.

Kabol didn't have time to explain his fear to the first officer. He quickly jumped into the ball turret below, without saying a word, and closed the lid. In front of him were miles of fog and cloud. Below him were ships with plenty of anti-aircraft guns, yet they held their fire.

The area was teeming with planes similar to his. Kabol felt crowded and cramped, even miles in the sky. His heart began to beat out of his chest. Anxiety ran through his blood faster than adrenaline and testosterone could keep up. His fingers twitched in anticipation. He almost choked on his own saliva. He tried to steady his breathing, forcing himself to inhale calmly. He couldn't hit anything if his hands were shaking.

He stared anxiously down the sights. All he could see were thick gray clouds. There was no sign of what he feared most.

Out of the thick fog, silhouettes of aircraft of Avonian design came shooting out as quick as a flash. Kabol could have blinked and missed it. It came past so quickly he didn't even have time to think about pulling the trigger.

It was an interceptor made specifically to shoot down without getting shot. On the bottom of the nose was a large cannon, and next to it were weapons that Kabol couldn't see clearly enough to identify.

Then another jet-propelled VTOL zoomed by—it was as fast as the first one—before more and more swarmed the sky, creating trails of bullets.

Kabol pulled the trigger, aiming at the jets, but every bullet missed its mark. The twin-jet VTOLs were too fast to shoot down. The turret couldn't move quickly enough.

Already, three of the cargo planes were on fire, ignited by rounds from anti-tank cannons. One of them had lost control of an entire wing of engines and begun to spiral downward.

Kabol still shot at anything he could, unaware of any damage to his plane. Not a single bullet had hit anywhere. The turret was so immobile it might as well have been stationary in this fight.

The leona turned his weapon toward the front hoping to deter any interceptors from targeting his craft first. It was pointless.

A cannon shot was a direct hit in front of Kabol. The bright flash made him turn his head, cowering, as glass shattered onto his body and face. The entire turret was filled with smoke and debris from the fire in front of him.

He couldn't breathe. The shrapnel from the plane had flown through the broken windshields with horrific effect, cutting his arms and other places the flak jacket didn't protect. Kabol tried to move the turret, but the rotors had been completely destroyed.

With no visibility, unable to breathe, and facing the constant threat of shrapnel penetrating him, he had to escape the confined turret or die.

He pushed open the hatch, and smoke spilled into the compartment. Hayden and Ben both grabbed the cat and yanked him out of the deathtrap.

Ben slammed the trapdoor shut, preventing any more smoke from entering the room.

Kabol had trouble breathing, and he felt lightheaded. Too much smoke had filled his lungs, and a shooting pain pierced his chest every time he coughed. He tried to move, but lost balance every time he stood up.

Hayden prompted Kabol to stand against the wall next to the cockpit and tried to get his attention. He was begging Kabol to stay awake.

Kabol's breathing was heavy, and his heartbeat was louder than his friend's voice.

The aircraft shook again, knocking Hayden backward off his feet. Kabol's back began to burn. He tried to lean forward. Thick smoke and fire emanated from the door of the cockpit.

"No!" was all Kabol was able to say. It took every fiber of his being to move toward the turret and grip a bar next to it.

In his ears sang the horrifying yell all diving planes create. He felt his body began to slide toward the back of the plane as gravity was no longer present. Kabol did his best to hang onto the only thing he had grabbed onto, sliding his arm all the way in as the plane began to spiral out of control. If he were to slip, his life would be forfeit. He wished he had prayed.

The twists and turns as the plane spiraled smashed his body, several times, onto the same hatch.

Fear turned seconds into a lifetime of horror and pain. He didn't experience the pain for much longer after he lost his grip.

⚬⚬⚬

"Ben?" Hayden called.

Throbbing, stinging pains ran throughout the cat's body. Kabol's eyes were heavy. He could open them for only a second. He saw Hayden limping and leaning on a destroyed cushion, looking toward a vast beach where the cargo holds had once been present.

Kabol was unable to stay conscious for much longer. Before he blacked out, he heard Hayden yell one last call full of sorrow.

"Inaan?"

25

Ziyad clenched his fist, feeling the trachea of his enemy break.

He released the corpse, letting it fall flat onto the concrete floor. Ziyad marched toward another group of conscripts, retreating into a pillbox on top of the wall.

Currently the most dangerous thing on the Sea Wall was the breeze that hinted at pushing him off. Ziyad scoffed at the words of his commander. Strongest fortress they had to offer? Yet here he was, singlehandedly responsible for killing half the garrison.

The hardest part of this assault was making sure every kilometer was clear of troops. It made sense that the tenacity of these leonas would convince them to build a wall as long as the shoreline.

He would make sure the beach ran red with the blood of the mutts and cats for annoying him with petty resistance, for taking his hand, and for offering useless ears to claim. This whole mission was, personally, a waste of time.

He might as well have fun.

He walked toward the bunker; its steel door was now barricaded. He could easily break it down, but they'd expect that. They'd see it coming. No. He wanted them to know, to experience what was like to not slow down death, how they could neither run from it nor fight it. He'd have them choke on their fear of how little they could do stop him.

The pillbox bore an opening, facing the beach and fit for a machine gunner's or sniper's nest. He marched toward the door and jumped two meters high, landing safely on top of it. He raced toward the opening to the beach. Below him was the glassless window. He turned so that his back was facing the beach.

Ziyad jumped down, grabbed the ledge, and quickly leaped over the edge. He landed with his talons inside the bunker.

Horrifying yells were heard as several of the soldiers pulled up their submachine guns and began firing at him. He shrugged off every bullet, only feeling pressure from the ones that hit the under-suit.

Without drawing a blade, he lunged and grabbed the nearest soldier, smashing his neck against a wall. Before the corpse could hit the ground, Ziyad was working on the next one. He grabbed the man's shoulder with one hand and his snout with the other and severed the skull from the neck without breaking the skin in a single jerk skyward.

One attempted to run, prompting Ziyad to pick up a nearby weapon and fire at her. It was remarkably fast, but inaccurate. Seven bullets missed before one found its mark in her back, just below the breastplate.

There was now only one left, a mutt cowering in the corner next to the wide slit Ziyad had climbed through. He must have missed him when he came in, focusing on the ones with guns. The Seraph went toward him.

For the first time, and against his better judgment, he decided to inspect the soldier. A brown retriever, it seemed. His eyes were closed behind his cowering wall of hands, and his hair was hidden behind a helmet.

A simple kill, but something in Ziyad's heart and mind told him to stay his hand. Whenever he looked at the mutt, he felt something. It wasn't the pity one would feel looking at a dying stray animal on the road. It was more akin to sympathy, like what one would experience holding a baby in their arms.

Something told him not to harm the mutt, lest he receive aggression from an equal. A thought of that Mary girl stung his mind.

He pushed the thought aside, grabbing the mutt by the collar, ignoring his wails, and turning him away. He wrapped an arm around the mutt, placing his elbow at the esophagus. He pulled his arm back, stopping the passage of blood to the brain. It only took a tenth of a minute before the man was unconscious.

For the first time, he didn't have the heart to kill. He wasn't sure why, but he imagined the cat at the hospital would frown at his bloodthirsty behavior. He wouldn't want that.

He returned to the barricade, removed the furniture in front of it, and unlocked the door. Nine Seraphs, each as heavily plated and armed as Ziyad, but none as experienced, were behind the open door. They only looked the part of one of the holiest of slayers, but after this endeavor they may have earned the title, depending on how many kills they'd achieved.

Considering they might as well be killing civilians, Ziyad planned on protesting against them earning anything.

"What took you so long, Commander?" Alexis jeered as they all entered the pillbox.

"I've killed an entire emplacement with my bare hands in half of a minute. You will show some respect."

"Nah, you missed one." Alexis kicked the leg of the pacified mutt near the opening. "Still breathing."

"Missed two." Renatus said holding down the whimpering woman, with a knee on her back, that Ziyad had shot earlier. It had turned out that the weapon was more inaccurate than he had thought, as the bullet had missed any organ. When the bleeding stopped, the wound would be as threatening to her life as a nasty paper cut.

As Renatus began to administer the pain relievers from his belt, Ziyad was beginning to think either he had lost his touch at killing almost immediately, or these two soldiers had been extremely lucky to catch him in a strange mood.

"What a view!" Alexis said.

She placed her hands on the ledge overlooking the beach. Ziyad took a single glance, noticing the crashed airplanes and debris, some of which still burned. The only thing he saw was a kill box.

"If it weren't for the people trying to kill us," Alexis continued, "I'd kind of like it here."

Ziyad ignored her, turning back to the Seraphs. "Alexis, Renatus, you stay with me. I want six of you to continue clearing out bunkers for our men. I want the last one to make sure machine gunners, maybe snipers, are in every one of these pillboxes."

"You sound almost afraid. Expecting something we can't handle?" Alexis joked and threw her hands in the air with a shrug. "Their guns don't even hit us half the time."

"They are calling in their soldiers, not just conscripts," Ziyad said. "Do you have any idea the numbers being reported? The number of troops New Albion is sending, who are on their way here?"

"One hundred and fifty thousand or so." Renatus used his knife to remove the bullet with careful precision and stuffed the wound with several small absorbent sponges that grew and clotted in the bleeding vessels.

The cat whimpered, "Th-thank you."

Renatus returned the gesture kindly by placing his hands on her neck, blocking the blood from her brain. She was soon unconscious.

Ziyad looked back at the beach. He took off his helmet, getting a whiff of the sweet scent of the cool breeze. He looked at the seashore calmly. He had never thought there was anything special about beaches. Where he came from, sand was everywhere. Adding a little water to it meant nothing.

But here? The wind carried away the smell of blood as if it were dust, and the sound of the waves lapping against the sand and metal surfaces sounded relaxing. Along with the seagull's song, it made him feel strange and nostalgic. He closed his eyes and felt like he was in a whole different place, a place far from yelling, and orders, and graves. A place far from war.

He felt at peace.

A loud boom in the distance yanked him out of the moment. He put his mask back on and looked at the horizon. A ship zoomed in, covered in fire, and was broadsided by a much more massive ship on its way toward the shore.

"Where are the machine gunners?" Ziyad asked over the radio.

"They're on their way," a foxen replied.

Ziyad stared at the beach and spoke to Alexis. "Take a good long look at that beach. It will not be recognizable by the next hour." His blood began to curdle and his fingers throbbed in anticipation. "Because anyone who steps onto that beach is going to die."

When Kabol woke up, he couldn't remember much of what had happened. His head throbbed with pain, and his aching arms were scarred. His fur was stained by his own blood, from his nostrils and limbs. His back stung with pain.

His legs were also hurt and bruised. He was almost happy about that; it meant he might be able to walk. He moved his legs slightly, shifting his position to sit up, and braced himself to lie back down if he were to experience severe trauma.

His breathing was fine, and he was able to stand with the wall propping him up. *I'm alive.*

He looked around for his Callum, and soon found it with the clip busted out. The bullets were everywhere, and around half were absent from the plane entirely. Even if he were to gather them all, the magazine was broken, and they would fall out again.

He hadn't even fired his weapon, and he had already lost a third of his ammunition.

He also noticed that Hayden was missing. He called his name—"Hayden? Ben?"—and limped toward the back of the plane. He passed his radio, which was now completely destroyed and spread across the ground, and walked through the arch of the now-missing cargo hold.

He fell lightly onto some sand. Tracks headed toward the ocean. Kabol could see some of the top of the cargo bay above the surface of the water. Next to the prints leading to the ocean were tracks returning. Only one set of feet.

Several battleships and troop carriers, only about two miles off, sat in the fog on the horizon, and the Sea Wall was too quiet for being under attack.

Kabol got back into the plane and noticed the door to the cockpit was slightly ajar. Maybe Hayden was in there? He limped and dragged himself there, careful not to scratch himself on any debris, and peered inside.

He wished he had chosen otherwise. The scent of smoldering corpses filled his nostrils before he saw the charred remains of Buttons smeared across the floor. That was all that was left of the deck. No controls, windshield, or seats or much ceiling remained. He didn't need to see any more.

Kabol backed away, hearing footsteps from outside. He went to the door to his right. Hayden was crawling from behind the turbine. His eyes looked dreary and even sorrowful. "Ben's gone. He's gone."

Kabol's heart sank. It was as if someone had coiled a rope around it and squeezed. He remembered the sight of Hayden calling out his friend's name. His gun fell from his hands. He staggered toward the mutt, and when he was close enough, he fell onto him and cried.

Hayden almost lost his poise, kneeling down with Kabol. "I… I never got the chance to apologize to him. Apologize for calling him a liar."

Kabol clutched Hayden more tightly, letting tears stream down his face. He almost cradled Hayden, trying to sway him from side to side out of force of habit.

He felt Hayden pat the back of his head. "I… I couldn't even find the body. I didn't see him when we hit. I… don't want to think what happened to him."

"Don't talk like that," Kabol sobbed. "Not now, mate."

Several booms were heard in the distance. Artillery shells from the Sea Wall, aiming toward the horizon. The ships returned fire shortly after being rained upon by missed rounds.

"Come on, get it together." Hayden patted Kabol's side. "Pull yourself together; we have a job to do."

Kabol had to force himself not to weep. "Ben…"

"I didn't find his body. Maybe he survived?" Hayden sounded like he was trying to convince himself more than he was trying to sway Kabol, but it still sounded hopeless. "He wouldn't let himself die before he saw some action."

It wasn't working. So much had happened. Kabol wasn't sure when he would next be able to weep on a friend's shoulder. First the plane had crashed, now his friend was dead, and the invasion had barely started.

Hayden was not going to have any of Kabol's sorrow. He shoved the cat off of him. "Soldier!" His voice was hoarse and cold, like an officer's. "Stand at attention! That's an order."

Kabol didn't listen. He wanted to, but couldn't. Hayden straightened his arm and slapped Kabol hard enough his neck hurt. The pain wasn't as effective at grabbing Kabol's attention as the shock of his friend's action.

"Did you not listen to me, Private?" Hayden pushed Kabol onto his back and placed a knee on his gut, grabbing his chin. "You will clear your mind of all but the battle. Do you understand me? I will not have an emotionally distressed soldier under my command. I am not prepared to have that kind of liability. Pick up your gun."

Kabol felt pressure move off his stomach as Hayden stood up tall and straight. Kabol crawled back and grabbed his weapon.

"Can you stand?"

Kabol nodded and got to his feet.

"Can you shoot?"

Kabol nodded and loaded his weapon.

"Then you are a threat to them. You can still kill. And kill you must, with extreme prejudice if you so desire. Do you understand me, Private?"

Another artillery round landed in the sea. This time it was much closer. Kabol took a long look at the channel. The ships were moving full speed ahead and would be on top of him within a few minutes.

Kabol looked Hayden in the eye. His grief had subsided, and his mind was in the present. There was one thing he would not let the Avon take. Hope. He nodded and spoke through his teeth. "I understand, Sir."

"Good," Hayden said. He reached into the back of the blown engine and pulled out a light machine gun stored in the cargo for actual soldiers. He didn't come back empty handed from his swim. He found a machine gun, one strong enough to actually hurt a Seraph. A rare weapon in an army of conscripts, and it was one he wasn't going to let sand in. Hayden spoke with more ire this time, lowering his voice. "What are your orders?"

Kabol was no longer sad, quite the opposite. His mind was swimming in irate passion. He held his rifle firmly across his chest, stock at the shoulder and barrel pointed down. "They killed him; we shall return the favor kindly."

Kabol saw that the landing crafts, small boats full of twenty men each, were less than a minute away. Hope shone in his eyes. The mutt and the cat were not going to be alone for long.

Any spark of hope was soon snuffed out by machine gun fire.

26

It didn't take long until the fury of hell was loose.

Artillery shells became more accurate with every shot, destroying transport craft before they could even dock. Machine gun nests were placed in captured pill boxes, mowing down troops before they could disembark from the boats. Snipers picked off stragglers before they could find cover.

Kabol looked behind him as the bloodshed stained the sand around the men unfortunate enough to be first on the beach. With every blink of an eye, ten more lives were lost. The only time ground was gained was when the machine guns reloaded.

The garrison of the fortress had removed blockades prior to the battle so the reinforcing ships could land. It had been a horrible mistake. The beach was now riddled with the carcasses of shot down planes and landing crafts along with foxholes made by mortar rounds.

Hayden held Kabol's chest against the engine of their plane as a nearby mortar spooked the veteran. They planned to use the advantage of numbers to avoid being picked off. Bullets ricocheted off the wing, forcing them to retreat or be pinned down. Hayden grabbed Kabol's arm and pulled him through the carcass of the plane.

He shouted an order, barely audible over the barrage of gunfire. "We have to do something about those pillboxes!"

"The damn radio is dead!" Kabol yelled back.

"Then we'll compromise." Hayden looked back to see a landing craft safely landing behind the downed airship he was in. Hayden released Kabol and ran back, gesturing to all twenty soldiers, as they disembarked, to run inside.

As they were nearing the shore, the boat was capsized by an artillery round.

Kabol got to his feet and ran toward the shore, ditching his gun and ammo on the ground. Hayden did the same. They both ran into the cold water and dived under the surface. Any bullet aimed toward them cracked into the water at a blistering speed for only a few inches before stopping dead and floating away.

The bullets were not the drowning troops' worst enemy—it was their packs. Hayden swam to the nearest one, unhooked a soldier's gear, and pushed past him toward the surface. The armor the conscripts wore was light and didn't weigh much underwater. Neither did the guns.

Kabol also unhooked a panicked soldier's belt, pushing past him and kicking him in the back to propel him to the next soldier. He repeated his actions, but this time the combatant's gear refused to unhook. Upon realizing this, the conscript lost his nerve and violently shook.

Kabol pulled out his knife and cut the straps off the mutt.

It was too late. The body was limp by the time Kabol cut the last strap. The leona he unhooked swam to the surface to take a breath, and a sniper's bullet snapping into the water ensured that it was his last breath. Kabol swam deeper and grabbed the limp body of the man, dragging him as he swam back to shore.

It was nearly impossible until Hayden dived in to help.

They dragged the mutt's body out of the water and removed his armor. Kabol did what he had been trained to do. He breathed into the mutt's mouth and pressed down on his gut. He was not going to let him die.

✦

Ziyad watched over the shoreline with a dispassionate smile. The gunners arrived just moments before the ships landed and not a minute too soon.

He admired the tenacity of the cats and dogs, working hand-in-hand to take back what was theirs. But he felt shame, pity even, that their efforts are futile. Not a single one had made it ten paces on the beach before being annihilated.

There was a major flaw in their plan: underestimating the might of Avon and his followers and thinking that the Sea Wall would stand up against anything. They were so trusting of their brothers-in-arms to hold the fort that they'd sent their troops on floating silver platters.

Their armor was weak, worthless; their weapons were inaccurate, worthless; their soldiers snapped like twigs beneath his fingers, worthless. That was the only way to describe the army of civilians and vagrants they had thrown at him: worthless.

He almost felt sorry for them, but it was so much fun seeing the high and mighty fall.

Ziyad stared over the kill zone with his goggles in zoom. The machine gun blared next to him, manned by Alexis and the other Seraph, who fed her gun a trail of bullets. To Ziyad's right was Renatus, helmetless with a sniper rifle, aiming down his sights but not firing.

"Renatus," Ziyad yelled over the firing machine gun. "Why have you stopped?"

The foxen didn't move or respond. He stared down his scope with wide eyes full of uncertainty.

Ziyad stood behind Renatus and activated the zoom function.

The foxen had been firing just fine earlier, what could have made him stop suddenly?

Ziyad saw nothing too special, just a downed cargo plane with troops hiding behind it and an overturned boat.

He then noticed someone, a medic.

A dark gray leona behind the plane, where the tail would have been. He was an easy target, one that a single bullet would put down. It wouldn't be too hard; he was performing CPR so his actions would be completely predictable. Considering he was attempting to save a life, he must not know his back was to a sniper.

Ziyad was about to order Alexis to take the sniper rifle and attack the target, to show Renatus how to obey orders, but he realized something. It chilled the Avian enough that his goosebumps felt like ice stabbing his bones and muscles: brown hair.

A leona, dark gray fur and brown hair. Could it be? Could Avon really have handed Ziyad this chance to wreak the holiest of vengeance upon the man who had taken his left hand? That out of all the shells and bullets this cat had passed, his life would be taken by Ziyad? He'd have to be religious to trust those odds. The only thing missing were the red eyes and white triangle pointed north on his face.

He would have to see his face.

Ziyad already knew what he would do with Red Eyes, what he'd learned to do to make a man truly die. The conscripts he had slain had been so quick to die that they might not have noticed it. He will make sure this cat suffered.

He was getting his hopes up. His heart began beating with pure excitement. He had to make sure. He reached his right hand over to the foxen, who still hadn't fired.

"Renatus, give me the sniper rifle."

The mutt coughed hoarsely, vomiting the water from his lungs. Kabol leaned him on his side and rubbed his back. "You're going to make it," Kabol reassured him. "Can you stand?"

The brown mutt nodded and got to his feet before vomiting more water.

"Where the hell are our tanks?" Hayden demanded.

"Bottom of the channel," a light gray leona answered. "Their gunships targeted them the moment they were visible."

"There's no way out!" a dark blue cat wailed. "We're dead."

"Calm down," Hayden said. "I don't need you inciting panic." Hayden looked at the light gray leona. "Where is your commanding officer?"

"He just joined the tanks." The leona pointed at the boat.

"How can you say that?" A red foxen in New Albion armor confronted him. "Show some respect."

"He was a sodding bastard and you know it," he snapped. "Good riddance to bad rubbish."

The dark blue cat wailed, "I can hear them scream out there. I can't take it anymore!"

"My name is Lieutenant Hayden Vargas. And you, Cry Baby…" Hayden grabbed the blue cat before smacking him twice on the face. "Buck up. And you, Aggro…" He pointed to the light gray leona. "Don't argue with Fox Fur."

"I have a name," Aggro snapped back. "I'm Private Williamson."

"It's Aggro now," Hayden retorted. "Aggro, Help Kabol get Brown Face to his feet."

"How come he gets to keep his name?" Aggro snarled.

"He just saved a life. He can be called whatever he wants." Hayden turned his gaze to the foxen. "Fox Fur, make sure Cry Baby here doesn't get himself shot. Kabol, come here."

All the troops listened to orders, and Kabol picked up his Callum and ammo before standing next to Hayden.

Hayden pointed toward another plane, a dozen meters away, that had been almost obliterated save for the front half. "Those turrets are made to take out emplacements and other heavier craft." He motioned toward two turrets on the nose of the plane. One was mostly in the dirt while the other had a clear view of the wall. "HEF rounds, most likely. Highly explosive fragmentation. Great for shooting just about anything. Those pillboxes are heavily armed and are shredding our forces. We need to get there and soften them up."

"All right," Kabol nodded and pointed to the wings and scattered metal. "Are we going to make a break for it? Or jump from cover to cover?"

"That's the part you're not going to like. We have to do a little bit of both." Hayden backed off and rallied the other forces in the plane. "Aggro, Fox Fur, Cry Baby, and Brown Face, listen to me. Our only chance to make it off this beach is to run to a nearby plane and use its turrets to take out the emplacements. Are there any questions?"

"No, sir," they all said simultaneously.

"Good, we're going to leg it." Hayden took a deep breath. "Follow me!"

Hayden dashed out from cover toward the plane. Kabol followed closely, carrying Brown Face with him. Aggro and Fox Fur were neck and neck, while Cry Baby took up the rear.

A trail of bullets ripped through the sand from the shore toward Hayden, who immediately fled to cover.

The gunner soon fixed his sights on Kabol and Brown Face. Kabol realized that he was between two pillboxes. One was behind him and another was in front to his right.

Kabol threw Brown Face inside a foxhole and dived in with him. The bullets kicked up sand but not much else. Aggro ran past the foxhole without stopping and made it to Hayden without a scratch on him.

Fox Fur wasn't as lucky.

The bullets cut through his legs and knees, making sickening snaps as they tore apart and shattered the bones. His painful and blood curdling screams were silenced as his chest was barraged with bullets.

The trail of bullets stopped and focused on a much larger target: the flood of reinforcements coming from the sea. There were now dozens of troops, perhaps almost a hundred, which had made it to the center of the beach where there was more debris.

Without a constant barrage of bullets to suppress the advance, the forces on that flank moved closer, drawing the attention of the gunner.

"It's clear, move!" Hayden gave the order.

Kabol got to his feet and helped Brown Face up. The cat shielded the mutt's blurry vision from the dead fox. Kabol slung the mutt's arm over his shoulder and carried him across the beach.

A snap was heard once again, followed by dead weight. A bullet pierced Brown Face in the heart from his back, completely penetrating his armor and blasting sand in front of Kabol.

The mutt dropped to the sand, grabbing Kabol's hand before the corpse began to twitch on the ground.

"Get over here!" Hayden yelled.

Kabol did as he had been ordered and was forced to abandon the mutt. He ran as fast as he could to cover. Another shot was heard, but Kabol was still moving. He made it next to Hayden and ran inside the plane. Hayden followed before quickly turning around.

"Get over here!" Hayden called from the plane. Kabol turned around and noticed that Cry Baby hadn't moved from some debris close to the first plane, "That's an order!"

"I can't! I can't!" the blue-furred cat called back. He poked his head over the debris and quickly hid again. "He's got my number. I know it!"

A loud clank tore through the air. A sniper round pierced the metal cover completely, entering the cat's back. He screamed as agonizing pain stung through his hide, and his spine curled back before he fell over.

He attempted to crawl back toward the plane, but another round went into back.

Hayden grabbed Kabol by his arm and pulled him out of the way. "We have to get on the turrets and suppress that sniper!" he said. "Shoot it until there's nothing left."

Aggro was already next to the turret almost buried in the sand. He spun the turret, shifting the sand until his feet were facing the ground and he had a clear view of the pillbox. By the time he was able to fire, Hayden was in the other turret shooting as well.

Kabol could see the pillbox through the front windshield. As the first rounds hit, concrete shattered like dirt clods. The trail of fire ceased to exist soon after the pillbox had been covered in smoke and ash.

Glass shattered in front of Kabol. The now familiar whiz of a sniper's bullet hit Aggro in the neck.

Chills ran up Kabol's spine. They were firing at the wrong pillbox.

"Get him out!" Hayden ordered and turned his weapon to face the final pillbox in sight. Kabol listened and ran to Aggro. He was unable to pull the lifeless body from the chair before another bullet was heard.

Kabol ducked behind metal, checking to see if he had been hit. His heart sank when he realized he was fine.

Hayden wasn't.

The mutt's suspended chair gave from under the pressure of the bullet and ripped it off of the already damaged hinges, leaving it hanging by only one thick screw. Hayden landed on his back and held his gut. His breathing became heavier and more sporadic. Blood gushed profusely from his wound, even when he applied pressure.

"Stay back!" Hayden held out his bloodied hand with his palm facing Kabol. "Stay back." His voice was weaker. He pointed to the other pillbox through the window.

"Hayden!" Kabol cried back, his chest heavy and his eyes filled with grief.

Hayden kept pointing his finger. "You stay the hell right there."

"I can help you." Kabol prepared to rip Aggro's clothes for a tourniquet.

"Don't you dare—" Hayden coughed hoarsely and lay on his left arm. He reached over his hips and pulled out his pistol. He held it against his own head. "Not one step closer… He'll kill you." He pointed it toward Kabol. "You stay there, and not a single tear."

Kabol stared at his friend. He couldn't believe what Hayden was telling him. "Why?"

Hayden either wasn't in the mood or didn't have the strength to answer. He held his weapon out to Kabol, wheezing and whimpering. "I'm scared. It hurts so much… I don't want you to hurt… I can make it quick…"

Kabol shook his head and wiped a tear from his eyes. "Hayden, let me help you."

"Shut up. Stay there," Hayden commanded and threw his pistol at Kabol. He grunted horribly as he crawled toward the turret. The wound on his torso looked as if his guts were spilling out. His intestines hung from the wound. There was no hope. Should he run or stand too long, his guts would spill out. Hayden pulled himself up and held onto the turret to catch his breath. The mutt reached over and prepared the turret to turn to the right. "He… zeroed in on you. Get. Out. Ready?"

"Hayden, please!" Kabol begged.

"What are your orders, soldier…?" Hayden cringed and held his gut, coughing up blood. "Regarding the Avon?"

Kabol swallowed a hard lump in his throat. "Kill them all…"

Hayden held the turret's trigger. "Get out."

⁂

Ziyad peered through the scope. His crosshairs were on the red-eyed menace who had dared to cross him. He was hidden, pinned down by him. The moment the cat went for his wounded friend, or retreated outside the plane, Ziyad would put a bullet in his back, then his head.

Now the only thing visible was the cat's snout and hand. Ziyad prepared himself, focusing on nothing other than his prey through his scope.

Just as he had anticipated, the cat made a break for it.

"Turret!" Renatus yelled and tackled Ziyad, making him pull the trigger with the sights on the sky.

The pillbox was bombarded with explosive rounds. Walls crumbled behind them. Alexis was fast enough to lie on the ground. The Seraph who fed her the bullets wasn't prepared and was hit.

The foxen was demolished by a single bullet piercing his stomach. The round immediately blew up, tearing the man in half.

Ziyad instinctively and quickly crawled out of the bunker and aimed his rifle at the turret. He shot. Behind the muzzle flash, the window was smeared with blood and the turret was silenced.

Ziyad quickly scoped around the beach looking for Red Eyes. He couldn't find him among an oncoming mob of New Albion troops. Ziyad felt his anger pulse up his spine. He'd had him! A chance that could have only been given to him by the gods, and Renatus had ruined it.

He pointed the rifle at the foxen and pulled the trigger on the unsuspecting creature, only to be acquainted with the sound of an empty rifle.

Ziyad threw it aside, preparing to draw the blades on his arms. A voice yelling on the radio got his attention. A commander was calling for retreat.

Ziyad opened the radio and responded. "Retreat? From what? The battle is ours."

"The right flank has collapsed. Two pillboxes are now out of commission. They're swarming us. We're going to run out of ammo."

"Commander!" Alexis called and pointed toward the shore. "They're reinforcing with Demon-class armor."

Ziyad looked through his scope to see that a transport bore a mutt in power armor. All around the beach, where the machine guns could no longer cover, conscripts and demons were now disembarking from transports.

"They've sent in their pawns first." Ziyad studied his surroundings. The bunker he was in had been completely demolished. The roof had caved in, there was no cover facing the beach, the prisoners were gone, most of the floor was honeycombed with holes, and all ammunition for their weapons had been destroyed. With no one giving coordinates for artillery it, too, was useless.

Ziyad held a foul curse on his tongue. He had failed in his mission to hold the stronghold, and his mission from Avon to exact revenge. He called on his radio, "We'll be overrun by the end of the hour. All forces are ordered to retreat."

27

Dinred stepped out of her room.

Several Avon soldiers were collecting their wounded and sick, moving them away from their rooms. The halls were crowded with Avonian soldiers. They tried to play it slow and casual, but it was obvious that they had never been in such a hurry.

Isabelle poked her head out from behind the arch. "What's going on?"

During the commotion, Dinred saw the familiar yellow-striped helmet of a Seraph. "I'm going to find out," she answered, "Isabelle, stay here."

Dinred tried to shuffle her way through the crowd. The Avon soldiers looked almost nothing like the Seraphs. They wore much less armor and bore white camouflage. Dinred wondered why they would dress in such a manner, but she remembered where they had come from.

Had New Albion really been that easy to conquer? So much so that they hadn't even given the troops proper armor to blend in to the environment? The more Dinred thought about it, the more she understood how the Avon thought. New Albion hadn't had an army since it was called Albion.

They had taken the opportunity like a hunter discovering a deaf rabbit.

Dinred managed to get to Ziyad, who was listening to orders on his radio. He moved into the waiting room, away from traffic. He must not have noticed the white cat coming toward him.

She squeezed between two people and entered a much less crowded room. It was the waiting room, the place she and Isabelle had hidden the night of the invasion. She barely remembered how it looked; she just remembered being scared.

"Ziyad…" Dinred forgot to say hello. "What's going on?"

Ziyad removed his finger from the radio and turned around, widening his arms for a hug. "Mary!"

Dinred ran up and gave him a hug, wrapping her arms beneath Ziyad's shoulders. This was the first time he ever offered a hug; she was going to take it. "What's with the grand greeting?"

"I'm glad you came to see me, I didn't think I'd have time to say my final hello."

"Final?" Dinred's ears drooped. "What do you mean?"

The Seraph took off his helmet and placed it on a nearby chair. "I didn't have time to find a good way to word this. I'll just say it." Dinred noticed he looked somber, almost as if he didn't like what he was about to say. "We're leaving, all of us. We're currently taking crafts back to the *Basilicas*. I'm going with them."

"You're leaving me?"

"Don't say it like that; it breaks my heart enough."

"Well, maybe it should." Dinred felt her own heart constrict. "I thought we were friends. You get me to like you, and then you just leave?"

"Friendship in a nutshell. Is that how you use that saying?" Ziyad took the lower beak of his armor off and rested it next to the helmet. "I'm sorry. I should have known better. We are friends though, Mary. I…" Ziyad stepped forward and grabbed her hands gently. "I would like for you to come with me."

"What?" Dinred was shocked to hear those words. She hadn't expected Ziyad to invite her to a giant warship to take off to who knows where on such short notice. "But, I'm not an Avon."

"You don't have to be," he urged. "The others won't have to know. Please come with me. You can bring your mutt. I mean, you can bring Lisa."

Dinred's tail perked, only for a moment. The Avon were leaving, so Isabelle wouldn't have to hide anymore. On the other hand, if she were somehow discovered to be queen on a massive ship full of people who wanted her dead…

She'd have to choose between Ziyad and Isabelle.

"Speaking of which…" Ziyad added and looked to his right.

The mutt was hiding was behind a chair, patiently waiting with her hands folded in front of her and embarrassed at how easily she had been caught.

"Lisa!" Dinred said. "I told you to stay in the room."

"It's quite fine." Ziyad motioned for the mutt to come closer. "I'm glad she's here. I would like to say something." Ziyad folded his hands behind his back. "I would like to apologize for the way I treated you. It was wrong."

"Ziyad!" a foxen called from the doorway. It was the red-furred fox in armor Dinred had occasionally seen. He looked quite cross and aggravated, with his fur standing on end. He looked like he was trying to keep his composure.

"Excuse me, Cypher," Ziyad growled at the fox. "I am having a moment. I do not need you, of all people, to ruin it."

The fox motioned toward the door. "The Father wants you on the *Basilicus*, now!"

"He can wait," Ziyad said. "What could he possibly want?"

"He wants you to stop running your mouth! What part of 'do not talk about the wolfen to anyone' did you not understand? I don't recall him stuttering."

"I haven't talked about the wolfen to anyone," Ziyad protested.

"Yes, you did! He said he spoke to a girl named Dinred. She said you started to literally preach about them."

Dinred's ears perked and her eyes widened when he heard her name being scornfully tossed into the conversation. She was stunned and began to worry. Would her secret get out? She glanced at Isabelle, who was gesturing for them to get out of the room.

"That just shows how much he knows about the leonas." As he continued defending himself, Dinred grew at ease. Ziyad was too stubborn to listen to Cypher. He added, "Dinred isn't a name; it's a formal greeting they used in the old times."

"Oh?" Cypher almost laughed. "You can't even comprehend how to use conjunctions, and you think you know more about New Albion and its language than him or me?" He straightened his spine and changed his accent to almost perfectly match one common around London. "Dearest feathered folk, ill and foul informed child. Thou know'st not the cunning of deep-rooted greets. A good-morrow, or dare nay, a fine evening are two simple chords often played. But Dinred? Thou hath alluded thyself to falsehood. You're being foolish, and I demand you stop."

Dinred was surprised that the foreigner had a vast knowledge of a language that even she had trouble with. He even spoke it as a means of offering a compelling argument that could convince even her.

It all fell on deaf ears.

Ziyad spoke like an affronted pastor. "You think you can trick me after you insulted me in front of my friends? I will not stand for this charade. This is why I do not like you. You take far too many things as childish jokes, games. You make the most annoying of banters. You do not understand what irritation you bring and to whom you do it. Are you listening to me?"

Cypher looked paralyzed by his peer's temper. His long petty frown looked almost mocking. "You don't like me?"

"Get out of my sight."

The foxen turned around with a retort, before heading for the exit. "I have about twenty-three thousand days left on this earth, and I'm not spending another minute arguing with you."

"I'm sorry." Ziyad turned to Dinred and Isabelle. "That man knows how to get under my skin."

"It's perfectly fine," Isabelle said, "and I accept your apology. But did I hear right? I heard you were leaving?"

"I am. And you're welcome to come along with me. I would like the chance to make up for how I treated you. I would like to leave this room with more friends than enemies."

Dinred felt flattered by Ziyad's actions. "Maybe you're already accomplishing that, and you just don't know it yet?"

Isabelle elbowed Dinred playfully. "Shh! We could get free stuff."

Ziyad smirked at the mutt's words; he almost even laughed. "I'll let you think it over. I must leave; the Father won't like it if I keep him waiting for too long. I'll come back." Ziyad opened his arms and hugged both of them.

Dinred closed her eyes, feeling happy, amazed at how soothing the hug felt.

Ziyad released the two and took a pace back. "I'll see you soon."

Dinred and Isabelle began to head out of the room with quite a lot on their minds. The leona stopped and turned around with sly smirk and a remark prepared.

Ziyad, however, wasn't concerned with Dinred anymore. He was focused on a wall with pictures of the hospital staff. The Avian was frozen stiff, and his fingers were separated like he had been spooked until he clenched them into fists.

"Are you all right?" Dinred asked.

The bird didn't respond. He stepped toward the wall, focusing on a single picture. "Who is that man…?"

Dinred wondered what he meant by that and took a few steps toward the Avon. "You're in the way. Which one are you referring to?"

Ziyad tried to remove the framed picture from the wall. It was budging but he didn't have the patience to figure out how to take it off properly. He reeled back an arm and punched it.

Dinred jumped at the sound of the glass shattering beneath his knuckles.

Ziyad, without grace, removed the picture from the frame. He read the inscription: "Kabol Anton."

Dinred's heart skipped a beat; then it felt like it was tearing itself out of her chest. He had spoken those words like a curse. She bit her lip, shuffling her feet, trying not to tremble. Dinred felt threatened by him. Any feeling of security had been gone the moment her husband's name was uttered.

"Whoa, Commander, was that you?" Another voice was heard behind Dinred. "And who's that?"

Dinred knew who that was. Alexis. She swallowed, wishing she had followed Isabelle out of the room when she had the chance. With Alexis here, she felt more vulnerable. The Ziyad who had been her friend was no longer there. She stepped back when the foxen walked past her, still talking.

"That name sounds familiar." Alexis took her mask off. "You know him?"

"He's the one that took my hand before running off."

Dinred's eyes widened and she silently gasped. *He's the one who harmed the bird? He got away? He's alive? He's alive!* Dinred almost jumped for joy. Her chest felt light and she smiled behind the backs of the two Avon.

Her smile was almost gone the next time Ziyad opened his beak to speak. "I'm going to kill him!"

No! Dinred's head ached with the barrage of emotions fighting for control. Fear, love, hope, and hatred all clouded her mind at once. *He's alive! But soon he'll be dead. Killed by Ziyad.* She couldn't let that happen. But what could she do?

"Hey, I know him," Alexis announced, looking at the picture. "I worked for him and his wife…"

Alexis froze as she was speaking. She looked up at the wall before her gaze darted to Dinred. Her mouth was agape and her eyes were wide. Her lips slowly curled into a smile and her brow lowered. Her finger, once pointing at the picture, wagged at Dinred.

Dinred wanted to scream for help. *How does she know who I am? What does she have against me?* There was only one voice, one plan inside her head: run.

Alexis placed her hand on Ziyad's shoulder and whispered in his ear. She kept glancing at Dinred, making the leona feel flushed with panic.

The two of them turned their heads toward the cat.

"A spy." Alexis smirked. "He trusted you. You really shouldn't have lied to him, Dinred."

28

Kabol held his gun to his chest and looked down the iron sights.

New Albion's plan was simple: shoot straight toward the capital before liberating the rest of the isle. Kabol, however, was done with the army. He'd seen how little his kind was valued.

Without Hayden and Ben, he felt alone. He'd decided he was going to leave. He knew where the conscripts were going after this: either against the Romans and their machines of war or the Avon and their zealous troops. Both were equally terrifying.

He had a plan of his own. Find Dinred and make sure she went to the safest place possible. He hoped she could leave New Albion, so that the draft would never pick her name.

After that, he'd either find the closest depot and turn himself in, or ditch the uniform altogether. If he was lucky, he'd run into a skirmish and tell the troops he had become separated from his squad and gotten lost.

Kabol was afraid he could not run from the fact that he was now a deserter. He had left the camp, under the cover of the night, right after the Sea Wall had been recaptured. He had also stolen a military vehicle. *Add that to the list of things to court martial me for.*

It was a shame there was zero tolerance for conscripts.

He wasn't dumb enough to drive a military vehicle into enemy-held territory. He had to leg it when he was a mile out. It had taken him a few hours of travel, but he was now in the streets of London.

He was still in armor, hoping the medic patches could make him a prisoner of war rather than an enemy. It didn't seem to matter. He hadn't found anything to replace it, or he would have.

The streets were bare and empty, almost to the point of being eerie. The full moon was still hung high above the street. The lack of light on the ground made the lunar glow incandescent among the rubble of buildings Kabol trailed silently through.

He had no idea where to begin his search. What had he been thinking? He was going to get himself killed! London was bigger than he remembered it, and now there wasn't much left to help jog his memory. No landmarks stood on the horizon that were taller than the dilapidated houses in front of him. The only thing that breathed life was an aurora of light blocks away, toward the center of town.

He wasn't heading there; that would be suicide. At least for now.

It wasn't until he heard a stream flowing that he recalled where he was. It was in the middle of a path, and the path itself was sandwiched between two rows of houses. Each one had once been two stories tall. All had markings of burnt ash and soot.

The once beautiful slate paths were now poisoned with black dust. The air felt somber and thick. Many memories had been made here, and now it was turned to cinders. Many of these memories were Kabol's, and no matter how glad he was to feel free of the suffocating atmosphere of decorations, he felt like it should have gone a different way.

A worse thought crossed his mind. How many people had been lucky enough to make it out?

He refused to think about it another second.

He heard a loud hum from far above. Planes. He looked up, unable to see anything. Turning around, away from the center of the city, he saw searchlights begin to appear in the distance. They steadily came closer until one appeared less than a kilometer away.

The aircraft were spotted very soon in the columns of light before being fired upon. The air raid siren blared like it had that fateful night. Within a single moment, the city was alive again.

Kabol hid in one of the houses when he heard the tread of tanks and steps of troops a block away. He sat down beside a staircase. His hands trembled. He was surrounded by enemies. He had to be. He should have known better than to come so close. The hospital was only a few streets down.

The cat turned around and looked up. He could see, through a hole in the roof, that the planes were dropping paratroopers and supplies rather than risking civilian casualties with bombs.

The nearby soldiers headed out toward the drop zones.

Kabol held his breath as the enemy marched by the house. Several equipped men and armored troop carriers passed. The infantry was having trouble keeping up with the vehicles. A few began to look through the windows of the building.

A soldier kicked in the door to another room, and the hinges broke under the pressure. The wooden slab slamming to the ground was louder than the sirens in the distance. Kabol retrieved the knife from his boot, ready to silently take on the man if he were spotted. His hand shook even more with anxiety about what could and would happen. He worried most about what would come of taking this man's life.

Another soldier yelled at the man to keep up with the squad, making the him turn tail and run back to formation.

Kabol held the knife tightly and picked up his weapon. He was glad the soldiers were in a hurry and didn't have enough time to search the houses. He was sure, even if he had the gall to stab a soldier, the troops would be suspicious when the dead man didn't answer.

He heard heavy footsteps from upstairs. He stood up, readying his weapon for anything that came down the stairs. The footsteps were heavy, and there was no mistake—it was a Seraph. Kabol took a heavy breath and tried to steady his weapon. He held still, facing up the stairs.

The footsteps sounded like they were still above him. Not on the second floor, but the roof!

Kabol turned around quickly enough to see what he feared most. A Seraph jumped down from the hole in the roof and charged him.

Kabol didn't have time to react and no clear angle from which to stab him. The Seraph was not hesitant. He smacked Kabol's gun out of his hands the moment he was within reach and swiftly jumped, placing the cat's throat between his forearm and biceps.

Kabol still hung on tightly to the knife in his hand. The Seraph acted too quickly, unaware of the threat Kabol posed and allowing the cat to have a clear spot to stab: the eyes.

Kabol swung the knife as hard as he could at the Seraph's head. A loud clank made the Seraph release him. Kabol lost his footing and landed hard on the stairs. Due to the speed at which he had been dropped, his helmet got snagged on the soldier's shoulder. It slipped off his snout onto the floor. The burnt steps below them snapped under its weight, and the Seraph toppled down with Kabol.

Kabol was the first on the ground and first on his feet. He pulled the knife in a position to stab when he saw the Seraph roll onto his stomach.

He missed his eye, gashing his forehead. The Seraph, rather than draw his blades, took off the mask entirely.

It was the foxen from a week ago, the one Kabol had saved.

He held out a hand and got to his feet. The foxen looked as

surprised as he was. All intent to kill had left the room entirely. The fox's stunned look didn't last as long. It turned to worry. "You… You need to get out of here."

Kabol shook his head. He had someone to get to.

"You need to go!" The fox tried to keep his voice down and grabbed Kabol's Callum by the barrel and slid it across the floor. "Before the commander sees you. Oh no." The foxen looked up. More feet were heard on the roof. He swallowed and shook his head, a look of guilt on his face. "I'm sorry. I'm so sorry."

He grabbed his helmet off the ground and turned his back on Kabol before darting into another room.

Kabol didn't pick up his Callum or his helmet. They were useless dead weight.

He didn't know what else to do but flee. It was either that, or he would curl into a ball and weep. So he ran.

The houses were full of twists and turns, even dead ends. The Seraph would be able to track his movements and get the jump on him. But if he were to run out of the houses, he would know the Seraph would only be behind him; he could run in any direction he wanted.

Maybe he could outrun him?

There was no other choice. He dashed out of the house, his boots grinding against the soot-covered slates beneath him. It was almost slippery, but Kabol wasn't careless enough to fall.

He could hear the gears and heavy steps of a Seraph clambering on the roof. Kabol glanced over his shoulder to see a new Seraph jumping onto a nearby roof and crashing through it.

Kabol still ran toward the frontlines, toward survival.

The Seraph jumped with enough momentum to skid on the ash and smashed through a brick wall in front of him.

Kabol stopped, blade drawn in shaky hands.

The Avian stood, back straight and weapons sheathed. Behind him an orange horizon of fire and lead, Kabol's current idea of safety, was blocked by an angel of death.

He reared his beaked head, and his eyes—those red slits—dug into Kabol's very soul. The yellow stripe across the beak scared the leona to his core, remembering the night when he had been at his mercy. There were no mistake—this was death here to claim him. The bird spoke with utter hatred. "You."

The Seraph jutted his arms and the blades sprouted from the gauntlets.

Kabol swallowed and steadied his hand. There was no retreat. He clutched his knife. If the Seraph moved in, he would be at a disadvantage and the sharp end of a blade. He had to strike first.

He charged forth, knife blade first.

The Seraph stood his ground and, with a single swipe, Kabol lost all advantage. The cat jumped back from the blade. He felt the pressure of the tip of the blade gliding and scratching his breastplate.

The Seraph jutted a shoulder into Kabol, knocking the cat on the ground. He reeled his foot up and prepared to stomp.

Kabol rolled to his left, toward the stream, and avoided the talon as it planted itself on a slate tile, obliterating it into smaller chunks. Kabol backed away; the Seraph lifted his leg once more. The second stomp almost crushed Kabol's tail.

Kabol quickly rolled back, keeping his knife in hand as he kept his feet in place. He was on even ground once more, as much of an even ground as one can find against a Seraph.

The Seraph marched toward Kabol without hesitation, like a hungry wolf after an infant.

"What do you want from me?" Kabol demanded.

The Seraph didn't respond. He trudged forward, preparing his blade to strike. He did not strike. He pointed to a nearby house and announced, "You're keeping Dinred waiting."

"What?" Kabol gasped. "What did you do to her?"

The Seraph retracted his blade and held his arms out wide, baring his chest and palms. "What I do to all heretics. She now sees salvation," he said, almost with sorrow and regret. "She now hears His voice!"

Kabol's muscles no longer told him to run. His mind no longer thought to hide. His heart no longer sought to heal or mend, but it and all parts of his being told him to protect Dinred against anything this monster had to offer. From his very soul was an order to kill.

Kabol, in a fit of fury and rage, moved his dagger to point down and rushed to the Seraph, placing all strength into a single stab at the neck. But the Seraph was ready.

The bird swung his left arm above his head, blocking the dagger.

All of the strength in that arm left Kabol after he heard a sickening crack as it slammed hard against the heavy metal. The blade fell right in front of him. Behind it, the Seraph jutted his blade out of his right arm, having a clear view of a cat's torso to stab.

"No!" the cat called, enacting the next part of his plan. He reached across his chest with his other hand and retrieved the falling dagger, and he plunged it into the Seraph's neck.

The Seraph gasped in horrible pain. Forgetting to stab the leona, he clutched the cat's arm and squeezed tightly.

Kabol twisted his wrist, hard. All of the force in the Avian's hands was drained instantly. Kabol twisted his torso, pushing the Seraph toward the stream. The talons slid easily on the ash, and as soon as the power-armored soldier leaned against the railing, the iron fence snapped apart.

The Seraph plunged into the stream and was submerged in its rapids. The only thing visible on the water's surface was blood and pockets of air. The latter soon disappeared.

Kabol dropped to his knees. The blood-drenched knife was still in hand. His heart was heavy, and his muscles were sore. He lay on his side and curled into a ball. The stress was enough that he was prepared to weep. It didn't help when he realized the horrifying truth: he had just killed a man.

His heart grew heavier when another thought came to mind. Dinred!

He ignored all his emotions. He had to. He threw the dagger to the ground and ran to a house. It was his house, which the Seraph had horridly pointed to.

He passed through the back door and up the stairs. His core shook as he looked through the rooms. They were all empty. Until he got to the dining room door. He reached for the charred handle and pushed the door open.

His heart sank and his eyes grew heavy with tears as he rushed to his wife.

On the floor was Dinred, dead. Her ears had been cut, removed, and claimed. Her eyes, her beautiful green eyes, had been cut from their sockets.

Kabol screamed and knelt down next to her. He lifted her limp shoulders from the ground and hugged her tightly. He cried, shaking his head and calling her name. Why would they do this to her?

Tears streamed down his face and dripped onto her shoulder.

He grasped her tightly, praying she'd move or respond. He begged for a response, anything to hear her soothing voice, just a whisper. He longed for one last chance to dance with her.

He bit his lip and cursed himself. He wished he'd let the Seraph take him.

That was the only prayer that was answered. Heavy steps found their way across the hallway floor. Steps of a Seraph.

Kabol didn't care. He welcomed it. He swallowed what felt like coal in his throat, able to croak out a last request without opening his tear-filled eyes. "Finish it. I'm already dead."

The Seraph was still for only a moment.

Kabol gasped as he was strangled from behind.

29

Kabol sat with his shackled wrists behind him.

His armor had been stripped from him, as had his shirt, leaving him bare and illustrated with new torture scars as his flesh bled onto his fur. He didn't know exactly where he was, other than imprisoned in one of their camps.

He occasionally heard propellers and engines flare up and away. He also heard the distant rumbles of battle. He was still in London; he couldn't have been out long.

Upon awaking, he had wept. They had taken her from him. They had taken everything. He sobbed until his eyes were empty, his tears stained his face, and his throat was dry.

He had failed.

The room was dark and cold. It was small, made mostly of thin metal welded together. Very little thought had been put into the process of making it comfortable or strong save for an iron door in front of him. He still couldn't get out by smashing on the walls. It was also isolated. Not much noise was heard anywhere other than in the distance.

He'd been inside for what felt like hours, alone with his thoughts. If only he hadn't stabbed the Seraph that night, she'd still be alive. If he'd let the Seraph take him, she'd still be smiling. If he had let him take Isabelle, her body wouldn't have been disgraced.

Isabelle.

Kabol's ears perked and his head rose. Isabelle was out there, scared and alone. Was she alive? A new surge of motivation ran through his blood. Kabol had to get out. He had to protect her.

He looked over his shoulders at the shackles that hugged his wrists. He wasn't just going to sit there and ponder what they could do to her. He had to get out, and there was only one way he knew how. He was glad the shabby prison had no chains to the wall.

Kabol pulled on his right hand and pushed with his left. His hand was still stuck, and his wrist and thumb started to become uncomfortable. He tried it again, this time harder and with more persistence. He wasn't going to let pain be a deterrent.

He placed his foot between the handcuffs, on top of the little metal gap that held them together. He pushed it down and used his foot to keep the cuffs anchored to the floor. He pulled once again, this time as hard as he could until his flesh ripped and his wrist bled.

He couldn't help but to wail loudly in stinging pain as he felt his bones dislocate under his skin. Blood became abundant enough to lubricate the cuff. Now his thumb was painfully jammed into his palm.

He heard a noise over his screaming and stopped as the metal door in front of him was unlocked and opened. He froze immediately.

A woman, foxen, entered the room. She was in fatigues, of average height, and moved at a brisk pace. "So, 'master' is finally awake."

Kabol looked sharply at her as she closed the door and glared at him. She noted his heavy breathing and smiled at his scars. She drew out a knife from under her shirt, the knife he had abandoned.

"Damn you." She leaned closer. "You've ruined everything. I needed the commander's word to finally become a Seraph, and you just killed him. You should really put a shirt on." She smirked. "We're civilized here."

Kabol instinctively growled at her, and a plan began to form deep in his emotionally weary mind. He continued to pull his hand out of the restraints. "Say that…" He let his head go limp. "To my face."

"I have other plans for that." She treaded closer and knelt down, drawing the knife to his ears. "I could claim you, like I did to your wife."

His head shot up. Anger flared in Kabol, giving birth to an unforgiving amount of hate.

"Lousy rich," she said, "but hey, no amount of money saved her, so I guess it worked out in the end." She moved the knife to his eyes. "Maybe I could blind you first. Would you scream just as loud?"

Kabol's breathing was heavier and filled with rage.

She placed the knife at his lips. "Or maybe I should start by cutting your tongue out? Or would that be too rude?"

Those were the last words she ever said.

Kabol slipped through his bindings. He simultaneously pulled down her outstretched elbow, bent it, and pressed the knife deep into her throat.

She gasped in shock, and her eyes filled with unspeakable pain. Kabol twisted the blade, making her squeal, before tearing it out of her throat.

He grabbed her by the shoulder and used her still-breathing corpse to help pull him up to his feet before pushing her down. He wiped the blood off the blade using the fur on his arm and then held it with his elbow. He used his left hand, still in the cuffs, to snap his thumb back into place. He'd need to seek attention for it once he was out.

He ignored her twitching, gasping body and stepped over it toward the door.

He opened it, revealing a row of makeshift sheds. They each had loops on top for an aircraft to hook onto. However, many of them were empty with the doors opened wide.

He heard whimpering from the nearest one, which was closed.

He went back into his room, hoping to find a key on the corpse of the woman. Satisfied with looting the dead, he opened the cell.

Isabelle lay sobbing on the ground; her ears had been removed and her eyes had been sewn shut.

"Isabelle!" Kabol rushed to her aid as her head shot up.

He grabbed her gently, making her wince, and rested her head on his lap. He was so glad to see her he had to restrain himself from hugging the air out of her. He placed an outstretched finger to her lips and hushed her.

"It's going to be okay," he reassured her and inspected her ears. He didn't touch them, but he was sure he could mend any damage if he got the right medicine. The eyes would have to wait.

He set her down gently on the hard floor and retrieved his knife.

Isabelle reached around the room blindly before grabbing Kabol's tail. "Dinred?" She held her head up and coughed, guessing where he was. "Is she safe?"

Kabol didn't answer. He held his blade firmly and said, "You have to let go. I have a job to do. I have to keep you safe."

"Where are you going?" She held him tightly, desperate not to be alone.

Kabol tugged his tail from her grasp and moved away from her. When he was at the door, he said the only thing he could think of, in blind, unspeakable rage.

"I have to follow orders."

⚍⚍⚍

The night was just about over. The horizon grew closer to Kabol, who sat and lay on the side of an unmanned bunker. The freezing air bit through his fur. He didn't mind, for lying against him was Isabelle, still blind and covered in layers of found clothing. He had found them on that one fox girl who had dared to taunt him.

Her ears, however, had been mended and replaced. Plastic ears from a medical bay were the only thing Kabol had found suitable to replace the lost cartilage. He had given her sedatives before sewing them on. He didn't dare attempt to free her eyes. Not yet. Not until she was somewhere safe.

Not until she was where she could no longer see him.

He was covered in blood, and very little of it was his own. His pelt, now red, was glistening in the light of burning vehicles and emplacements.

He was at the base of a fountain, lying on the bloody plaque that sat under the gaze of Cerberus.

He couldn't feel anything other than his hand against Isabelle's shoulder, pressing her against him whenever a noise was too loud, injecting her with more painkillers so she could no longer hurt.

He felt dead. He couldn't feel his heartbeat. A few times, he had to place his hand on his chest before convincing himself he was still awake and alive.

He didn't know what to think, so he didn't. All he had planned was to wait for the wall of fire and gunshots to reach him. What would mean death for him would be life for her.

A vehicle drove up, armored and carrying troops. It was a

silhouette in front of the fire surrounding him.

Kabol picked up a blood-soaked pistol, ready to kill whoever stepped out.

It stopped a few meters away from him, outside the metal fence of the palace courtyard. A man stepped out, from the passenger's seat, before several more followed.

Kabol aimed through the iron sights with steady red hands.

The soldiers lifted their rifles and placed their fingers on the triggers. One of them didn't. Instead he ran in front of all the troops repeating, "Nein! No!" in a thick German accent.

Kabol pointed the weapon toward the hound's head.

"Er ist… Shell shocked." The mutt motioned to Kabol and waved his hands, batting away their guns. He turned around and stepped closer, holding out his hand. "Kabol. Ich heiße Ansgar."

"Ansgar?" Kabol felt a rush of relief. He dropped the gun and all the soldiers moved in closer. He felt sad. Rescue had finally come, but he wished it were someone else. "Why did it have to be you, Ansgar?"

The mutt ran to his aid, and Kabol patted Isabelle's side.

"Take care of her for me," he told the mutt in German. "Promise me."

"What are you talking about?" Ansgar carefully picked up Isabelle.

One of the soldiers walked past the three, toward the new hell Kabol had created. He didn't want to see any of it. He was sure he would be joining Dinred soon. In one final attempt, he pleaded, "Ansgar, promise me you'll take care of her!"

"What the hell is this?" the soldier said, seeing the horror behind the statue.

"Promise me!" Kabol said before the soldier returned and grabbed him by his shoulders.

"What did you do?" The soldier pushed him against the plaque.

"I don't know!" Kabol wailed at him.

"You're under arrest." The soldier grabbed Kabol's arm and almost dragged the weakened cat toward the car. "Private, Corporal, get him to report to base camp. Do not let him leave your sight."

Another soldier grabbed Kabol's other arm. The Corporal guided him toward the armored vehicle as Kabol heard a new, familiar voice.

"Kabol? Ol' buddy, ol' pal, is that you?" Ben called, walking out from behind the transport. His fur was no longer yellow washed away, perhaps, by the waters of the beach. It was pure white in contrast to his gray hair, and both were almost completely covered in blood.

"Ben?" Kabol was too out of his wits to be shocked, but he still had to ask. "You survived?"

"I know." The cat bared his terrifying Cheshire cat grin, and his white eyes, the only part of his body and clothes that were unstained, stared into Kabol. He placed his hands on the gray cat's jaws, focusing Kabol's gaze on him. "Crazy, right?"

30

Imprisoned once again, Kabol sat with his hands chained to a table.

He had been locked away in a cell for three days. The Avon had returned to Swethin.

He had gotten almost no sleep or food for that matter. He was no longer among allies or friends. He had been left alone to rot, a preamble to the consequences of the sins he had committed.

Now he sat in a cold room, constrained to a table that was bolted to the floor.

He had no more tears. He was no more awake or alive than the chair he sat on.

He knew what happened in this room. Beside him was a two-way mirror, and in front of him was a steel door locked from the outside. They were going to interrogate him, get him to confess to what he'd done.

Soon the door was unlocked and opened.

Kabol felt angry and alive again when he saw the man who had walked through the door was none other than Kai. He stood up, causing the chains to yank his hands back to the table.

"You really know how to screw up spectacularly." Kai looked over documents in his hand. Kabol sat back down as Kai walked over and placed the folder on the table. He put a single finger on it. "Thirty-six people. I'm impressed."

Kabol stayed silent, glaring at the mongrel in front of him.

"Disgracing the bodies though?" Kai continued, keeping his voice calm. "Wow. I couldn't even find the words to describe one of them. I've never seen so many stab wounds on a single corpse. Just what the hell were you thinking?"

"I wasn't."

"Obviously." Kai grinded his knuckles against the folder. "But you had to have had something going through your mind."

"I was following orders."

"Orders? What orders and from whom?"

Kabol wasn't going to say Hayden's name. He wouldn't have wanted that. But he knew who would have. "You."

"You're lying."

"You gave the order. In boot camp. It's how you trained us. It's what you wanted from us."

"This is my fault? I trained you to kill soldiers. I've ordered you to kill soldiers. These were—!" Kai stood up and, in a fit of rage, threw the folder against the mirror and yelled at the top of his lungs, "Those were not soldiers!"

Kabol's heart sank as his ears drooped and his eyes widened. "What?" No, *he's lying. He wants me to confess to crimes* I *haven't committed. I only killed birds in Avonian armor.*

"This is just as surprising to you?" Kai asked honestly, still angry. "Who gave you the order?"

Kabol yelled back, "I wasn't thinking! I was mad, but I only killed soldiers, damn it. You trained me and ordered me to kill them all."

"The point of that training was for you to figure out how to control your anger." Kai pointed back. "For you to realize that emotion will endanger you and everyone around you. If your deliberate hatred of me will get in the way of you being honest, I will leave now, empty handed, and you will be court martialed and sentenced to death."

Kabol clutched his chains. "New Albion doesn't kill prisoners."

"They're willing to make an exception for mass murderers," Kai said, sitting back down. "Especially when Deutschland says it'll help with paying their debt. So far, the only person who is defending you is the queen herself. How did you possibly get on her good side? She must hate them as much as you."

"I don't know what you're talking about," Kabol spoke as honestly as he could. He didn't know a queen.

"You listen to me, and you listen well for once. I am your savior. You need to tell me what was going through that head of yours and who gave the order. Then I'll tell you how to get out of this mess without getting strung up like the animal you are."

Kabol was silent. He rested his forehead on the table, letting a tear drop from his eye. "They took her away from me."

"What was that?"

"They took her away from me!" Kabol repeated. "They cut off her ears. They cut out her eyes. They claimed her like an animal. Hayden is gone as well. I thought Ben was dead. I had to kill them. They were going to take the only person I had left."

Kai nodded. In a calm voice he spoke. "Extreme distress under pressure from a traumatic event, intoxicated by a sleep-deprived mind and the night, as well as twisted and deluded forms of information while training. Now who gave the order?"

"I didn't know the officer's name," he lied, unwilling to bring his best friend into this. "He was a mutt, though. His last orders were to kill them all. I didn't think. I followed them to the letter." Kabol lifted his head. "Just like you taught me."

Kai was quiet now, nodding his head. He stood up and kicked around a few of the papers that had spilled from the folder. "I see. So it is my fault. Now it's my turn to give you a few options." He held out his hands. "In this hand, you can accept what the council and parliament have decided. Stand trial, be found guilty. You will be hanged for your war crimes. On the other hand…" He placed the arm behind his back. "You're as much as an asset as a liability. Great in lifting spirits and rallying troops. You've been seen exiting a vehicle that destroyed two emplacements on the beaches, saving hundreds of lives. Singlehandedly slaying an experienced Seraph, among other things. Even managing to save the queen, of all people, from being taken away.

"This war needs you." He lifted his other hand toward Kabol. "You will join a penal battalion, newly developed, under my command. Tactical Auxiliary Personnel. You will be forced to fight for the rest of the war. Without pay or commendations. Front lines and suicide missions all year 'round. One order: kill them all. But just the soldiers, to clarify."

"Auxiliary?" Kabol asked.

"Just a fancy way of saying you're completely disposable. You're not the only one with war crimes on your head. Just ask Ben and his collection of scalps. But after the war, you're a free man granted amnesty. And you'll get to go home with a clean record and soul." Kai held out both his hands, "Either way, they will have a body."

"So I'm a dead man?" Kabol said.

"Yes."

Kabol already knew that answer. For three days he had known that answer. He regretted the decisions he'd made, and they would live with him his entire life. He could feel his heart beat softly, too gently to convince him he was alive. Dinred was gone. Hayden was gone. Ben could take care of himself. And Isabelle was safe. There was nothing else for him to live for. He was already dead.

Nothing to live for but a single, last, and solitary goal. He would die in this war. Kai's words from boot camp echoed in his mind. Who should be blessed, who should be cursed, and who should be hated most? He understood now.

He opened his mouth and spoke clearly. "I'll kill them all."

www.ingramcontent.com/pod-product-compliance
Lightning Source LLC
Chambersburg PA
CBHW071748190726
48292CB00003B/912